# HE'S SO POSSESSED WITH ME

# HE'S SO POSSESSED WITH ME

COREY LIU

LITTLE, BROWN AND COMPANY

New York Boston

Cover art by Jenny Kimura. Cover design by Jenny Kimura.
Cover copyright © 2025 by Hachette Book Group, Inc.
Interior design by Jenny Kimura.
Birch trees on front cover © Dome Life Thibaan/Shutterstock.com; back cover birch trees © Borisovna.art/Shutterstock.com; sequins © Sonia Goncalves/Shutterstock.com; gems © Katflare/Shutterstock.com.

Interior art credits: Bluebell flower © Irina Anashkevich/Shutterstock.com; anatomical heart with arrow © Esqoty/Shutterstock.com; droplet © VELvector/Shutterstock.com; birch tree forest © veter LV/Shutterstock.com; emojis © SEJWAL123/Shutterstock.com; sparkling lights © Leigh Prather/Shutterstock.com; textured wall background © STILLFX/Shutterstock.com; sparkle © Daily Beaters Studio/Shutterstock.com.



Little, Brown and Company
Hachette Book Group
1290 Avenue of the Americas, New York, NY 10104

Visit us at LBYR.com

First Edition: October 2025

Little, Brown and Company is a division of Hachette Book Group, Inc. The Little, Brown name and logo are registered trademarks of Hachette Book Group, Inc.

The publisher is not responsible for websites (or their content) that are not owned by the publisher.

Little, Brown and Company books may be purchased in bulk for business, educational, or promotional use. For information, please contact your local bookseller or the Hachette Book Group Special Markets Department at special.markets@hbgusa.com.

Library of Congress Cataloging-in-Publication Data
Names: Liu, Corey, author.
Title: He's so possessed with me / Corey Liu.
Other titles: He is so possessed with me
Description: First edition. | New York : Little, Brown and Company, 2025. | Audience term: Teenagers | Audience: Ages 14 and up. | Summary: "A boy must save his best friend from a demon that wants to steal his heart—literally."
—Provided by publisher.
Identifiers: LCCN 2024057047 | ISBN 9780316571845 (hardcover) | ISBN 9780316571869 (ebook)
Subjects: CYAC: Gay men—Fiction. | Best friends—Fiction. | Friendship—Fiction. | Demons—Fiction. | Supernatural—Fiction. | Chinese Americans—Fiction. | Horror stories. | LCGFT: Gay fiction. | Paranormal fiction. | Horror fiction. | Novels.
Classification: LCC PZ7.1.L5839 He 2025 | DDC [Fic]—dc23
LC record available at https://lccn.loc.gov/2024057047

ISBNs: 978-0-316-57184-5 (hardcover), 978-0-316-57186-9 (ebook), 978-0-316-60200-6 (international)

Printed in Indiana, USA

LSC-C

Printing 1, 2025

*My first gaysian friend*
*High school was a scary bitch*
*But ha, so were we*

# PROLOGUE

I WAS LESS THAN THIRTY-FIVE SECONDS OLD WHEN THE universe decided I was ugly. Or at least, my mom did.

She still tells me the story, like a lullaby or a Grimm fairy tale before bed. How, seventeen years ago, I was born at Women's Grace Hospital, just a few ticks before midnight. How she held me in her arms, all six pounds of crying, splotchy boy. How she brought her nose to my forehead and breathed in her love of me. How she then cooed into my ear, like a prayer, "Oh my lord. *You are one ugly baby.*"

She didn't say it to be mean. It was a blessing. An amulet, made out of words, to ward off the evil.

"So, is evil scared of ugly things?" I asked her once. I was eight at the time, and we were in the kitchen—back when the two of us still lived in the one bedroom in St. James Town. Mom was washing the rice. Cockroaches scuttled across the parquet floor like little elves' feet.

"Not scared," Mom replied. Her words still had the accent

from back home in Kolkata, which confused all my teachers. Because if we looked Chinese, we should at least have the decency to sound like it. “Evil things—demons and spirits—they want pretty things.” She placed the pot in the rice cooker and flicked it on. “So, I called you ugly and they left you alone. Because when they heard me say it out loud—‘you are ugly’—they didn’t stop to ask questions.” She winked. *You’re welcome.*

I teased, “Maybe one day I’ll grow up to be pretty like you, Mom. Make my hair and lips all fancy. Make all the evil in the world fall in love with me.”

A cockroach scuttled onto the counter. Mom smacked it flat with her palm. “Colin. Never say that again.” She didn’t look at me when she spoke.

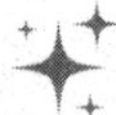

I used to close my eyes and imagine Mom standing over my crib, like the fairy godmothers do in *Sleeping Beauty*. All protective spells and enchantment. And the promise of something more—a kiss from Prince Charming.

Lately, I wonder if Mom cursed me instead. Crushed that horrible word onto my face like a stubbed crayon, drawing everything wrong. My eyes, too small. My nose, bulbous and long. Lips so chapped that no boy would ever want to kiss them.

*Ugly.*

I got older. Mom used the word less. Then, one day, she didn’t use it at all. She didn't need to. *Ugly* was already written all over my face.

Well, Mom got what she wanted. The evil things never came for me. Neither did the things that would fight them off. The white knight. The prince. The woodcutter with the big, calloused hands. Why should they?

When the evil things won't touch you, neither will anything else.

# 1

BEFORE ANYTHING ELSE ABOUT HIM—HIS EYES OR ARMS, that thick neck—I notice his hands. They're bigger than mine. Much bigger. With rough cuts and hair scattered all across the knuckles. *Daddy hands,* Ren would call them. Hands that make you feel safe but also that much more breakable.

I wouldn't mind being broken, if it was because of those hands.

"He's cute," I tell Ren, trying my best to sound blah. Which is hard when you're yelling the words over Cyndi Lauper.

"Cute?" Ren laughs. And the sound is so magical that, I swear, even under these dim blue spotlights I see the glitter around his eyes fall off like fairy dust. "Colin, he's cuter than cute. He looks like Keanu."

"He's, like, forty," I say. "He's old enough to be our dad."

"*Everyone* here's old enough to be our dad."

I look around. Fair point.

It's Friday night and we're at Fulcrum, the gay club on the corner of Church and Wellesley. Ren's eighteen and I'm seventeen, meaning we're both too young to be here with everyone else: the older, fancy Suit Types on Bay Street who slip in at night to become leather bears and otters, silver foxes and brown-haired stags.

Earlier, when the barrel-chested bouncer asked for our IDs, we whipped out two driver's licenses Ren borrowed from some friends in Kitchener. Tonight, we are Chester Chao and Phillip Ma, two engineering students at Waterloo.

Mr. Barrel Chest looked down at our IDs, then up at us. Same heights. Same weights. Same kind of Asian. Close enough.

"Thank you, Chester Chao," I whispered to my ID as we slipped into the music.

Ren said, "And thank *you,* White Person Who Can't Tell Asians Apart." At the time, I could barely hear Ren, the synthesizers were so loud. Could barely see him, too, in this dark and tangled mess of sweaty bodies—his coiffed white hair bobbing between them like sea foam. Ren grabbed my hand and led us right into the pulse. *Thump thump thump.* It was like being swallowed by Middle Earth's gayest dragon. Like we were listening to its heartbeats.

Ren asks, "What should we do now?" We've been standing alone at the bar for ten minutes, and no one will buy us a drink. Even worse, the bartender with the handlebar mustache is eyeing us over the tap, like he's in on our secret. "Should we start dancing?"

"Are we allowed?" Somehow, dancing doesn't feel right when no one's asked you to first.

"We should do *something*," Ren moans. "Or I'm wearing my Slut Shorts for nothing."

He's not joking, but I laugh—two helium-filled *hah*s that float over to the table of Ken dolls sitting six feet way. I hope the sound will pop over their sandy heads and make them look over. They don't. Probably because they can tell how badly I want them to.

I pull down the sides of my shirt until they stretch. "Maybe I should've dressed slutty, too...."

"Shut up. You look hot."

I gesture to the T-shirt design I'm wearing over my cutoffs: a giant tufted pineapple wearing sunglasses. When I first put it on, I thought it'd make me look adorkable. Now I see it just makes me look stupid.

*Ren* looks hot. Last night, when I slept over, I rubbed a box of Molly Moonshine into his hair, the pearly white one with flecks of silver and rose gold. Splashes of aquamarine. Now, whenever Ren sweeps the bangs out of his eyes, the whole world crackles with K-pop.

The DJ changes things up. It's "Ashes." Club remix.

"Is Celine Dion queer?" I ask.

"Deadpool likes her," Ren screams back. "And he's *violently* queer."

Ren steals another look at the man with daddy hands, who, we decide, should be called Papa DILF. He must feel us looking at him because now he's looking right back. He winks.

At Ren.

I can't blame Papa DILF. Everyone looks at Ren, even the seniors who make fun of us at St. Brandon's. Sometimes I even catch the straight boys stealing looks: during art with Ms. Paul; before morning mass; in the cafeteria line on pierogi day. I guess that's what happens in a grody all-boys' school. Straight boys are so hungry for pretty they start finding it in other boys.

My pants vibrate.

"Is that him?" Ren asks.

I pull out my phone. No. Message from Mom.

Where are you son call me back now.

Ren snatches my phone before I can text her back. "Is that Ferris? We agreed, Colin. This is a safe space from all confused, mediocre straight boys."

I show Ren the text. "It's not him."

"Oh." Ren chews on his lip. "Should we go?"

The smart answer is yes. Maybe Mom figured out that Ren and I aren't in his room, watching reruns of *Sailor Moon*. Which is only slightly less gay than the actual truth.

*Yes, Ren,* I should say. *Take me home to my bigot mom before she traces my phone's location and screams half this club out of its neon crop tops.*

*Yes, Ren,* I should say. Because I'm smart, and that's the smart answer.

Only tonight, I don't want to be smart. I want to be rid of this dried spider's husk Ferris has left in my chest. I want to channel the power of our Lord and Savior Celine Dion.

*Can beauty come out of ashes?*

Yeah, Celine. Damn straight it can.

I take Ren's hand and pull him onto the dance floor.

"That's my girl," he says.

At first, we're like the cows in that old movie *Twister.* This vortex of music bumps us into trucks and barns and sweaty man bodies. Then Ren and I are laughing and by some magic *we're* the ones moving everything—feeling the song between our fingers, bumping it off our hips.

We are not Ren and Colin anymore. We are the old Chinese ladies who do tai chi in the park every morning. We are Gohan turning Super Saiyan when the dust settles. We are Mario, high on Flashing Star—no one here can touch us.

We are mighty. Indestructible.

We are dazzling.

Ren presses his forehead against mine. "I'm so happy you came out tonight." And I'm about to say "So am I," except Ren is looking past me now.

At first, Papa DILF just hovers around us, looking from Ren to me. Like he can't figure out what we are—to each other, mostly. Then Ren smiles back, and Papa DILF takes this as some kind of permission to slide in between us.

*He dances like a dad,* I want to whisper to Ren.

But they're both so into each other they forget all about me. I shrug, mostly to give myself something to do. And then I feel pathetic just standing there, so I squeeze past the other bodies and head for the bar. "Ashes" is over, anyway.

"Having fun?" someone asks when I grab the stool next to him.

*Wait. Is a cute guy talking to me?* I chew on my bottom lip, the way Ren does when he talks all flirty to Plopping Dave. Then I see who it is.

"Oh," I hear myself blurt. "You're in my class."

I almost don't recognize Blair without his Brandon's blazer and tie. Not that he looks any different sitting here. Formal wear seems to be his default. Like always, Blair Prince is the yearbook picture of Black Goth chic meets Ruth Bader Ginsburg, with frostbite-blue lips and cat-eye glasses. He's even wearing a collar ruffle, which he's fidgeting with now.

"So," I start, "did you also break the law to get in?"

Blair takes a sip from his drink, so poisonously green it must've been ladled from a cauldron. "My cousin is friends with the bouncer."

"You mean Mr. Barrel Chest?"

"Excuse me?"

"Nothing."

Blair takes another sip. He doesn't ask me how I got in.

Of course he doesn't. In all the years we've gone to St.

Brandon's, Blair's never said a peep to me, even though we've taken all the same classes. Even though I usually sit two or three seats behind him.

Gay solidarity, sister?

Okay.

Blair fidgets with his collar again and I notice a tattoo on his wrist. A crimson upside-down heart with an arrowhead aimed at the sky.

I grin. "Sailor Mars."

"Who?"

I point to his tattoo. "Sailor Mars. You know"—I press my hands together and mime shooting liquid flame out of a water pistol—"Mars Fire, Soul! *Pshoo pshoo.*"

"Actually," Blair says, "it's the mark of Ares. The god of war? And of—"

"Agriculture," I finish, a little rudely. "Yeah, I took Classics, too." Then, even though no one has asked, "I got an A."

Blair tugs at his collar again. He got an A+, and we both know it. "Sorry," he begins. "What's your name? Colin, right?"

"Colin Ong."

He cups an ear. "Dong?"

*What.* I take a deep breath and tell myself Blair probably didn't mean anything by it. Only I don't care. I've heard it three thousand times before, ever since Coach Krevz mispronounced my last name during roll call in gym, freshman year.

Ong, which sounds like Dong, which means my name is two degrees away from an overused Asian penis joke.

"Uh, no," I reply. "Not that."

Blair seems to realize what he's said. "Oh, wait. No, that came out wrong."

"Forget it."

"I couldn't hear—the music." He's frazzled, his fingers playing tug-of-war with his collar. "Although Dong is a common Vietnamese name..." He changes the subject. "Hey, isn't that your friend?"

I follow Blair's pointing finger to where Ren is still dancing. Next to Papa DILF, Ren looks small. *Like David rubbing up against Goliath,* Ferris would tease.

Ferris.

His voice slips into my head so clearly it makes me want to cry. *No,* the reasonable part of my brain says, *Ferris doesn't want me.* Not anymore. Maybe he never did. But at least I have Ren. Except right now he looks perfect and a part of all this and I hate myself because why can't I be happy for him?

Blair fidgets in his stool, like he's catching my bad vibes. "Are you okay?"

"Better than okay," I lie. Then I fold up the edges of my Sad Boy Thoughts and head for the door. "See you in class."

"See you," I hear Blair mumble.

When Ren waves at me, I wave my phone back. *I should go.* He mouths, *You sure?* Then Papa DILF wraps his arms around Ren's waist, and I wonder how nice must it feel, to have someone want you *that* badly they won't let you leave?

Or maybe it's creepy. Maybe it's both?

Ren breaks away from him. "Where are you going?" he asks, grabbing my wrist. He tries to pull me back onto the dance floor. *"Come on."*

"I'm so tired." I emphasize my point by giving the world's greatest yawn. "You stay. I'm going home."

Ren pouts. "But what about your mom?"

"Don't worry about her. I've got a plan."

Which I don't. Mom closes the restaurant on Friday nights, meaning I've got an hour before she gets home to wash off. But say she already knows I lied about staying in? Say she already knows where I am?

Here's my plan: I'm fucked.

"I'll be fine, Ren. Just promise me two things. One." I gesticulate to Papa DILF, who is dancing to Robyn on his own. "Do not leave with that guy."

"Well, duh," Ren starts, but I talk over him.

"And *two,* text me when you get home. Okay?"

But when I reach the big steel doors, I feel a hand on my shoulder, five fingertips clawed like a crouching spider. It's this thing Ren and I do, our sign to each other since seventh grade, stronger than any pinky promise.

*"I'll be fine,"* I tell him again. "I know my way home. Stay. Have fun."

Before I can say anything else—protest or laugh, because the spider-hand thing is so stupid—Ren says, "I'd rather talk about anime." And he skips out the door.

It's a little past midnight when we arrive in Markville. It's the suburbs, so almost everyone is asleep. The 53 bus route drops passengers off at Birchmount and Steeles, ten blocks away from my house, eleven blocks away from Ren's. We don't mind walking the rest of the way. We pass the Esso gas station. The plaza with Green Grotto, open twenty-four hours, littered with sleepy-eyed undergrads hunched over their MacBooks, clicking through lecture notes.

"Know what I love most about *Sailor Moon*?" Ren suddenly asks, hugging his bare arms. Even though it's late spring, this is not crop-top weather. "The show feels so soft."

I grin, then respectfully tell Ren he is wrong, just to get a rise out of him. "What's so soft about it? Sailor Moon kicks ass."

"But she never hurts anyone unless she *needs* to. Even then she uses healing-based attacks first."

I take Ren's point. In season one, the Dark Kingdom turns the citizens of Tokyo into youma, and Usagi uses Moon Healing Escalation to lift the curse.

"That's why she's the champion of *love* and justice," Ren continues. "She's not like the Avengers or the Justice League. Sailor Moon doesn't have throw-downs with monsters. She makes humans out of them."

I roll my eyes. I keep on listening, though, because whenever Ren gets hyped up about something, it builds and buzzes inside him like kinetic energy. Then it touches you and sparks.

He asks, "What's your favorite attack?"

"Love and Beauty Shock." That's when Sailor Venus blows a giant heart-kiss at her enemies.

Because shouldn't love feel like that?

Bright and spinning, strong enough to break through walls?

We walk past the hot pot place where, last week, someone tossed a brick through its window. By now, it's all patched up, but the restaurant still looks sad. Or maybe that's just me. Because I cut our night short. Because I forced Ren to leave the club.

Ren says it's all right. He says *talking* about dancing with hot guys is as much fun as actually dancing with them. An obvious lie. Ever since we left the club, Ren has been humming "Ashes" whenever things get too quiet. Like one of those wind-up music boxes you buy at the Disney Store. He wants to replay the magic.

"All those guys were into you," I say, because I think Ren needs to hear it.

"They were not."

"They were, like, *looking*." I bump my shoulder into his. "Just watch. Those artsy boys at MCAD will eat you up, too." Maritime College of Art and Design, only fifteen minutes away from my dream school, King's U. Ren and I are already looking into off-campus housing so we can live together.

"No one was looking at me." Ren pulls the neckline of his shirt so far up I can see only the top half of his face, blushing. "And before I forget: Thanks for leaving me alone with Papa DILF. He was probably a serial killer."

Ren has good reason to be upset, but I know he isn't. By the time I can see St. Brandon's in the distance—a towering slab of concrete peeking over the trees like a tombstone—he says dreamily, "It *was* fun...."

I don't think Ren is really talking to me. I think he's reopening that small music box in his head where he keeps everything safe. Those shiny things. Those moments.

Lingering looks by cute boys. The smiles. The confession that, one day, a lover in college will write for him.

Whenever I see Ren get like this, it's hard not to feel a little sad. Because when will I get a shiny thing, too? Just a piece of it.

"Eleven eleven," Ren says, pocketing his phone.

We've reached school grounds. To get home, we should cut across the soccer field and keep going straight until we hit my street, then his.

We don't move. We just stand there, looking up. Ren takes one of my hands so we can keep our palms warm.

There are more stars here than in the city. Not *enough* stars, and none as bright as we need them. That's why we squint until the passing airplane lights above us blink back like a white dwarf. We make stars so we can make wishes.

I wish for my first kiss. I wish to be *kissed*. I wish for this person to have a six-pack, and for him to let me run my finger along each bump. I wish for Ferris to ask me to prom (and after that I wish for the abs again).

Mostly, I wish for a shiny thing. One I can slip into my pocket before high school ends. I wish for this last thing so hard it feels like there's nothing else inside me. Nothing but this wish.

Stupid, airy, weightless thing.

Then I stop wishing. Because someone is following us.

# 2

Ren drops my hand. Then I hear it. Laughter—drunk and wild, almost angry. A laugh that sounds more like a warning.

"Dukes," Ren says. "Two of them."

You can always spot a Duke from the sounds they make when they're in public. Boys, presumably straight—the loud, obnoxious kind who slur *gaylord* out from their windows when they drive by like tossed soda cans. Boys who kick down restaurant signs on the street or smash pumpkins on Halloween. Boys who take up the whole sidewalk with their sounds because they can't with their bodies.

*Fake Big Dick Energy* is how Ren would describe them. But right now, he's quiet. The Dukes are behind us.

Only now they're not laughing.

And I know—somehow, I know—without turning back, that they're looking right at us.

My hand hangs cold and limp. I'm thankful Ren had the foresight to drop it.

The footsteps behind us get louder. Quicker. Gently, Ren pulls my arm until my whole side is leaning into his. We let the Dukes pass. I smell vodka, root beer, cigarettes. And that's when I do something stupid.

I lock eyes with one of them. The Duke closest to me.

He looks our age. Tall. With a crooked nose and a square jawline spiked with little brown hairs. He's handsome, in that gruff, toxic masculine kind of way you might find sexy one moment and terrifying the next.

His gray eyes glide over me, taking in my painted face, my pineapple shirt. Something in those eyes lights up, and for a second, I wonder if he might start flirting. So, I do a second stupid thing: I smile.

That's when the look on his face twists into something else. I am a centipede he's found curling at the bottom of his mug.

"Yup," the Duke whispers audibly to his friend as they pass by. "Nothing worse than a Chinese fag."

Certain words can cut you like a ninja sword. You don't realize you've been sliced in half until you're already falling to pieces.

Before I can pull myself back together, Ren is already leaving my side. "Um. What?!"

*Oh no*, I think. *Please, Ren. Let them go.* My thoughts bounce off his back, weightless as paper balls.

"Hey, you piece of shit!" he shouts.

And the Dukes stop. They actually stop. And they wait for him, amused, as he marches over to them, short shorts flouncing with each giant stride.

"What did you just say to my friend?" he demands.

Duke One's eyes trail down Ren's pearly white hair and linger somewhere around his lips, slicked pink like a candied heart. "Uh-oh," he sneers. "She's mad."

Something about the way he's looking at Ren moves my legs forward. Makes me grab Ren's arm and yank him away. "Let's just go." *Home,* I want to say. *Let's go home.* Only where is that? I don't know. Right now, I don't know anything. Just that there's no one else on the street. No headlight in the distance from an oncoming car.

Now Duke One is staring at me again. And I wish I could shrink into my oversize T-shirt until it swallows me whole. Until the grinning pineapple is as big as the sun.

"Listen to your boyfriend," Duke One tells Ren. He tries to make his voice sound like mine. Harmless as helium. And Duke Two chuckles stupidly. I get a better look at him, too. About six feet. A black mop of tightly curled hair, likely permed, poking out from underneath a baseball cap.

"C'mon," he says to Duke One. "These two want, you know. *Alone time.*" It's an insult, but I don't care. I want them to leave, too.

Duke One takes another step toward Ren. "You're disgusting. You know that?"

"Aw, darn! Am I?" Ren pouts. Then it's his turn to give Duke One the look-down. "Like I care what you think, Pencil Dick."

Duke One's cheeks flush pink. For some reason, this slip in his bravado makes my insides spin electric blue and red. I look around again. No cars, no people. Every star in the sky, hidden as help.

And then I see him. On the other side of the grassy field, standing so still next to the goalpost.

A boy.

The tree line of Birchmount Forest towers behind him. I'm not sure how long he's been standing there. How I could have missed him? He's wearing gray trousers that stop a foot above his knobby knees, with clean white stockings pulled tightly around his calves.

*Help,* I think to this stranger, because now Duke One is taking a step forward. Close enough to punch Ren. Or kiss him.

In response, the Boy in Short Shorts holds both his palms out before his face and makes a rectangle with his fingertips. Like he's framing this moment.

"Oh, what?" I hear Ren say. "Are you gonna hit me?" And in the three microseconds it takes to look to Ren and back, the Boy in Short Shorts is gone.

Duke One tilts his chin. At first, I'm not sure what he's doing. And then I see it—a bubbly white glob dribbles out of his fleshy lips. It lands right onto Ren's shoulder without making a sound.

Duke Two laughs into his fist. To him, his friend's saliva is the world's funniest punch line. And Ren—

"Stop."

I don't remember pulling it out. I don't remember turning the camera on. Suddenly, I'm holding my Huawei cell phone out in front of me like a crucifix wrapped in *We Bare Bears* skin: praying for some powerful force out there to hear us. God or Google or the Chinese government Mr. Kinsey swears is listening in on my phone.

Four unread messages from Mom.

Two missed calls.

"Leave." I try to force my words to come out of my belly like Puppy Chow once coached me. Deep enough where no one else can hear the fear. "Now! Or I'm posting this."

"Are you serious?" Duke Two says. He turns to Duke One. "Is this guy serious?"

On my screen, Duke One's face blinks back at me in night mode. Wolf eyes.

I've seen enough doxxing videos online to know how things escalate. Bigots are like evil spirits from those found-footage horror movies—they don't like being caught on camera. They don't like feeling *caught*. And all Duke One has to do is leap forward and smack the phone out of my hands. He could grind it into a million pieces under his scuffed runners. Do the same thing to me.

Instead, I see the boy on my screen smirk and back away, hands up like white flags. As though I'm the unhinged one, and why can't I take a joke? "*Thorry,*" he lisps, and he turns around. Duke Two follows. And then they're gone.

I wait until they're light-years away.

"Hey," I finally say, quietly. Because all this time, Ren hasn't said anything. And then I realize I'm still recording, so I turn my phone off and pocket it. Except I still don't know what else to say, so again I say, "Hey."

Ren starts to respond. "He..." The answer tumbles out of him like a clump of rose petals. He looks around us, at this deserted street, searching for something he lost. The right words, maybe. "He got my shirt."

Ren starts wiping at the wet patch on his shoulder with his thumb. Since I don't like the thought of Duke One on his skin, I use my own thumb to rub at the stain. For a long while, we just stand there, saying nothing, me wiping at the stain, trying my best to clean tonight off him. I know this will be the last time I ever see Ren wearing this shirt.

When I'm done, he says it's late and we should go home.

I say sure.

He asks which way.

The Dukes are gone, but we can still hear their joker laughs, ringing out from somewhere on the other side of the school. That means they're using the same path we wanted to use. Which means now we can't use it.

"What about the trail?"

Ren looks uncertainly down the hill, at the pathway cutting through Birchmount Forest. Every noon, before the bell rings for third period, I see Puppy Chow and the other twelfth graders duck behind those trees to get high. It's not a deep forest, just a loop trail, a five- or six-minute walk. And we can use our phones as flashlights.

I tell Ren all this and he just nods.

Together, we glide quietly across the soccer field. Once we arrive at the wide gap between the trees, where the trail begins, I leave my hand hanging between us. Ren doesn't take it.

# 3

IN OUR NINTH-GRADE ASTRONOMY UNIT, WE COVERED dark energy, learned how it can cause whole galaxies to drift apart in space. I can feel that cosmic force right here with us now in Birchmount Forest, pulling Ren away from me.

I talk to Ren about prom. I talk to him about Puppy Chow's broccoli haircut. I talk about the biology handout Ms. Kincaid assigned us, on trophic levels and apex predators. Each new topic is a glowing white rock I place in the dark for Ren, hoping he might pick one of them up and find his way back to me.

And because he's Ren, he tries. No, he hasn't worked on the handout yet. For sure, Puppy Chow looks better with a shaved head. Oh, do people still go to prom?

His answers are half-hearted, and maybe that's because his other half-heart is still somewhere on that grassy field, where Duke One spat on him. Now there's mostly this heavy silence hanging between us, wet and balled up.

Ren finally breaks it. "Fantastic," he says, wiping his eyes. His cheeks are streaked with mascara. "Look at my makeup. I'm a mess."

"You look great."

"Those guys didn't think so."

"Who cares?" I say, remembering the way Duke One looked at him. "I bet that guy was closeted."

Ren keeps walking.

It's not as though we haven't been called stuff before. Boys will always find a way to make you feel bad when they hate you enough, or when they're bored. Still, I wish I could forget that look on Duke One's face, as though the sight of me was something disgusting. The balm Ren dabbed onto my lips. The gold-leaf eye shadow that took me thirty minutes to apply. When I get home, the first thing I'll do is wipe it all off.

Something crumples under my heel. I shine my flashlight down onto the dirt path and see broken glass and pine needles. A Skittles wrapper reminding me to taste the rainbow.

And next to it, bright burning wicks of blue. When I kneel down for a closer look I see it's a single stem of flowers, each one shaped like a bell.

Bluebells.

It isn't growing out of the trail. It was plucked and laid here, like it was left for someone to find.

"Pretty, huh?" I ask Ren, holding it out for him.

He takes it and inhales. "Fresh. Like damp moss." Then he lays it back down where we found it, and we move on.

A few feet ahead, Ren lands his flashlight on a birch tree, his beam sweeping down its smooth white trunk. It stops at a scar. "Creepy," he says. "Like an eye."

"It's a lesion," I point out, recalling our field studies section in eleventh-grade bio. "You get it when the branches tear. Or if they freeze off during winter."

Ren has nothing to add to this, no follow-up questions, so we turn right.

By the time we reach the trail leading to the exit, I stop and turn to Ren. "Look. I want to respect your mind-space. But for the record, Ren, you were really impressive tonight." I lay my claw-hand on his shoulder, hoping for a smile, a cringe. "Seriously. You were so *brave*."

I leave that last word in the air because I want Ren to laugh. It's a joke between us, ever since Clarissa Wong called Ren brave—breathlessly—in seventh grade because his nails were painted cotton candy blue. Also, from that time Ren and I walked together downtown, and a Mini Cooper honked at us. The family inside nodded their approval at our skintight jeans and paisley jackets. As though we were doing some great service for our country. As though we were dressing for war.

*You're so brave.*

Well-intentioned hetero nonsense. Ren and I are never trying to look brave. We are trying to look hot.

I hope this memory will pull Ren back, but he isn't laughing. "Do you ever get tired of it, though?"

"Tired of what?"

"Being brave."

Before I can ask what he means, he stops walking. Because up ahead, something huge is blocking our path.

Ren squints. "Did a beaver make that?"

I shine my light on it. "I don't think that's a dam."

It sits there, a white tangled mass of shrub and fallen branches from the surrounding birch. A beautiful wreckage pulled out of a child's dream.

A thicket. Almost taller than we are.

"Whoa," Ren says.

Up close, it's as though we're standing before something dead. A small whale, washed ashore, meat picked clean off by the crabs, leaving behind glittering bone. It's the kind of white you're left with once you strip everything else away. Pure, close to nothing. It sits there and waits.

"Colin," Ren starts, inching closer to the thicket. "Has this always been here?"

"Maybe someone in art club put this together?" I reply. "It could also be one of the seniors." Gabriel, Jonah, Puppy Chow. They'd been flexing their pre-graduation muscles all last week with pranks. Streaking through the third-floor corridors. Supergluing a pink wig onto the founder's statue. This time I'm not sure what the joke is.

"We'll walk around it," I say. And I'm about to skirt off the path, down the sloping hill, to join the skeleton leaves.

Ren doesn't follow. He circles the thicket, curiouser and curiouser, like he's playing *Pokémon GO* and there's something rare on the other side.

"Look," I hear him say. "There's a tunnel."

I follow Ren's voice and find him kneeling in front of a crooked opening under the canopy of branches. I shine my light inside, and it lands on nothing. Maybe the St. Brandon's boys dug a hole.

"It goes deep," Ren says. "Really deep."

Deeper than it has any right to be. Deeper than looking inside a well. Suddenly, I'm aware of how dark and quiet everything is. No crickets chirping or howling wind or rustling leaves. And I can't help but imagine it's because of this hole. That it has devoured all the sounds of Birchmount Forest.

This doesn't feel like a prank anymore.

"We should go, Ren."

Ren must feel it, too, because he's already rising to his feet and brushing the gravel off his knees.

"Wait." Ren grabs my shoulder. We freeze.

Ren puts a finger to his lips and I stop breathing. A whimper, quick and muffled. Then nothing.

Ren turns to me. "You heard that, right?"

"It's probably just Jonah, taking a dump in the woods." Ren knows I don't believe that. The whole forest knows. I'm about to tell Ren we should go again, *we should go*, except he's not paying attention.

"What is that?" he asks, pointing. "Right there."

"Ren, *please*."

"I'm serious." Ren walks a few paces, bends down, and picks something up. He returns to me and holds it up to our crossed beams.

A black dress shoe, its skin frayed at the toe area. Ren turns it around in his hands, using only his fingertips, like the shoe is a sculpture blown out of glass so thin even light can shatter it. And that's when I remember him.

"The Boy in Short Shorts."

"Who?"

"Before, on the field, with those guys." The guys made of terror. The boy who was watching, who gave me the idea to record the Dukes on my phone. "I saw someone. I think this is his."

We slowly turn our faces back to the thicket. Could the boy be inside?

Ren returns to the opening and shines his light through the gap. "Hello?" he calls. "Is someone down there? Should we call for help?" When no one responds, Ren drops to his hands and knees. "I'm going inside."

"I'm sorry," I snap. "Have you lost it?" I drag Ren back to his feet by the forearms. Because Ren is not a himbo. And neither am I. We are both on honor roll. "Ma'am, you are not climbing into a mysterious hole. Use your head."

Ren bites his lip. "You're right." Then he bends down and reassures the hole with a quick "Hang tight. We're calling for help."

Ren fumbles to unlock his phone. That's when I notice the scars running along the bent branches that arch around the hole. I see the eyes again.

Except they're not eyes. Because they're not scars. These lines run sharp, more deliberate.

Hearts. Little ones scratched onto the bark. The edges are splintery. Like an angry knife hacked into its white flesh again and again.

I hear Ren curse as he bends down to retrieve his phone. In his haste, he must have fumbled and dropped it.

My shoes crunch into dead leaves and carry me away from Ren, around the thicket. More hearts. And I see there are scraggly lines inside them, too, thin as whispers. And those whispery lines make letters. No, not just letters.

*Isaiah.*

A name.

"And now my screen is cracked!" Ren whines. "My IU wallpaper looks like she has a mustache."

My orb of light uncovers as much of the thicket as it can. Every inch of white is split open with those hearts and names, gray scabs carved all over its skin, letters and writing—all done by the same hand.

*Isaiah.*

*Isaiah.*

*Isaiah.*

Who wrote this name? My beam stops at one, sliced into a heart at the end of a branch. The cut looks deeper. Fresh.

I get a closer look. Am I reading it right, those letters? That name?

"Oh, wait," Ren says slowly. "I think I see something moving inside."

*Ren.*

He's kneeling by the opening again, neck beaded with sweat. Close enough for the hole to clamp down onto it. "You okay in there?" he calls out. "Are you able to speak? Hello?"

And before I can bark at Ren to get away, before I can pull him out by his sleeve, someone answers.

"Ren."

His name stretches out to us like an echo. Not hurt or whimpering. Not like any voice we know.

We should run. I know this. Then why am I edging closer to Ren's side? Why am I looking into the hollow?

With a shaky hand, Ren shines his phone light inside.

I don't know what Ren sees—just that suddenly my nostrils and lungs fill with something rotting and the phone slips out of his hand and click-clacks to the ground. Just that Ren jumps to his feet and seizes my wrist and pulls and pulls. Away from the thicket, from the path home. And we're running and I'm asking, *What is it, what is it, what did you see?* And there are trees everywhere because the trail is gone, and I hear one of us sobbing as the branches cut and tear at our shirts, our arms, our faces. And the trees tower like bare-naked people, watching with those eyes. All those eyes.

Ren begs we have to go, now, now, we have to go now we can't stop okay.

Only we do, because Ren's shirt gets caught in a white branch, twigs spidery quick, and it clings and drags—it actually drags Ren back with such force that his hand is torn out of mine. And for the first time that night, Ren screams, and I scream. The branch twisting into the back of his shirt is a human hand.

Then they're gone. The hand. Ren.

Gone before I think to hold onto him.

Gone before he makes a sound.

"Ren?" His name sounds so clear coming out of my mouth, like it's the most tangible thing left of him.

He doesn't respond.

I call out for him again. Still nothing.

*Where is he?* Ren wasn't dragged off, thrashing and screaming. He was here, and now he isn't.

I reach for the air where, moments before, he stood facing me. *Maybe this is a trick of the light.* A trick of the dark. My fingers need to close around something—the smooth bareness of his shoulder, the mesh fabric of his shirt.

*Should I call for him a third time? Isn't third time the charm?* But his name snags in my chest when I look down. When I see glowing petals by my feet.

Bluebells.

Like the ones we found earlier, plucked and laid out, but not where we left them.

And then I hear him. *Ren.* Not from the bluebells but from up the hill, from the direction we came.

Is he singing?

I can't make out the words, but it's him, I'm sure of it. The leaves chitter overhead as I climb up the hill, past the roots bursting from the earth like bulging veins, back to the trail.

When I find him, still as a mannequin in front of the thicket, he stops singing. His back is turned to me, his arms hanging slack by his sides.

He is looking inside the hollow.

"Ren?"

He doesn't reply, doesn't show any sign he's heard me. He just stands there, swaying a bit in the breeze, his pearly hair dull in the moonlight. Duller than dandelion fluff after the yellows fade. The wind picks up, rustling leaves, and for a second it seems strong enough to take Ren with it, scatter him across the forest into a thousand wishes.

"Ren," I try again. I scan the trees on our left. The trees on our right. I squint at the brambles growing in thorny hedges off the path, bleeding with poison berries. We're not alone. "We need to go now. Before he comes back."

I move forward and Ren startles, his head snapping up toward the starless sky. Then, in that same dreamy voice I heard down the hill, he sings.

*"'Cause I've been shaking, I've been bending backwards till I'm broke. Watching all these dreams—"*

He stops singing, and when the seconds creep by, I realize it is for my sake. That Ren wants me to finish the song.

Ren turns his head enough for me to catch a pale sliver of his cheek. "Colin," he says, his face a fingernail moon. "Can I show you something?"

I've had enough.

"What do you mean, *Can I show you something*? What's going *on*, Ren? What happened to you?"

I listen for it again. A stranger's footsteps—but there is only silence. The forest is thick with it.

"It's just us," Ren says, reading my mind, finally, turning to face me. "We're safe. Don't worry."

But I do. I worry as he walks over. I worry as he takes my hands. "I saw someone."

"Who?" Ren's palms are warm, but they don't feel safe. "Colin. Look around. There's nobody here."

"The man. He grabbed you like this." My fingers dig into Ren's wrist. Because maybe his flesh will remember. Maybe Ren will stop smiling at me like none of this is real.

He doesn't even wince. "There's nobody here," Ren repeats. "It's just us."

"But what about this?" I gesture to the thicket. "We heard someone. Didn't we?"

"I don't hear anything now."

Ren moves closer to the hollow, pulling me by the arm with

him. "Listen. Nothing. And you said yourself, someone probably left this to be funny."

"I saw your name on it."

"My name?"

"Here!" I shine my phone light on the spot. The two of us squint at the overhanging branch, at the blank space. *Ren* isn't there. None of the names are. I flinch when something lands on my shoulder. But it's just Ren, doing the Claw. "You are such an Asian lightweight. We need to build up your tolerance—"

"Stop." I swat Ren's hand away. "I didn't drink tonight."

"Are you sure?"

I pause. Did I drink? No one bought me a drink at the club. It's the forest where the details become hazy—where the images sear away in white like when a projector overheats. Blisters a hole right through the reel.

I want to cry. "Am I going crazy?"

"*No,*" Ren says, and he gives me a hug, the same kind Mom used to give to chase the nightmares away. "Nothing is wrong with you," he hushes in my ear. "Maybe you're tired. Or maybe you're in shock? Because of what happened, with those boys? Maybe you're imagining things?"

I stare at the back of his crop top, stained with dirt. Am I sure it was a hand I saw there, twisting into it, and not a branch? But what about Ren? How he was standing there one second, gone the—

Ren tightens his grip (or am I imagining that, too?). "Maybe," Ren starts again. Then he stops, his body tensing against mine. He breaks our hug when we hear it.

The trees. They sputter alive for a second, branches bending and cracking as they sway above us, leaves rustling in dry, angry whispers. It seems strange that there should be rustling at all when at this moment there is no wind, not that I can feel, not so much as a cool breeze gracing my face.

When the sounds have stopped, when it is just me and Ren and the unbearable silence again, I say, "Maybe."

A smile blooms across his face. "Come with me."

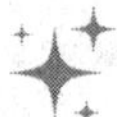

Ren's fingers are threaded through mine when he leads us into an overgrown clearing. I've never been to this part of the forest before.

"Look." He points to those bright, dreadful wicks of blue dotting the grass. They glow like will-o'-the-wisps, or the hottest part of a flame. Bluebells, setting the whole clearing ablaze. "More of them. Like he said."

"Who?"

But Ren releases my hand and wades into the overgrown field until he is knee-deep in flowers. "Look how many there are!"

I join him. "Can we go?"

"Look at the petals." Ren plucks a stem and brings a droopy bell to my face. "Look how they dip their heads away from the moon." Ren kneels and gathers fistfuls of flowers and bunches them against his chest. "*As blue as a bit of sky come down.* Where did I hear that before? In a children's book?"

"You want a story?" I pull Ren up by the underarm and drag him along. Bluebells tumble off his lap. "Once upon a time, two boys left the creepy woods and one of them took a really long, hot shower."

Ren sighs as I steer him back onto the pathway. "The book I mentioned wasn't a fairy tale."

"So not the point."

Ren twirls a bluebell, the one he managed to hold on to. He brings it to his nose. Breathes it in. "Magical. He said that, too."

This time I don't ask who "he" is. The author, probably.

But later, once we have reached the end of the trail—the streetlamp on the main road a shining lighthouse—I say, to break the silence, "Wait. *Magical?* You told me the book *didn't* have magic."

"I said it wasn't a fairy tale," Ren reminds me, that dreaminess crawling back into his voice. "But there's magic, Colin. You'll see. This story will drip with it."

# 5

IS IT TOO LATE TO START AT THE BEGINNING?

The first time I saw Ren, I was with Mom. We were in her car, and it was the summer before seventh grade. I don't remember where we came from, just that we were heading home. Our AC was roaring in the sweltering heat. Mom rolled to a stop on Alberta Street and Bucket when I heard something. Faint, polite. A bell.

*Ting ting.*

He breezed by on a Barbie-pink bike, its handlebars glittering with gold streamers. The boy looked to be around my age, in shorts that were so short they were more like cutoffs. He was smiling up at the sun. Even though our windows were sealed shut, I could tell he was humming.

Mom shook her head. "Look at him," she said with a *tsk*. "Bànge Gung-ma."

I winced. *Bànge Gung-ma* is Hakka for "gay" and literally means "half-man-woman." But it wasn't the intended slur that bothered me. It was the gleam in Mom's eyes when she used it. The same gleam she had when she saw men who sashayed as they walked, men holding hands with other men. Sometimes I wondered if part of her wished that flinging such a word would have the same impact as chucking pebbles or empty water bottles at someone's head. Disdain just hard enough for the other person to feel.

I always felt it.

Somehow, the boy did, too.

He skidded to a stop in front of our car and squinted at us through our windshield, like he could sense we were talking about him. There, backlit by the sun, his eyes met Mom's for three defiant seconds.

Then he stuck out his tongue and wheeled away.

I wanted to laugh. I should have.

"Did you see?" Mom sputtered in Hakka, long after the boy and his tassels whipped out of sight. "Did you see that disrespect? And what Asian mother would let her son go out dressed like some—some—megaslut?!"

Even now, Ren still laughs at that one.

Two months after I saw him, we became friends.

It was on the same day Peter Chen threatened to whip a handball at my face. Another recess in seventh grade. The

Creamsicle sun had melted down the whole playground into a pool of sweet, sticky orange.

That recess, I sat at the top of the big slide, my sketchbook cracked open on my knees. All twenty-four of my pencil crayons were hiding inside my Keroppi foam case. I chose that spot because Samantha Vo always hung around with her two girlfriends. At that moment, they were perched on the rickety bridge of the jungle gym, giggling and swinging their legs over the sand. Floating above everyone else.

The girls were far enough that they couldn't see what I was drawing. But close enough that I could hear their conversations. What answer did Clarissa Wong bubble for question six? Did anyone catch that episode of *Riverdale*?

But I didn't care about any of that.

I just wanted to hear them talk about the boys. The boys who played handball against the side of the school building every recess. The boys I turned into manga characters inside my sketchbook.

"Look how cute he is when he scratches his head," Clarissa said.

Joy Park confirmed his cuteness by adding, "So smol," and all three of them sparkled with laughter. I laughed, too. On the inside, though, where no one could hear.

Clarissa was talking about Danny Lee, whom she had claimed for herself two weeks ago on that very bridge. And Joy had said she approved of this because she liked Aaron Shin better, but at the time I could tell she was lying because she barely spoke again until the bell rang everyone inside. As for Samantha, we all knew she had eyes for Taylor Naranjan, who could sprint the fastest and still do sixty-eight push-ups.

I watched the boys. But I also watched the girls watching them. Which only now I realize sounds creepy. It was their intensity, maybe. Or that they all had something to share with each other. Little hearts scribbled around a cute boy's initials. Love poems penned during class. Laughing whispering longing sighs.

One time I caught Samantha writing Taylor's name in her geography binder. *Taylor, Taylor, Taylor* again and again, an incantation written all across her map of Canada. And then Samantha showed her Taylor Map to Joy and Clarissa, and their sunshine laughter made me smile even though I'd never felt more lonely.

To everyone else, they might have looked silly. Especially to the teachers. But back then I wondered if grown-ups forgot what it was like to be young, to have that feeling make a home inside you. That brimming ache, too enormous for any one person.

You need someone else to feel it with you.

"Can you fucking leave?"

I jumped. Peter Chen was looking up at me from the bottom of the slide. How long had he been standing there?

My notebook snapped shut. "Sorry?" I blinked and blinked. Because Peter said *fuck* to me. Because his friends had stopped playing handball and were watching us now. Because the girls had stopped, too. Because the whole playground was listening.

"I said leave," Peter repeated, more slowly.

"Or *you* could leave," Clarissa barked. "Colin's not doing anything."

"Yeah, Peter," Samantha chimed in. "Go back to your game and we can keep ignoring you."

"He sits there, every recess, looking at me. It freaks me out."

My grip tightened around my sketch pad. In fact, I hadn't been looking at Peter Chen. I had been looking at Peter *Chow*, nicknamed Puppy for the way he panted while running circles around everyone else in PE—tongue wagging, so exhilarated to be alive he might start humping your leg. People joked about that, but Puppy was a real gentleman. He had raven hair that swept across his eyes and loaned me his kneaded eraser once during art when I lied about not having one. Sometimes, when I sat behind him in class, I could see a little sweat sprinkled along the nape of his neck.

In my sketchbook, I was drawing Puppy as an anime character, with a flowing black cape and sparkle effects. Holding out a bouquet of pink roses.

"Go away," Peter growled. Only this time his arm was slung back, a blue rubber ball clenched tightly in his fist. Peter was an excellent server.

I gathered my sketchbook, my Keroppi foam case, and clanged down the slide.

"You're such an *ass*, Peter," I heard Joy sneer.

When I passed the boys playing handball, they said things

to me, too—except for Puppy—though mostly in Cantonese. Which they all knew I couldn't understand.

I took my book and supplies to portable sixteen, where Mrs. Driscol taught us music on Thursdays and cried when she realized our lack of talent was beyond saving.

I didn't like being here during recess. Sure, it was always empty and had air-conditioning, but the carpets were mildewed with dried spit from the woodwinds. Well, here at least I would have privacy. Here at least I would—

"Hullo," a voice said from the corner. It was squeaky, like the words were forced through a chipped reed.

He was sitting in the chair closest to the back window. The way he looked in that moment, orange sun pooling around him, making his edges softer, fuzzier—he was like a fairy photographed in a garden, or something else made entirely of light. Too stunning for direct exposure.

Because even then, *I knew.* Ren Hsu was beautiful. I'd known ever since I saw him that day on the bike. Shortly after, everyone else knew it. From the moment Ms. Coy led him to the front of the class and explained how he'd transferred from public school and Ren bowed—actually *bowed*—his happy, crescent-moon eyes directed at no one. His round face a glowing peach.

All the girls wanted to be friends with him because they said he was smol. And then Puppy got really quiet, like even he could see it.

On that day, I vowed to hate him.

In the portable, he said to me, "Oh. Are you making art?" He glanced at my sketchbook.

I said nothing and took the seat farthest away from him.

Then I opened my sketchbook and filled in the roses. By the time I'd reached my sixth rose, I heard a voice over my shoulder say, "Cool! That looks like Puppy."

I jumped. But before I could stow my artwork away, Ren was already bending over it. He took my 4B pencil and, with it, rounded the edges of Puppy's eyes. "Maybe his face needs to look more open."

I had to admit, Puppy did look better this way. Which only made me hate Ren more.

"Can you fucking leave?" I asked.

"Huh?" Ren blanched whiter than those models in the Korean face cream ads.

I didn't stop. In portable sixteen, I cussed Ren out, calling him a sissy, a gaylord, a dumb bitch. Every hateful insult Peter Chen and the straight boys had ever thrown at me, I unleashed onto the new kid with all the force of a killer serve. The new kid, who peeked at my secret. The new kid, who touched it and made it prettier.

Ren took a step forward. I braced myself for him to give it all back. Instead, Ren's words got twisted and lodged in his throat. "I," he began, cheeks flushed, practically choking on the word, "am *not* a dumb bitch." Then he buried his face in his hands and cried.

I don't remember why I hugged Ren—was it out of guilt or

something less noble, like fear of him tattling? Whatever it was, my arms wrapped around him and my chest felt slick with hot tears and snotty, muffled cries. "No, no. Please don't." I hushed over his sobs. "*I'm* the dumb bitch. *I'm* the dumb bitch."

Two days after the portable incident, Ren arrived to school with a box of sweet lemon tea. We took turns sipping from it during recess, safe in the big shadow of a leafy maple.

A year after that, on a Saturday, Ren came over to watch *Sailor Moon*. It was the first time I had another boy in my room.

"What's this?" he asked, tapping his bare foot on a hardened, discolored lump on our carpet.

I scrambled to explain how it used to be a soy sauce stain; how, in a panic, I caked the spot with baking soda like the cleaning blog said, but it only got worse. How when Mom felt the lump, I braced myself for one of her fits. But she just shook her head, so tired, defeated, to find another thing in our house that I'd ruined.

Ren looked like he was listening, but his eyes flicked around, landing on my curtains, which Mom make-shifted out of *Lion King* bedsheets; my light switch, split down the center with a huge crack we didn't have the money to fix.

*Mom is doing her best,* I thought, glaring at Ren. *Don't you dare judge us.*

But Ren didn't say anything about my curtains or my huge crack. Instead, he flopped onto my bed. "So what's this life-changing thing you want me to see?"

I logged on to Mom's old laptop, a Dell that overheated if you had too many applications open at once. The trick was to give the laptop enough breaks and never leave it on your actual lap. "Ready?"

There, belly-down on my mattress, shoulder to shoulder, Ren and I watched *Sailor Moon* with subtitles on. Or Ren did. I mostly peeked at him for his reactions; his nose, wrinkled at the muted colors ("Whoa, it's *so* nineties"); his eyebrows, knitted when the theme song played.

"Waiiiit," he whined, tugging on my sleeve. "Please pause." Ren needed more time to read the lyrics.

*But I have a simple heart, so what can I do?*

*My heart is a kaleidoscope.*

I blushed and said the lyrics made no sense, but Ren held a small fist to his chest. Like he could keep the song in there with him, safe. Absorb all its colors.

Later, the Dell's fan whirred and whirred, exhausted. I worried Mom's laptop would shut down, break whatever spell the show held over him.

"Do you like it so far?"

Ren didn't reply. A mystery man swirled in with a black cape and top hat.

“Who’s that?” Ren asked. He had a cool, casual tone that didn’t match how much he was leaning in.

“Tuxedo Mask. He pops in randomly to tell Sailor Moon to believe in herself. But he doesn’t save the day. She does. Because this show is for feminists.”

“Huh” is all Ren said, and he got really quiet.

It occurred to me then, while Tuxedo Mask leapt out of frame, that Ren might have been feeling the same humming, warm feeling I had in my belly when I first saw him, or whenever I stood close enough to Puppy Chow to smell his sunscreen.

“He’s so cool!” I blurted. “Tuxedo Mask. Isn’t he?”

Ren didn’t respond immediately. Which is how I knew he knew.

Knew *cool* meant more than cool.

Knew *cool* was a confession I had left on the cushion between us like a hard candy. My hands trembled and my heart hammered for a thousand years before Ren finally said, “Cool.” He tried the word out. Tasted it. “Yeah,” he said, a bit out of breath. “He’s cool.”

Suddenly, it didn’t matter that my curtains were bedsheets, that there was a massive, sad lump in my carpet. Ren Hsu thought Tuxedo Mask was cool.

It wasn’t just me anymore.

# 6

WHAT'S THIS?" MOM ASKS WHEN I FIND HER IN THE laundry room, unloading the dryer. No *hello.* No *happy Monday*. Not even my name.

"What's what?"

Mom waves my tufted pineapple shirt in front of my face. The shirt I left in the dryer, that I wore to the club three nights ago. At first, I'm not sure what it is Mom wants me to see. Until I see it. Twinkling on her thumb. Sprinkling my collar.

Glitter.

I blink, to buy time. Mom never found out about Friday night. Not about the club or the borrowed IDs. How could she when, it turned out, she was too busy playing slots at Casino Niagara with Auntie Lily and Carmen and Rose? The first missed call was to say Mr. Huang let her off early. The rest were to ask for my favorite number, my locker combination, my predicted AP scores. Lucky numbers for bingo.

We got away with it, I texted Ren. Lucky us. But for some reason, I didn't hit send.

"Well?" Mom says. She pinches off more glitter.

*Say it's for an art project,* I think wildly. *Say you got glitter bombed!* I fumble for a better excuse, a white lie, a thread of plausible deniability. Then Mom folds her arms, eyes flashing, and everything unspools around me.

"It's Ren's," I hear myself squeak.

Mom narrows her eyes.

"It's true!" I insist, because it is. Glitter is Ren's thing, not mine. But even days after seeing him I'll still find the stuff clinging onto me. Winking off my skin in the shower. Dusting my pillow. I used to pretend it was leftover magic, proof Ren and I had slipped into Narnia or Neverland, somewhere Not Markville. But now, seeing that glitter reminds me of Dukes and spit. The woods. A thicket.

A white, white hand—

"Are you listening?" Mom's voice brings me back. "You said you were studying Friday night." Mom plants her hands on her hips, what a parent might do if they smelled alcohol on your breath or found a joint in your pocket. She might have preferred that. Better for your son to be a stoner than Tinker Bell. "What were you two doing, *really*?"

"Nothing!" I clasp my hands in front of me like a pious Pilgrim in a witch trial. Goody Colin, wrongly accused. "We *were* studying. Ren just likes makeup. For, you know, the vibes..."

Mom just keeps staring. She does this for such a long time, without blinking, that I realize she is examining my face. Not for evidence of lies but for traces of lipstick. Eyeshadow. And she is so obvious, so shameless about it, like she *wants* me to feel studied. Like it is her right.

I want to scream—at her, then at myself for not screaming.

"You know I don't like this," Mom finally says. She unloads the rest of the dryer.

Ren lives on Sweet Pea Road in a house the color of a robin egg. As I round the corner, I see the tip of its gabled roof peeking over the white fence, then the huge bay window looking into Ren's room. His blinds are up, so I see his childhood bike in there, too, pink as ever, hanging down from his ceiling like an art installation, or a Christmas ornament. Suspended on chicken-wire fairy lights.

When I squint, I see the bike's silver bell, too.

I break into a smile once I find him waiting for me on the veranda, sitting on the top step. School blazer. Black tie. I'm about to yell his name. But something about seeing him there, alone, hugging his knees, stops me.

Ren and I haven't talked since Friday night. Not about the woods, the Dukes, or anything else. Not a single DM. What was there left to say when, according to Ren, I had imagined that hand, those names? Because names don't just vanish, and neither do strange men. If only I had been told that I imagined the rest of it, too.

The Dukes, leering.

Ren, dropping my hand.

Ren, leaving it there while my fingers got cold.

Now, on the veranda, he still hasn't seen me. He's too busy fiddling with something long and thin, holding it up to the light. A twig?

No...he's plucking things off it, one by one. My breath hitches when I see what they are. Petals. *Bluebells.* Did Ren return to the forest to pick more of them?

I clear my throat to get his attention.

Ren's head snaps up. He breaks into a smile. Then he tosses aside the naked stem and flies down the porch steps.

"'Sup, slut?" Our standard greeting, while he links an arm through mine. And we head off, like always. Like nothing has changed. Why would it?

Ren cackles after I've updated him with my morning report. "All that drama for *glitter*? And thanks for throwing me under the bus."

"I panicked! I'm sorry."

Ren gives me an imperious look-down. "You are forgiven. Because unlike you, I support homosexuals."

We wait at the stop sign at Honeysuckle Road and Princess Street. Ren uncaps a tube of Kissy-Kissy Butter Balm and, per our morning ritual, moves in with it to consecrate my lips. But then a van crawls to a stop beside us, and for one wild second, I imagine the Dukes in there, sneering. But by the time I see it's just a mother driving with her kid in the back seat, swiping his iPad, I've already pulled away. Ren doesn't say anything as he recaps the tube.

"Nooo!" I fuss, hating the hurt look on his face. Hating that I put it there. "Give it. Please. I need my lips *juicy*!" I pucker them and, with a playful sigh of exasperation, Ren starts dabbing again. It tastes like browned butter.

"My dad gave me a morning lecture, too," Ren says, though, unsurprisingly, it didn't seem to take. His eyelashes are already curled, his cheeks dewy with his blush of choice, Peachy Fucking Keen. A rhinestone sparkles above his lip like a beauty mark. Since tenth grade, Ren has flittered out of his home in jewel tones and metallic sheens and feather cuffs—even when the Hsus have begged him not to go out dressed like a slutty hummingbird. Which, for Mom, is the problem: that his parents *beg*. That they even *ask*.

"Are they white?" Mom demanded of me once, in her car. "*Let's make this a family discussion.* No," she said, smacking the dashboard. "Sometimes you have to *tell* them. Be a parent. Or your kid ends up looking like *that*."

*We should all be so lucky,* I think as Ren tilts his heavenly face at me, admiring his technique.

"Want me to do your eyes?"

"You better."

Ren produces a vial of clear mascara. "Parents are so irrational." He tuts with a twist of his wand. "And *we're* supposed to be compassionate? *It's not their fault. It's trauma. They all have trauma!* But I'll tell you what I think." Ren leans in, eyes twinkling with wisdom and periwinkle shadow. "I don't think it has anything to do with intergenerational trauma. I think our parents are just assholes!" He caps his mascara. "Ready?"

I blink. My eyelashes are fluttery. Full.

"One second." I dig into my knapsack for my slip of gold stars. I peel off the shimmeriest one and press it below my eye like a teardrop. "Ready."

Ren squints at my sticker. "Please don't tell me you still give yourself gold stars."

"Only when I get full marks."

Another exasperated sigh. "Oh, Colin. How will I protect you from bullies when *I* want to bully you?"

The trek to school is less than ten minutes. Luckily, time dilates when Ren and I walk together, meaning we have the luxury to talk about everything.

At 8:15, it's game theory.

"Hypothetically," I start, while Ren jabs the button for the crosswalk, "if Kirby swallows a sexy muscle man, will he *become* sexy?"

By 8:18, anatomy.

"I *swear*," Ren cries, pinching the flabbiest part of my elbow. "This is called a weenis!"

Four minutes later, when we arrive on campus, Ren is deep into political philosophy. "So let's say we're on a gay cruise and we get shipwrecked on an island," he postulates. "Our key to survival? We *organize*. Tops are hunters. Bottoms are gatherers."

"What about verses?"

Ren's already thought of that. "Administration and sewing."

"What about me?" I skip up the stone steps leading to the entrance, two at a time. "On this island, what's my role?"

"Flesh-light."

*"Rennn!"* I move to whup his shoulder, but he ducks away, laughing his tinkling laugh that makes me laugh, too. How did I ever think a couple of bigots could change *this*?

By the front doors, Ren takes a step back and looks up at the building. "Can you believe it?" he asks fondly. "Just two more months..."

"Whatever. You hate it here."

"Do not!"

I bump my shoulder into his and look up at the building with him. Look up at the cross-shaped window on the third floor, where the chapel is.

Ours is not the school you read about in books or manifest on vision boards—gothic towers with spiral staircases and great halls. Gargoyles craning their necks over lintels, guarding the students. Built in the eighties, St. Brandon's sits at the top of a muddy hill, slablike and gray. The first time Ren laid eyes on the sad concrete building, he said it was like standing before someone's grave, where love of learning comes to die.

I didn't hate it, and still don't. Not the brutalist architecture. Not the green mold staining the side of the building that, in good lighting, one can mistake for spilling ivy. Not the linoleum floors squeaking under our shoes as we enter the lobby. When we pass the trophy case, Ren wonders out loud why we don't have more trophies. But I'm not looking in there.

I'm looking at *them*, huddled by the doorway leading to the stairwell. Towering and beautiful, grinning like Labrador retrievers. The Big Spoon Boys. Boys like Jonah, Dillon, Puppy Chow. Boys who peel their sweaty shirts off in the summer to play soccer on the pitch in the blistering sun. Boys who share gym motivation videos on their socials, with titles like "Pain Is You, Getting Stronger."

One time on our walk home, Ren waded through the comments section of a video Puppy linked, a mash-up of an Arnold Schwarzenegger interview and the Lazarus Pit montage in *The Dark Knight Rises*.

"What is it with straight guys and Batman?" Ren had asked me, baffled. When I insisted maybe Puppy Chow wanted to be dark and mysterious, Ren snorted back with, "Last week I saw him stuff Jonah's face into his armpit!"

Which made me unspeakably jealous.

Puppy never tried that with *my* face.

Right now, the Big Spoon Boys are hugging one another in that bro-ish, noncommittal way that triples as a high-five and a firm pat on the back. It is a shame. Because what must it feel like, to get a *real* hug from one of them? To become swaddled in those toned arms, to sink your whole face into their pumped-up pecs? We call them the Big Spoon Boys because we see all that potential for snuggles, wasted.

As Ren and I draw near, I can feel the heat coming off their bodies. Or is that me, my face, burning up? I tug each sleeve of my St. Brandon's sweater until they look oversize. Until I become petite.

Ren glances at my stretched-out sleeves. "Who's a smol, sexy baby?"

"Shut up," I mutter, pinching his weenis.

"Guys like *confidence,*" Ren decrees as we leave the Big Spoon Boys behind. "At least make direct eye contact with them."

I don't dignify this with a response. Because Ren doesn't get it. It's easier to pretend boys are looking at you when you don't look back. Easier to pretend they're like Weeping Angels in *Doctor Who,* or ghosts playing peekaboo with Mario. Cute boys who only reach for you desperately the second you turn away.

But once we've climbed the top of the stairwell and I hear one of them coming for us, I wonder if my make-believe has turned real.

"Hey, Ren." A Big Spoon Boy taps him on the shoulder.

"Oh." Ren fixes a smile. "Hi, Dave."

Aka Plopping Dave, because Ren says his personality is like

the sound a spoonful of plain yogurt makes when you drop it back into its cup.

*Plop.*

Right now, Plopping Dave's eyes have the half-lidded, glazed look of someone trying too hard to look bored, even though he's out of breath.

"How was your weekend?" he manages to ask Ren (with exaggerated non-feeling).

"Good," Ren answers (with just a scooch more).

Then he chews on his bottom lip.

"Good," Plopping Dave repeats, his glassy eyes never leaving Ren's mouth. "It's good that you're good." He balls his hands into fists that bump into his sides. One after the other, back and forth, like Newton's cradle. Ren surveys him with scientific interest.

"Mine was good, too."

"*Jesus,* Colin!" Dave says, just noticing me. He clears his throat. "Well, okay. Nice to hear." Then, when all of us just stand there, smiling, Plopping Dave murmurs, "Bye," and takes off.

We wait until he's out of earshot, until the two of us have flown deeper into the corridor, our insides frothy with pent-up giggles, and by the time we reach Ren's locker, we're exploding with it. A group of juniors nearby throw us a withering look.

"Dave's adorable," I say, ignoring them. "You should ask him to prom."

*"Plopping Dave?"* Ren enters his locker combination. As he turns the dial, the numbers play inside me like a love ballad.

66-86-22. Ren gave me free rein over his locker in freshman year, when they assigned me the rusty one next to Peter Chen. "Dave's nice, but he's not my type."

"Then don't bite your lip at him!" I cross my arms. "Your behavior is both sexy *and* cruel."

Ren flashes me an impish grin over his shoulder. "It was barely a nibble. Besides," Ren continues with a fierce tug on his locker door. It's jammed. "Plopping Dave doesn't even acknowledge you when we're together. So minus thirty points."

"Aww." I mime catching Ren's words and stuffing them inside my pocket. "You're a solid friend."

"I'm a *great* friend."

Ren gives his door a final tug and it squeaks open, spilling out his geography textbook, a protractor, and a pocket-size French dictionary. These days, I can't muster the strength to look inside Ren's locker. It's always been messy, but now it's like a game of *Tetris* where all the pieces stack on top of one another without locking.

I segue. "Please note that when we live together, all *this*"—I gesture to the chaos—"is unacceptable."

Ren sticks out his tongue.

This is our plan: After graduation, the two of us will move to the east coast. We'll live downtown and rent something affordable, like a one bedroom or a studio. We'll take classes in the day and at night groove at the gay club called Mirror; or sit wide-eyed through poetry readings about sapphic love at the feminist bookstore. We'll co-parent a lop-eared bunny and call him Rabbit Downey Junior.

I will pay my half of rent with a combination of scholarships, student loans, and work placements offered through my department. Or maybe I'll stack and shelve dusty old books at the university library.

I hope by then Ren will address his hoarding problem.

Right now, he is trying to pull something out of his locker without triggering an avalanche. When he is successful, I see it's his sketchbook with the collage cover. It has SpongeBob stickers and *Seventeen* cutouts and fortune cookie slips with useless fortunes.

*You like Chinese food.*

*You will drive a car.*

"Back to the topic." Ren pouts at his magnetized mirror. "According to Baby Gap, Plopping Dave says he doesn't even like guys." Ren slams his door shut and clicks his lock. "At most, he's curious. And what did we say about confused, mediocre straight boys?"

But Ren stops. Because there mine is now, on the other side of the corridor, talking to our Latin teacher, Mrs. Reid. His hands are stuffed into his pockets and he's rocking back and forth on his heels, like a big kid.

Ferris.

Before he can turn his shaggy head in our direction, before I can see his eyes, light gray, *piercing,* Ren grabs the front of my sweater and yanks me with him, into the chapel.

"Get your paws off me!" I huff, smacking them away. "I wasn't going to *talk* to him."

"You had that look," Ren says, flouncing down the aisle between the benches. He peeks into each row to make sure no one is eavesdropping. Once he confirms the chapel is all clear, that it is just us and the Holy Spirit, judging our life choices, Ren turns to me, fingers tented, almost in prayer. "You two aren't good for each other. Ask me why."

Big sigh. "Why?"

"Because he's insufferable." Ren reaches over and tucks a fly-away hair behind my ear. "Colin, he's a man who wants to major in *philosophy.* I don't want that life for you." His voice cracks with exaggerated heartbreak. I crack a smile back, to humor him. "He's not worth it."

*I know,* I'm about to say, but Ren interrupts. "And don't tell me 'you know.' You don't believe me yet, because you don't want to. But one day you'll see. He's not worth it."

I look up at the window, shaped like a cross, just to have something to look at. Everything inside me becomes small. "Then why does it hurt so much?"

"He rejected you," Ren says gently. "Of course that hurts."

I flinch at that word, *rejected.* Like I'm an old stuffie Ferris has tossed into a pile, with all the other things he's outgrown.

Our story—if we had one—is hard to summarize. A good summary distills the main points from the minor ones. The details that don't matter. But when I think about Ferris, all I remember are the details. Not just big events, like the first time Ferris sat across from me in Latin. Everything. The goofy smile when he explained his name's etymology (not Ferris like the wheel but like *Bueller's Day Off).* How, whenever we met at the Green Grotto to review conjugations, he always found a reason to lean in and read the drills over my shoulder. How after a month of us studying he reached for my hand under the table and squeezed it—*actually squeezed it.* How he said he wasn't sure if he liked guys, but maybe he could see himself dating one, dating *me.* How Ferris said this thing between us—whatever *this* was—needed to be a secret, for now. And I loved the sound of that word, *secret,* falling from his lips. Small, delicate, a photograph you'd slip into a locket and wear around your neck.

How that afternoon, I told Ren everything on the bleachers and he asked me, practically bouncing on the steel bench, "How do you feel?" And I said, "Pocket-size." Like I was something Ferris wanted to keep safe in a gilded cage. Perched on a soft cushion.

Pretty. Was that how he saw me?

If I had closed my eyes long enough, would I have seen it, too?

And then Ferris stopped. Two days after he held my hand. Stopped the meetings, stopped messaging. Stopped before our secret could even start.

How, right now in the chapel, Ren says it again. "He's not worth it." Like maybe this time I'll believe him.

# 7

I REMEMBER WHAT IT WAS LIKE TO BE A ROMANTIC, WITHout being hopeless. To want love the way other boys wanted to be astronauts or deep-sea explorers.

Two weeks before eighth-grade graduation, Ms. Edith told our class the human mind is a powerful organ. That if you picture something hard enough you can manifest it. She was talking about things like straight As in Calculus. The perfect hamburger essay. Boring stuff only I wanted to picture. But Ren had a better idea.

"What she said made me think of this really old movie," he told me later that day. We were in his bedroom, and his eyes were flickering, *electric*. "It was about witches."

We were kneeling on Ren's bed as he unloaded everything we had pillaged from Ms. Edith's supply closet. Glue and glitter and that month's edition of *Crushd*. This was when Mr. Hsu still forced us to leave the door open. But this time Ren kept it shut.

We needed privacy.

We were about to conjure something.

"There's this one scene with the two characters," he said. "The Owens sisters? Played by Nicole Kidman and that actress from *The Proposal.* And they make this collage of the perfect man. All the right features. The perfect nose. Perfect mouth. A jawline for days. And years later, one of the sisters meets him. Like her magic brought him to her."

"Wow," I breathed.

I looked around Ren's Strawberry Milkshake Room. I called his room that because, even then, there was pink everywhere, in his artwork, his linens. Not huge swaths of it, but blushes, accents. Ren had always loved pink as much as I did. Pink tufts of cotton candy. Pink frosting slathered on birthday cake. Pink you devour and keep devouring, even when it makes your teeth ache. Mom never let me own anything pink, so as a kid, I got my fix of it here.

"That stuff with the witches sounds like a horror move, Ren. Don't people like us die in those?"

"Not in this one." Ren ripped a picture of Dylan Sprouse right out of the magazine. "In this one, we don't die."

That night, under a fingernail moon, we snipped and tore and glued pieces of our favorite boys together. Mine had the boyish, wide-eyed look of Felix from Stray Kids and the plush lips of Tom Hardy. Then we printed out every love song that made us quiver with tears and mashed up the lyrics.

*I can't breathe*
*Can't get you off*
*I feel your love,*
*Please don't say*
*It's second hand.*

We chanted our lyrics to each other again and again.

"Isn't it tragic?" Ren said with a sigh.

I nodded. "And beautiful."

We made copies of these words and cut them into bite-size fortune cookie slips. We pasted them onto our collages, stuffed them into our boyfriends' parted lips as speech bubbles or attached them as tear-drop-shaped poetry leaking from their eyes.

When our faces were done, we laid them onto Ren's mattress like Frankenstein's monsters. They wanted to be made alive.

"Tell me about him," Ren said, holding up mine. "What's his name?"

I closed my eyes so it would come to me. "Cheddar."

"Cheddar?"

"It's what his friends call him. He's in a band."

"Well, okay. How did you two meet?"

I said at one of his shows, backstage. Cheddar played the guitar and I would soon learn that he read Byron and was still just a junior at St. Brandon's. By the time I started there, I would be the ingenue freshman Cheddar would feel this inexplicable urge to protect.

"Protective, yes!" Ren said, penciling the word down into our list of Good Boyfriend Qualities.

"Like—like—like," I continued, catching his hype, "like if Peter Chen tried picking on me, Cheddar would pull up a chair and wrap his big arm around my shoulders. Pull me right into his body, with everyone looking."

"And, um, he would smell like sandalwood."

"And I would feel petite."

"Also," Ren whispered, a hungry look in his eyes, "he's *possessive*."

*Oh, yes,* I thought. That hungry-for-you kind of possessive. The possessive that says, *You're mine,* out of fear. Because Cheddar *would* be afraid. No matter how much tougher he was than me, how much stronger, how much more of a man. He would be afraid of me leaving him. Love, sex, fear—to my eighth-grade brain, they were all the same. I guess they still are.

Possessive, yes. We needed to add that.

"Will he take you to prom?" Ren asked (back then, we still thought prom was cool).

I nodded, taking my collage from Ren and practically wrapping it over my face so Ren couldn't see my cheeks flushing. "And there..." I whispered this into Cheddar's mouth like I was breathing life into him. "...on the dance floor, I'll make my confession."

"What will you say?"

"I love you."

I heard a barely disguised *pffft.* "Everyone says that, Colin. Be original."

"Not *I* love you," I enunciated. "Ai love you. *Ai.*"

I thought about the Chinese dramas Mom watched late at night, where actors with heartbreakingly beautiful faces professed their love for each other under the rain. They used that word, *ai.*

In Mandarin, *ai* means love.

"So . . . *love* love you?" Ren untucked his ankles from under his bum and shook out the pins and needles. "Isn't that redundant?"

"It's an intensifier." I stared up at Ren's popcorn ceiling and imagined it was blooming with cherry blossoms—pale, pale white before they turn pink and fall. "Two loves for one boy. But I don't explain it to Cheddar. It's just for me. Because even though I'm saying it to him, it's still *mine.* My heart. My double love. You know?"

"I know," Ren said, so quickly but quietly that I believed him.

Then Ren showed me his. His first collage was called Billy. But Ren said when he finished making it, he didn't like it as much. So, he made a second.

I don't remember all the celebrities he used for that one, which parts. Only Robert Pattinson's nose because Ren liked *Twilight.* The weird thing about this second face was, it didn't have eyes. Ren said it was because he couldn't find the right ones. "And the eyes have to be perfect," Ren explained. "They're windows to the soul."

*Then this man is soulless,* I thought with a shudder. Because as Ren held the face up to the light, something about it seemed wrong, this lack of eyes, like holes in a mask.

*"I like watching you sleep,"* Ren said, staring through them. *"I find it fascinating."* He was doing his best impersonation of Edward Cullen, constipated with vampire lust.

I laughed even though his collage still scared me. "What's his name?"

"Marshall." Ren didn't even need to close his eyes to think about it. The name just dropped into his lap.

Marshall. I wrinkled my nose, thinking about men in helmets, men with guns. But Ren said the name reminded him more of marshes and castles and knights.

I wanted to be supportive. "How did you meet him?"

That's when Ren closed his eyes. Not like he was manifesting something but like it was actually happening. Like he was tuning this world out and peeking into the multiverse. "We're in a meadow. And he comes riding in on a horse."

"There's a *horse*?"

"He gets off it," Ren continued, eyes still closed. "Then he's holding my hand. His palm is rough, calloused. The kind of hands you have when you're good at yard work. And he's leading me up to this tree." Ren's words were spilling out of him faster, and I worried we would both slip on them. "And the branches, they're bleeding with apples. I want to taste one but I'm too short. I can't even reach the lowest-hanging one on my tippy-toes. So, Marshall leans over and picks it off for me."

And I swear, I heard it—the pluck. The rustle of wet leaves.

I heard the two of them laughing as dewdrops sprinkled over their heads. I saw the apple in Ren's hand, perfectly round. Candy red. Redder even than the one Eve bit into when she gave up Paradise.

At some point, I closed my eyes, too.

"What kind of apple is it, Ren?"

"The kind for wishing."

By the time I opened my eyes, Ren had his opened, as well. He was looking down at his collage. I thought I might see a sparkle in there, some glimmer of that magic remaining from the world we'd just left. But his eyes were tired without being dreamy. Like he was sad.

Sad he wasn't still in the meadow with Marshall.

Sad he was only in the Strawberry Milkshake Room with me.

We lidded the box and pressed both our palms on top. Closing our eyes, we channeled the power of the human mind. Of the Owens sisters.

We used our hearts, too, because we had both read in a children's picture book that when you love something hard enough you can make it real.

Ren doesn't take Religion with me because he had it last semester, a blessing he thanks God for every day. He says Religion is just a one-hour reminder for its students that they're all going to hell.

"All you kids care about is being cool and different," Mr. Frank hissed at us last week. "But do you know what would make you truly *iconic*?" Mr. Frank asked. "If, every day, before lunch, you did *this*." Mr. Frank folded his hands before him in prayer. "Show gratitude, for once in your lives!"

With that, our assignment: to memorize a speech about the power of God's Grace and recite it.

In front of everyone.

As I enter class, thoughts still swimming with Ferris, I hug my Catholic Youth Bible to my chest. The St. Augustine passage I printed out and memorized is sandwiched between its pages in Proverbs.

*I have a great deal of difficulty in climbing the rope of grace, and yet I do not let go.*

There's more, so much more, but if I hold his words to my heart long enough, maybe they will leave an impression there. Maybe I won't choke.

Mr. Frank hasn't arrived yet. Neither has the majority of class. This means I'm free to take my favorite seat at the back, near the window overlooking our founder statue's bald head. On the whiteboard, someone has written *Truly Iconic* in dry-erasable red. Peter, probably. Last week, he snuck up to the bulletin board and pinned an index card under Jesus's Eight Beatitudes: *Blessed are the porn stars, for they get paid to have sex.*

Before I can snap a picture of the whiteboard for Ren, Baby Gap is already wiping it clean. He doesn't like Mr. Frank, but he likes vandalism even less.

"Colin!" he says, seeing me. "I like that star on your face. It's real pretty." Then, before I can stutter a thank-you, "Are you going to prom? I didn't see your RSVP."

Baby Gap is our year's social rep. His name used to be Victor. Then, in tenth grade, a boy from St. Michael's broke his heart, and Baby Gap threw himself into weight lifting. Bulked until his deltoids ballooned into melons and his chest expanded two sizes too big for his medium-size golf shirts. Which, to this day, he continues to wear. (Another blessing Ren thanks God for every day.)

"I'm not really a prom person."

"Oh, but you have to go! We'll hang out. It'll be fun."

I titter, not for his thinly veiled grab for my prom fee (Baby Gap and I have *never* hung out). But because as he speaks to me—"Okay! Just think about it!"—he suddenly starts dribbling. Behind the back, under the leg.

But there is no ball.

Ren and I have observed this phenomenon before, with the Big Spoon Boys: where, in mid-conversation, they will inexplicably start bouncing or batting or tossing a phantom ball only straight boys can see. Or, in Baby Gap's case, the straight-passing.

"And wait till you see our venue," he says, taking a jump shot.

I assume it went in.

"Venue?" a voice says with a scoff.

I look up to see Blair trickling in with the other boys. He slides into the chair two tables ahead of mine. "Can we just call it the school gym?"

Baby Gap beams. He and Blair have been besties since ninth grade, the brawn to his brain. "It'll be spectacular. You'll see. When you inevitably decide to go."

"Absolutely not." Blair cracks open his textbook—*Campbell's Biology*, thirteenth edition. "I have a field studies project due the next morning. Blame Kincaid." With that, Blair flips ahead to our next section on keystone species (which I already read). Up close, I see he has fastened a rose to his collar, like a bolo tie. Not a garden rose, but the wild kind you find in meadows. It makes me think of Daphne, the nymph who sprouted into a tree to escape Apollo. I wonder if she looked a little like Blair. Which is wildly unfair. Beauty, brains—you should only get one.

Blair catches me staring. "Yes?"

I fumble for something, anything, to not seem like a creep. "I don't remember Kincaid assigning us a field studies project."

"Extra credit." Blair returns to his reading. "Wildflower diversity in Birchmount Forest."

Baby Gap's eyes flit between us. "You both need lives outside studying. Why don't you..." But I don't hear the rest.

Because now I'm looking outside.

Past the founder's statue to the tree line hemming in our campus grounds, Birchmount Forest looks as it always has during the day. Rows of pale trees with pale eyes. I shudder from the sudden draft rattling the windows. Or from the sense, prickling somewhere in my lizard brain, of a person out there, waiting in the trees, looking back. The windowpane rattles again, as though small hands, many of them, are knocking. *Come outside and play.*

Baby Gap taps me on the shoulder. "Take my word for it. Years from now, you'll regret not going to your prom."

"Ren and I were gonna stay in."

Baby Gap knits his brow. "Really? That's not what Ren said."

I'm about to ask what he means when Mr. Frank lumbers in. "Mr. Nguyen, put that away," he snips as he dumps a briefcase onto his desk. Mr. Frank means the protein bar Baby Gap has finished unwrapping. It smells like egg breath and fart. "You know my policy on eating in class."

"But, sir! My one-hour window!"

"And, Mr. Ong," he says slowly, his gaze drifting my way like a glacier. "Earlier, in the corridor, did I see you carrying that?" He eyes the Youth Bible I'm still hugging to my chest. When I nod, he drawls, "Next time, keep it in your bag between classes? If you drop it into a puddle or lose it, what then?" He uses that *isn't-it-obvious* tone some teachers save exclusively for students—because they know kids are the only ones who will let them get away with it.

"Now," Mr. Frank continues. "*Assignments.* Your orals! Oh, grow up, Mr. Chen," he groans when Peter snorts. "If anyone wants to volunteer to read out their assignment, please do. If not, I will happily do it for you."

A long, painful pause from everyone. I shrink into my chair. Even though I'm staring down at my shaking hands I can feel Mr. Frank's eyes land on the top of my head. "Why don't we start with Mr. Ong—"

But then a chair scrapes and Blair is already making his way to the front of class. The classroom walls go *click-click-click* because of his heels.

"Mr. Prince," Mr. Frank calls out. "Let us hear it."

Three rows to my left, Peter Chen snickers. He leans back in his chair to whisper something into Luca Ferrari's ear. Loud enough for me, for Baby Gap, for Blair to hear. "Nice *flower.*"

Blair throws him a look made of rattlesnake venom. "Where have you been?"

He says it in such a low voice, leveling Peter's stare, that at first we all think these words are meant for him alone. Then Blair practically screams to the heavens, "Where have you been! *Where have you been?!*" and we realize this is part of his act. He jabs a finger in Peter's direction: Peter, who isn't laughing for once or smirking. Peter, who stares back blankly.

Blair folds his arms and says nothing more. He allows this silence to stretch on and on until it goes taut. Until Peter realizes he is meant to break it.

He asks more than says, "I'm . . . here?"

Blair tosses his head back and delivers a wretched laugh. "And where were you twenty years ago? Ten years ago? Where were you when I was new? When I was one of those innocent, young maidens you always come to? How dare you," he hisses. Then shrieks, "*How dare you!*" His eyes start welling.

Something about Blair's performance, it feels like recognizing a face at a coffee shop without quite placing the person. From where in the Bible did Blair pull this passage? Psalms? Proverbs? It's only when Baby Gap snickers into his knuckles that I'm brought back to story time in second grade, when Ms. Nichols played *The Last Unicorn.* Blair is acting out the scene where Molly Grue meets the unicorn for the first time. I look around, but no one else, not even Mr. Frank, seems to twig.

As for Peter, his eyes flit across Blair's fingernails, slicked bloodred, like they might soon be bloodier. Like Blair means to dive at him and use them to tear him apart.

Instead, Blair falls to his knees and dips his head with a swan's grace so we can see nothing of his face. Only hear his voice, whittled down into something sad he drops into his cupped hand.

"How dare you come to me now"—his voice is a sigh—"when I am this?"

He doesn't move. No one does. The whole world is still.

And scene.

"Whoa."

I say this before I can stop myself. It shudders out of me and ripples across this classroom, this school. The whole city of Markville quivers, or I do. Then I'm clapping and Baby Gap is clapping, and why are we the only ones clapping?

Blair doesn't care. He rises and saunters back to his seat. He didn't do this for the applause. He did this for the A. There is no question on his face he has earned it.

"Well," Mr. Frank says at last. "The assignment was to discuss God's Grace. How it moves you." He waits for Blair, St. Brandon's star pupil, the boy who captained Crystal Chemistry Club in our sophomore year and can memorize the first eighty-six digits of pi—Mr. Frank waits for this boy who is smarter than all of us to explain himself or apologize. When Blair only stares back, fiddling absently with the wild rose in his collar, Mr. Frank clears his throat. "That reading—where was it from?"

"Book of Peter."

"I— Is it?" But Mr. Frank does not challenge this. He just scans his attendance sheet to call out the next student.

And I should volunteer, after seeing Blair put Peter and Mr. Frank in their place. Like the time Ren did that to Mom years ago on his bike. I should feel empowered seeing boys like Ren and Blair, glittery boys, flower boys, boys like me, thriving.

But I look down at my hands as Mr. Frank calls Mark Warren up. Ren and Blair are nothing like me. Boys like them shine. Boys like me stay hidden.

# 9

During lunch, I look for Ren in the chapel. Long ago, we gave up on eating in the cafeteria, where the seniors at the time would scream "HEY!" to jump-scare freshmen clueless enough to pass along their table. But the chapel was quiet, always empty of worshippers. Under its tapered ceiling and the light filtering through the cross-shaped window, dust motes swirling, Ren and I found our sanctuary. For the last four years we've been sneaking in our lunches and eating them in the pews, Jamaican patties and strawberry-cream Pockys and boxed chrysanthemum teas. One of us keeps an eye on the door in case old Brother Ambrose wobbles in. He did catch us eating the one time, but all he did was wink.

Now, as I enter the chapel, I see just one person seated in the nave, the back of his pearly head a shock of white under the light.

I'm about to join Ren, about to unload my armful of books into the pew next to him, when I hear him talking to himself.

"Wait" and "please" and "just a friend"—muttered under his breath.

Is Ren praying?

He can't be. He's not religious.

Then he says "Stop," and I do; I freeze by the doorway, even though he's not talking to me. Even though he doesn't know I'm here.

Praying or not, this feels like an intrusion. But as I move to slip out, my one free hand wrapped around the door handle, I hear him speak.

Not Ren.

Someone else.

"Don't."

Everything spills out of my arms and clatters around me in a mess. I bend down to gather them into my lap—my Norton anthology of Shakespeare, my flash cards for European history. My mechanical pencil with the Bao push, rolling to a stop at the font.

"Colin? Is that you?"

I look up. Ren doesn't turn around after he's called for me. He remains seated on the bench, staring ahead at the pulpit. Something about his stillness—like a statue, like the Virgin Mary looking down at us from the altar through her marble eyes—makes me want to become still, too.

"'Sup!" I cry out.

Ren doesn't respond, doesn't move an inch as I squeak down the aisle to his pew. And once I'm standing in front of him, facing him, Ren still doesn't move. Doesn't even flit his eyes up to meet mine.

"Were you spying on me?"

"I wasn't," I start. And when Ren finally turns his head to look me in the eyes, unblinking, I add, "It's *true.* Anyway, who were you talking to?"

Ren makes a show of scanning the room. "We're in the chapel, aren't we? So that must mean I was praying."

I wince. It's the *isn't-it-obvious* tone Mr. Frank used on me in class, a tone I never thought I'd hear from Ren. "I thought I heard—"

"What? What did you hear?"

"Someone else." Someone new but also familiar.

"I don't see anyone here but us," Ren says simply. "Do you?"

The chapel, of course, is empty. But I heard someone else, didn't I? A deeper voice.

Ren rises from the pew and squeezes past me. "I'm starving. Let's get lunch." His voice is warm now, sweet, sickly honey.

I look down. There, scattered on the bench where Ren left them.

Blue petals.

"Colin?" I hear him call from the exit. When I look up, he's watching me, his back leaning against the door. "You good?"

"I'm great." I even smile as I say it. I try to ignore that prickling again in my lizard brain. It is the first time I have ever kept something from Ren: the suspicion that, for once, he is keeping something from me.

LOOK WHAT I FOUND," REN SAYS, LEADING US INTO HIS bedroom. School ended on a ho-hum note, but the walk here was fun. "I dug it up last night."

The smoldering face of a man looks up at me from Ren's hardwood floor. Striking. Familiar. He has hollow cheekbones and full, girlish lips. I don't remember the magazine where we found his face, just that when we did, we felt shivers all over. We knew he'd be perfect for our shoebox lid.

"Our Boyfriend Box!" I cry. "Are the other faces still there?"

"Check."

I slip off the lid and find three human faces inside—Billy, Cheddar, Marshall. Identical to how we left them five years before. I re-lid the box, blushing. *Remembering.* "Oh God. We were such horny eighth graders! Where did you find it?"

"Back of the closet, with my piano certificates. Spring cleaning."

I look around Ren's room. It *does* look cleaner. Ren has even framed some of his artwork. I see his latest pastel drawing hanging over his desk, the one of a duck wearing a pink raincoat and pink boots.

"Got my grade back for that." Ren sighs. "B plus."

I think it's lovely. "You should make a million prints of it and sell them on Etsy." Something gold winks at me from Ren's nightstand. I light up when I see what it is. "Oh, Ren! Your kaleidoscope. I thought you lost it!"

"Are you about to get nostalgic about everything?"

"Obviously. It's our final year." I hold up the kaleidoscope. It's tiny, barely the size of a lighter.

The first time I held it I was just a freshman, high off the first paycheck I'd earned from our school's peer tutoring program. I took the subway downtown to a thrift store called Box of Delights and peeled through racks of acid-washed jeans and mesh tops. I dug through dishes heaped with mood rings and power beads.

Then I found the kaleidoscope. I looked through its fish-eye lens and rubbed a thumb along the spidery engraving on its brass tube.

*Wondrous.*

I thought, *Ren would love you.*

And he did, for all of two months.

"My heart broke when it went missing," Ren says.

"You mean when you lost it."

"I thought Peter stole it! But it was under my bed the whole time. Still works like a charm, though. Look."

I stare through the eyepiece and see many Rens, waving back. Spinning. It reminds me of that question, *How many angels can dance on the head of a pin?* Only now there's an answer:

About two hundred angels, every one of them beaming. And they all look like my best friend.

"I bet Halifax has a ton of thrift stores," I say. "Ooh! We should spend a whole day hunting for them."

Which is when the Spinning Rens stop smiling. All two hundred faces turn away from me. "About that..."

Then he cuts off when a hundred new faces swim into my field of vision. A man with Ren's perfect eyes and perfect nose. I lower the kaleidoscope.

"This is yours," Mr. Hsu says, dropping a cream envelope onto Ren's desk. I sit up straighter and fold my hands into my lap, a sign they have no intention of undressing his son. It's been years since Mr. Hsu asked Ren to keep his door open when it's just the two of us in his room. Still, I keep my hands folded for him to see.

"Your deposit," Mr. Hsu tells Ren with a tap of the envelope. "Remember to mail it by tomorrow."

For some reason, Ren flashes me a look before waving his dad out. "Okay, I will. Byeeee."

Mr. Hsu frowns. "Ren, this is important. Green College won't hold on to your spot if this arrives late." Then, before I can react, before I can even process this bombshell of news Mr. Hsu has lobbed into my life, he turns to me. "Colin."

"Hello, Mr. Hsu," I hear myself say.

Ren pretends he isn't shivering from my icy glare while his dad powers through the Asian dad pleasantries. *Are you still getting good grades? Did you pick a university? Win any scholarships?*

I answer in the affirmative to all three. Then Mr. Hsu says Mom must be very proud and I say she is (even though she isn't) because I want him to leave. And he does, muttering something about melons on his way out.

As soon as he's out of earshot, I round on Ren.

"Now, Colin," he starts, waving his hands in front of me like two white flags. "Before you totally queen out—"

"Green College?"

Ren winces at my shrill pitch, as high as a banshee's wail. But can anyone blame me? If it feels like something inside you has died, why shouldn't you herald it? Why shouldn't you scream?

Ren's eyes flit around the room, in search of a glittery distraction to lob my way. "Have I ever told you how gorgeous you are?"

"Green fucking College in *Vancouver*?"

*"Shhh."* Ren presses a finger to my lips. "Hush now. You're pretty."

I swat his hand away. "Stop trying to make me laugh. I don't want to laugh! What happened to Halifax? Me, King's. You,

MCAD." I point between us. "What happened to living off campus, together? We had a *plan*."

"I *know*," Ren says, sounding miserable. "I know we had a plan. But then they sent me this pamphlet and..." Ren slides open his desk drawer and produces the document with a shaky hand, like he's handling a murder weapon. "Their illustration program is *really* good. Please don't be mad, Colin."

I realize he's holding out the pamphlet so I can take it. And I do, to block his face. I flip through its glossy pages without looking at any of them.

Green fucking College. Green like the magic on poisoned apples and cursed spinning wheels.

When I reach the end of the pamphlet, I ask, "This is what you want?"

"Yes," Ren says without a smidge of hesitation. And my heart snags on it, this one simple word.

"Then..." *Liar! Traitor! How could you make this decision without telling me first?* "Okay."

"Okay?" Ren asks. "You mean it?"

I feel myself nod.

Ren closes the gap between us and pulls me into a hug, before I can duck away from him. The pamphlet crunches between our chests.

"Okay," I repeat. My reply feels hollow but heavy at the same time. "This is a good lesson in not being, you know, codependent."

"But you can *visit*," Ren insists, releasing me. "On long weekends or holidays. You don't have to come back here to your mom. You can stay with me. Oh, and you'll love it there, Colin. We're right on a peninsula!"

*Peninsula.* It conjures images of palm trees and a glittering open sea and stupid, beautiful people strolling along stupid beaches with orange flowers pinned into their stupid hair. "Have fun being Moana."

Ren gives a dry laugh. "It's *Vancouver.* Or, sorry, 'the Pacific Northwest.'" He corrects himself with air quotes. "Oh, and Ms. Paul put me in touch with someone there, a former student. They said there's this pathway to this grove, and at night, if you listen closely, you can hear owls talking to each other."

"Suspicious behavior, I'd say."

*"And in the summer,"* Ren talks over me, "you'll find starfish along the harbor. And sea lions, too, poking their whiskered heads out of the tide." Ren bites his lip. I forgot how weirdly excited he could get about the sea. Ren's dream is to be an artist, but his first love was marine biology, the classic pipeline for intellectual hotties.

I try to sound happy for him. "This place sounds great, Ren. Truly. It's so exciting."

"Yeah?" Ren smiles down at the pamphlet. I smile down at it, too. We both sit there, smiling at no one. "You forgive me?"

"There's nothing to forgive. I'm happy for you."

Maybe it's the way I say *happy,* like I'm not, that makes Ren fold up the pamphlet and leave it on his desk. He walks over to his bike hanging by the window and looks through its spokes, at the open road outside.

So I can't see his face.

So we can both pretend the whole ocean wasn't just in his eyes.

"I really do want you to visit," he says quietly. "I'll visit, too. Ms. Paul says it's normal to be sad about change."

"I'm not sad," I say too quickly. A half lie.

I'm not sad about change. I'm sad about what was lost. Ren and I are each other's support system, our found family. We were supposed to cobble together a life with what little we had, and it wouldn't be glamorous or cheap, but it would have been ours.

At what point did he stop wanting that?

Why does this feel like a breakup?

I don't say any of this out loud. I just say, "I hope this means I won't have to live on campus. Share a bathroom with the whole floor..."

Ren nods like he gets it.

When the house gets this quiet it feels haunted. Especially the kitchen. This is, after all, where I came out to her, where our relationship died. Four years later, I can still hear her crying.

*"I don't want this,"* she sobbed to me in Hakka, again and again. She accused me of being gay just to spite her.

I should have screamed. Instead, I asked, "Do you know how hard this is for me?"

"Do *you* know how hard this is for *me*?" she echoed. Mom did this a lot in arguments: turned herself into a talking mirror. As though repeating my question could make me mistake my pain for hers. As though she was the only real person, and I was the reflection.

"This hurts. The way you're acting right now, Mom. It *hurts*." My voice sounded so small, and I hated myself for it. Hated myself for calling her *Mom*. Hated myself for thinking this would move her. "Don't you see you're hurting me?"

"Don't *you* see *you're* hurting *me*?" Mom folded her arms and gave a sickening shake of her head.

*You are a child,* I thought. *You are a child, when all I want right now is a parent.*

After that, Mom started disappearing.

I'd wake up on a Saturday morning and hear the absence of dishes clinking in the kitchen or the dryer roaring. Later, I would discover she was off on a day trip with Auntie Carmen or Rose at the casino, or across the border in Buffalo. I'd find things like toothpicks and receipts and hard candies strewn about and wonder if she had left them for me to find. A trail of Easter eggs pointing to all the other places she'd rather be than here with me.

On the first Saturday she disappeared, Ren let himself in. He found me ducking under my covers, where I had tried to swaddle myself, baby-style.

"That bad?" he asked.

When I didn't reply, didn't move, he slipped a hand under the covers and pressed it into mine. He squeezed until they both felt warm, became one sweaty hand. "What happened? What did she say to you?" And, when still I said nothing, "How is your heart?"

So I told Ren all of it. My whole wretched tale.

By the time I was done, Ren had already climbed into my bed. We sat across from each other, sheets draped over our heads like a circus tent, our faces glowing in the blue light of Ren's phone. "Oh, Colin. I'm really sorry."

"I feel…" I choked. I didn't know what I was feeling, because there was so much of it. It felt enormous and inevitable. I'd always known this would happen, hadn't I? I'd known Mom's love wasn't simply conditional, but borrowed. That at some point I would have to give it back.

"I know," Ren said. He pressed his forehead against mine. Like he could take some of that wreckage away. He wasn't out to his parents yet (it would be another year before that). But he understood, as queer kids do.

"I can't do this."

"Do what?"

"All of it. With my mom. Everything. I can't face all of it alone."

"You're not, you dumb bitch." Ren clasped our hands again. Tighter.

I looked at Ren's hand in mine, both equally small. Sissy-boy-smooth. They could have belonged to the same person. I thought of every cruel thing the other boys had called me, that

Mom saw in me but never said out loud. Soft, weak. A half man. But, there with Ren, I wondered how any of those things could be bad, when my hands looked like his?

I said none of this to Ren. But he sensed it. He responded with the world's saddest smile.

"Oh, Colin." He laid the Claw on my shoulder. "Classic Cancer sign."

Then he held me. We sat like that forever, until the blue light on his phone dimmed and turned black. Until the wreckage Mom left inside me still felt enormous, but at least had an end—in that tiny, warm space where my body met his.

Now, in my room, I fold my hands together and pretend one of them is Ren's. A part of me had always known I'd never find a boyfriend. That the gay fairy tale wasn't meant for boys like me. But who needs a boyfriend when they have Ren?

*I can't face all of it alone.*

*You're not, you dumb bitch.*

Did he know that he would leave me, too, even then?

# 11

I CAN'T." I THROW OUR TWEEZERS DOWN INTO OUR DISSECtion tray.

It's not the look of the dead frog that makes me heave, that putrid yellow underbelly. Not its slippery skin, snagged between my scissors, the sound of tendons going *snip-snip.* It's the smell. Once I pull it all back with a pair of tweezers, easy as unrolling a rubber glove on my hand. Formalin. Pooling the insides of our frog's cavity. Its three livers are greasy with it.

"Can you cut its heart out?"

Ren blinks at me from behind his safety glasses. He doesn't say anything, has barely said a word to me all day.

Which is fine. I don't care.

But when Ren cradles his chin into his palm, like the mere effort of holding up his head is too much for his neck, I ask, "Are you okay? You look..."

Ren gets there first. "Like Kayako? Sadako? A stringy-haired ghost girl?"

*"Tired."*

But ghostlike covers it. Under the stark halogen lights of AP Bio, Ren is a wilted thing. His eyes have deep hollows, his pearly hair has lost its shine, its bounce. Everything about him is wispy, pale, gossamer thread.

"I didn't get much sleep."

"Fine. I'll start." I scan our handout. "First item: determine sex." I bend over the frog's carcass and search for white granules salting the insides. And when Ren doesn't even attempt to lean forward, doesn't even pretend to look, I mutter, "Guess I'll do everything."

*"Pffft."*

I stop. Did he just *pffft* me?

The injustice simmers in me to a boil—my tweezers almost shake with it.

Why is *Ren* pissed? In four months, he'll have Green College, with its hooting owls and starfish and peninsulas. He'll have the attention of West Coast Boys who play Ultimate Frisbee in courtyards and jog shirtless along seawalls and call bubble tea *boba* and do whatever else it is West Coast Boys do.

"You're upset," Ren says, reading my mind—which doubly upsets me. Because why couldn't I read his? How did he manage to keep Green College a secret for so long? And why—here, my fury spoils into that prickling, lizard-brain fear—*why* do I feel Ren is keeping something else from me, even now?

"You told me you were happy," Ren continues. "But you're not. Are you?"

I look down at Mr. Frog's husk. Did he have a gay roommate named Mr. Toad? What if Mr. Toad is waiting for him now at their riverbank, wringing his webbed hands, frantic, but here Mr. Frog is on our tray, gutted, drowning in formalin? And maybe that's what it is about the smell that gets me: its unnaturalness, its cruel sterility.

Maybe it is better to let a thing rot.

"I'm disappointed," I murmur at last. "I just wish you had told me about Green College sooner." I choose my next words carefully, ones that will hurt. "I just wish you had been...a better friend."

Ren blinks. He sits up straighter and swipes the bangs from his eyes. There, tucked behind an ear, like a pencil, bluebells. A long, wilting stem of them.

"I," Ren starts, defiant, squaring his shoulders back, "am a great friend."

I cross my arms. "A *great friend* wouldn't have lied to me. A *great friend* would've told me he changed our life plans. If anything, *I'm* the great friend, because I forgive you!"

"Oh, this is you *forgiving* me?" Ren crosses his arms, too. "Well, if I'm such a terrible, awful friend, maybe don't use my makeup anymore? Buy your own butter balm!"

"*Fine,*" I choke. "Since I'm a great friend, I'll wipe it off right now!"

"Do it."

"Watch me!"

I search our workstation for a napkin, an extra handout,

something not splattered with Mr. Frog. When I can't find anything, I sneer, "And what's with the bluebells? You *always* have them on you. What, are you gonna start tying them into a crown? Play Sad Girl Songs on the ukulele? Is that what all the cool guys do in Vancouver? *What?*" I snap at Blair, who has just drifted over.

He doesn't even flinch. Just picks at his collar ruffle. "Someone's in a mood."

"Excuse him," Ren says, flashing Blair a smile like confetti. Ren emphasizes *him*, knowing I'll hate it. Knowing it's a trigger when people refer to me in third person when I'm standing right there. "*He's* been like this all day." Ren shrugs. "But forget *him*. How can *I* help you?"

"I've got a yearbook-related question. Mr. Brett wants me to take photos of our senior science classes. Show off our STEM facilities." Blair holds up a digital camera. My stomach drops when I realize what he's asking. "Can I take a picture of you two?"

"No," I say, while Ren says, "Sure!"

"You can have one of me," Ren offers brightly. Then he leans in close to Blair and whispers behind a cupped hand, loud enough for me to hear, "*He* doesn't take pictures."

After Blair snaps some photos, he glances at the bluebells tucked behind Ren's ear. Blair purses his lips, like he wants to ask a follow-up question but decides against it.

Once he takes off, Ren's arms are still folded, but that spark has fizzled out of his eyes. He even tries to say something, but

I hunch over our lab report and pretend I'm too busy filling it out to listen. When I reach question five—*How does an amphibian differ from a mammal?* (answer: Unlike a mammal, a frog will not betray his best friend)—I hear a rip. Then scribbling. Then a note slides under my nose.

Please don't be mad at me.

Under that, Ren drew a smiling egg wearing a baseball cap. It's the main character on that Canadian show about imaginary friends. Before my heart can soften, I crumple the note and flick it to the side.

A chuff. Then more scribbling, angry scratches this time. A fresh note appears.

Wow. I literally apologized???

I write under that:

*You literally did not. Here's the receipt.*

We swap the note back and forth until the page crinkles into a furious crosshatch of Ren's bubbly snipes over my loopy ones. They crawl all over each other, clawing for the last word.

Well I <u>am</u> sorry! God!

*You made your choice. Have fun at Green.*

sdfjhgewadhhyjty

*The time you spend HANDWRITING random sequences of letters can be better used for our assignment. Just FYI.*

Why are you being like this? I'm allowed to choose a different college. I don't need your <u>permission</u>.

*And I'M allowed to be disappointed when the next four years of my life have changed because of YOUR decision. But you just want me to say I'm 100% fine so it makes you feel better. You always do this!*

When? Name seven other times I've done something like this!

*Why seven?!?! Why does it only count when it's SEVEN?!*

Ooooh. That face you're making right now <u>chills my blood</u>.

*Whatever, traitor.*

Ho

*ALL HAIL THE POTATO QUEEN.*

**Drink water, you dehydratedtwink.**

I'm in the middle of drawing a veiny purple dick and labeling *Ren* on its mushroom head when Ms. Kincaid swishes over in her lab coat.

"I hope whatever this is relates to animal anatomy," she says, plucking the note from my hand. Ren and I look on in symbiotic horror as she squints at our back-and-forth, the halogen lights reflecting off her safety glasses. Even under the lens flare, I can make out her eyes, widening.

"Mr. Ong!" she breathes, looking between us, her face blanching white like her hair. "And Mr. Hsu! Some of these comments are just…" She traces the word *Potato Queen*. I pray she lacks the interest to look it up on her phone. "Do I need to send the two of you to the principal's office?"

"No!" Ren and I cry in unison.

"We were kidding," Ren insists.

"It's the way we communicate. Our love language."

"Yeah, it's not bullying."

"We're just being boys!"

Ms. Kincaid examines the two of us like she is weighing our

words. Testing them. She sighs. "No more of this. Let's focus on the lab?" She slips away with a swish of her cloak.

Ren sighs. His mouth quivers into a half smile. When I don't return it, he leans in and says flatly, "I suppose what they say is true. *Men can't be friends.*"

He waits for me to grin or, better, to laugh—he'll settle for the ghost of either. And my lips *do* twitch, but I look down at my knees before he can see.

"*Come on,*" Ren pleads. A shy nudge from his foot under the table. "I really am sorry." Even though I'm not looking up I know he is running a hand through his hair. "You're right. I sprung Green College on you. And I'm extra touchy today. I haven't been getting a lot of sleep and..."

Ren trails off, sounding miserable.

I look up. Suddenly, he looks small and afraid. I tread carefully. "And what?"

Ren hesitates. I can tell—he *wants* to tell me.

"'Sup."

Plopping Dave saunters over and leans a casual arm on our lab bench. I would think it was cute if it wasn't for the timing.

*"Dave."* I almost spit out his name. "We're busy."

"Totally," he replies without listening. He's not even looking at me when he says, "This lab, right?" He gives a tired shake of his head. "Why are we even learning about frog anatomy?"

"Because. It's. *Biology?*" I punctuate each word through gritted teeth.

Dave whistles a dry laugh. "Well, I wish it wasn't mandatory for health sciences. Maybe if I tell myself I'm having fun, I'll believe it."

"'There is no war in Ba Sing Se,'" Ren says. He gifts Plopping Dave a weak smile.

Plopping Dave gifts a blank look back that says, *I have never heard of* Avatar. "Right," he says feebly. "Good to hear—because war is bad." And when I look down, when the secondhand embarrassment is too much, I hear Plopping Dave ask, "Ren, can I talk to you privately?"

I see his shadow glide across our lab bench.

Ren scrapes his chair away from our table so fast it shrieks. When I look up, he's rubbing his wrist like it was splattered with hot oil. Like Plopping Dave tried to hurt his arm, not touch it.

"Sorry," Plopping Dave mumbles. When Ren is still rubbing his hand, again he mumbles, "Sorry. Did I hurt you? I didn't mean to."

"Please," Ren says. "Don't touch me."

He's not looking at Plopping Dave as he says it. He's looking outside the giant window, even though there's nothing outside. Nothing but the tree line and the trailhead leading into Birchmount Forest.

Wolf eyes and cigarettes.

A thick rope of saliva, dribbling onto Ren's shirt.

"Sorry," Plopping Dave chants a third time. He's on autopilot. "I just wanted to ask you something."

"Carve it somewhere." Ren says this in a low, dangerous voice. I never knew he could sound like that.

Plopping Dave shuffles back to his table, with Puppy Chow and the other Big Spoon Boys. His dress shoes are caked with dried mud. For some reason, this makes me feel bad for him.

I turn to Ren. "Are you okay?"

Ren doesn't answer. He lays his head down on our desk. I lay mine there, too, so our eyes can meet. "I'm fine" is all he says.

From this angle, I can see every freckle on his neck.

Ren doesn't have freckles.

"What are these?" I ask gently, running my finger along the trail of pink and purple flushing his nape. They look like a rash.

Ren lifts his head and touches the marks like he can rub them away. "Mosquitoes."

*Another lie.* I know this because when I look closer, I can see what they are.

Love bites.

In fifth grade, I gave them to myself one recess—planted my lips onto my inner arm and sucked and sucked until the skin turned raw numb. Whoever left these marks on Ren did the same. Like the boy tried to devour him.

Only there can't be a boy. Because if there was, Ren would tell me about him.

"Hey," I start. "What's going on with you? Is something wrong?"

Ren stares at me hard, like the truth is right there on his open face, and he's giving me permission to take it.

"Nothing," he says finally. "It's nothing."

I lay the Claw on his shoulder. It means when he's ready, I'll ask him again.

The rest of the period drones on. But when Ren and I are three-quarters into our report—*How does the structure of the frog's heart compare to that of other vertebrates?*—a prickling on my neck makes me look back.

Two tables away, Puppy Chow is showing a tattoo to Mark Ly and Adam Papadopoulos. Plopping Dave is there, too, but he isn't listening. He's staring at Ren.

"Don't look," I whisper, ensuring Ren does.

When they lock eyes, I expect Plopping Dave to look away. But he goes on staring.

"Ignore him," I mutter, waving our attention back to the report. "Hot take: Some guys don't handle rejection well. They're creepy."

*But is* creepy *the right word?* I wonder, glancing at Dave again. He looks crushed, like it aches everywhere inside just to look at Ren, but he can't stop. I know that look because I know that feeling.

"Whatever." Ren stabs his scalpel through Mr. Frog's gallbladder. "Oh! Wait till I tell you what happened in English."

Ren talks but I'm not listening, because that prickling is back on my nape. And when I turn around a third time, Plopping Dave is staring at *me*. His hands are gripping the sides of his stool. His knuckles are white.

I try to ignore it, try to laugh along with Ren and catch snippets of his story like falling leaves into an open hand. But then someone behind us says, "Where's our scalpel?" and a shadow spills across our workstation, drenching our lab notes, our dissection tray, Mr. Frog. The shadow creeps along Ren's arm and up his neck, and that's when Ren notices—that's when he finally looks up and fixes his eyes on something over my shoulder.

"Dave?"

A smile freezes on Ren's face, a joke made millions of years ago, trapped in amber.

"Dave, what are you—"

It's the rustle that makes me look back. Dave's arm is raised, and I see a flash of something clenched in his fist, glinting sharp and silver, before he brings it down.

Ren screams, or is that me?

It sounds like one of us is coming up for air.

I duck over our tray, nose inches away from Mr. Frog, that sterile stench.

*My neck*, I think wildly. *My neck is exposed.* I brace it to feel the quick sting of the scalpel, but it never comes, just the sprinkle of something warm and wet.

"Mr. Livingston?"

I hear the swish of Ms. Kincaid's lab coat as she crosses over to our lab bench. "What are you—" she starts, and stops. All the slicing and snipping and scribbling of pencils—all of it stops.

I uncover my face.

First, I see Ren, peeking through his latticed fingers. Like me, his instinct was to cover his face.

Next, I see Blair, watching in shock from his station, a hand pressed over his mouth.

Finally, I see Dave, his back turned to our table, bending over something—I don't know what. Whatever it is, the students in front of him, the ones with a full view, they shrink away.

"Mr. Livingston!" Ms. Kincaid starts forward, horrified. "Stop!" There's a quick skirmish, like the two are wrestling for something, then she yelps and crashes into a desk, cradling her hand. The students in front of Dave throw themselves out of their stools and there's clattering and scraping and then Dave turns to me, and I see why.

In movies, when someone is stabbed, you hear friction. Blade against something hard, like it's being sharpened. But with Dave, each cut glides along his arm, as fluid as slicing through air, blooming a fresh trail of red. Dave makes no sound through his clenched jaw, eyes spiked with tears. And this more than anything is what horrifies me, to know a body can suffer so much in silence.

"Dude." Puppy Chow approaches Dave like he's a wild animal. He reaches for the blade, careful, uncertain—what if Dave turns the knife on him next?

Then Dave lashes his bleeding arm out to Ren like an offering, and Puppy and two other boys leap forward. There's scuffling and grunts as they pry the blade out of Dave's fist and soon practically the whole class is on him, pinning him down onto the linoleum floor so he can't reach for the scalpel again—the scalpel someone kicks, that slides a few feet and comes to a stop by my shoe. The same shoe that, moments before, Ren nudged with his.

The blade's tip is red.

Dave collapses under the weight of everyone, but not with the look of someone who has given up. His eyes are closed and he is smiling with the satisfaction of a job well done. Then he opens his eyes, and they dart around until they find Ren.

*Did you see it?* his eyes seem to say.

*Did you see what I made for you.*

*Did you see how I listened.*

I can tell from Ren's face he did see. Because I saw it, too. On Dave's arm, when he offered it, like a gift. Carved again and again in glistening red.

*Ren.*

*Ren.*

*Ren.*

# 12

THE BELL TOLLS THE END OF THIRD PERIOD, BUT WE were dismissed before that. A few boys lingered behind with Dave while Ms. Kincaid pushed the rest of us out. Then an ambulance parked in front of our building, by the accessible ramp.

I gather my textbooks from my locker and head out to the quad, where the air is damp. I want to ask Ren how he's feeling. I need to know he's okay. But he ran out of the lab so fast, faster than I could catch him. As I pull out my phone to shoot him a text, there is the slightest tug on my sleeve.

"Colin?"

*He's not worth it.*

I cling to Ren's words, Ren's voice, because I want to believe it. But how can I, when Ferris is standing right here, looking down at me?

Was he always this tall?

"Ferris Hale," I hear myself say, and immediately regret it.

Ferris *Hale*? Why does it sound like a silly school crush, saying both his first and last name?

He breaks into a wide, toothy smile. Then he ducks his head, shy, like always, his light eyes blinking under his shaggy bangs. "Colin Ong." When he rises to his full height—a whopping six foot three (so Ferris says)—I glimpse the graphic T-shirt he's wearing underneath his dress shirt. The gray one with the bust of an old dead white guy, captioned *Marcus Aureli-YES!*

"How've you been?" I ask, hating myself for genuinely wondering.

And Ferris Hale says, "Forget about me. What about you? I just heard about Dave. Aren't you in that class?"

Ferris doesn't call me *man* or *bro* like he does the guys in Yearbook Club or Debate. That meant the world to me. I suppose it still does. I look down at my shoes.

"I think Dave's fine. I heard his cuts"—*cuts,* I saw a guy *cut* himself—"missed his arteries and nerves. Surface wound." *I saw him cut* Ren, Ren, Ren, *all across his arm.*

"But how are *you*, Colin?"

"I'm fine."

"*Are* you? You're shaking." This makes me look up. Ferris is still watching me. He's always been good at that. Paying attention and being gentle about it. Like I'm something small with a broken wing he can cup in his hands. Then Ferris extends an arm like he wants to do just that—or rest his palm on my shoulder. And I wish he would, but he shoves it into his pocket. Then he rocks back and forth on his dress shoes like a big kid, like I saw him do in the corridor just yesterday with Mrs. Reid, and for some reason this makes me feel brave.

"Ferris, where..." I start, and suddenly all that courage evaporates. I try again, making sure to keep the hurt out of my voice. "Ferris, why did you..."

*Stop.*

*Vanish.*

*Why did you stop liking me?*

I know I shouldn't ask these questions. They're too awkward. Too vulnerable. Ren would scold me for tipping my hand. More than that, it's not the time. Not when Dave is carving Ren's name onto his skin. Not when love bites are bruising Ren's neck; not when there are bluebells and Dukes and thickets and a white, white hand; and the feeling that Ren knows something about all of this, that he's holding the weight of some terrible secret. All of these things are more important than a broken heart.

And if I was older and wiser, if I wasn't so *basic*, I wouldn't just know this, I would *feel* it. But Ferris is here now, and I need to ask him before he disappears again.

"Ferris, why did we stop hanging out?"

He stops rocking, like even he's surprised by my nerve.

"I wanted to," he starts. He looks away from me. "I wanted to text. Wanted to see how you're doing. Check in."

*Then why didn't you?*

Ferris glances at me, and maybe he sees the question on my face. He starts rocking again. "Anyway. How *are* you doing?"

"I'm fine," I reply, my own question left unanswered. "I snuck into a club."

Ferris raises an eyebrow. "A club. *You?*"

"Why?"

"Nothing," he says hastily. Then, "Did you . . . meet anyone?"

Ferris looks away as he asks this. Is he jealous? Or is he just acting that way?

"It was fun," I say vaguely.

Ferris nods. I want him to ask follow-up questions. I want him to keep this conversation going for hours, for days, to make up for these last few weeks, the horrible silence. But he pulls out his phone and declares, "Fourth period's about to start. We should . . ." He trails off and tips his head toward the school, as though I need help with directions. He even hooks his thumbs into the straps of his knapsack, like he's raring to go.

I tell Ferris to go ahead of me. I tell him I'll catch up.

I watch his figure recede as he crosses the muddy field.

Will heartbreak ever stop feeling like the end of the world? Maybe when it's doomsday or Armageddon. The literal end. Even then, I would just close my eyes and throw my hands up to the burning sky. I would welcome the dazzling white light of a supernova to swallow me whole—this dead feeling inside.

# 13

I don't bother calling out for Mom because she isn't home. She just left. I see the telltale signs of her absence right here in the kitchen, scattered across our ceramic tiles. Toothpicks in plastic wrappers. Crinkled receipts. A hard candy, still in its strawberry foil. Tiny things that must have dropped out of her overstuffed purse as she rummaged through it in her haste to leave.

I pick up the strawberry candy she dropped and hold it against my ear like a seashell. I imagine hearing Mom's voice in it, asking me what's wrong. And I want to tell Candy Mom. Everything. About Dave cutting his arm. About Ren moving to Vancouver. I want to tell her about the Dukes, the things they said that now live inside me. I want to tell Candy Mom about how everything feels *wrong* after that night in the forest, but Ren says nothing happened and he wouldn't lie to me but what if he is?

I listen, listen, listen to the candy cupped in my hand.

Ferris once told me that when you hear the ocean inside a shell, it's actually the blood pressure in your ear. It's a lovely thought: that the sound of something as deep as the sea is an echo of you. Still holding the candy, I wait for a voice inside me to say, *It'll be fine.* But it never comes.

Instead, my phone dings. A message from Ren.

Slumber party?

As I cross the Hsus' manicured lawn, past the shrubs popping with pink dahlias, the garage door grinds open and Ren's dad marches out. He's wheeling a trash bin to the edge of his lawn.

"Colin!" he says, seeing me. "How was school?"

He asks this so pleasantly, his arm leaning casually on the trash bin, that I know Ren hasn't said a peep about Dave.

"School was great," I lie. "Did Ren mention I'm—"

"Staying over?"

I shuffle my feet. "If that's okay."

"Of course. You're welcome here, Colin. *Always.*" Then: "I, uh, guess your mom is out again?"

"Working late," I hear myself say, instead of the truth—which is she's probably at the casino. I can't help but cover for her. Something about the way Mr. Hsu talks about Mom, while giving a warm welcome to me—it's like chewing into a brownie and finding salt grains inside.

He nods. Then we stand there on the lawn, and I mostly listen as he segues predictably into the glory of China. Ren said his dad's obsession piqued during the Beijing Olympics. Now it's *China this* and *China that* and *Don't believe everything you read in the Western news.*

*There are practically yellow stars in his eyes,* Ren said, and in this moment I see them, too, twinkling on Mr. Hsu's face.

"And you should see their railway system!" he gushes as I help him carry the blue bins to the driveway. "Their trains are fast and they take you anywhere—not like our subway."

I make a *mhm* sound, but I'm only half listening. When I peek into the recycling, I see a shoebox in there, painted electric blue with glue trails shaped like stars, sprinkled with glitter. I see the smoldering man on the lid. It's our Boyfriend Box.

"Does Ren know you're throwing this out?"

"He asked me to."

My chest seizes. It sounds silly, but it feels like Ren asked him to throw *me* away.

As I rummage into the bin to pull our box out, Mr. Hsu asks, "Do you know if Ren is seeing someone?"

The question is so out of the blue, I wait for him to elaborate. When he doesn't, I ask, "What do you mean, 'seeing'?"

"Is Ren dating?"

I look away. Didn't I see love bites flushing all across Ren's neck? But he *said* they were rashes. Ren wouldn't lie to me.

Right?

"Colin?" Mr. Hsu takes a step forward. He asks me, again, "Is Ren dating?"

"No, Mr. Hsu." I look up at him. He's another step closer. Now he's practically towering over me. "I don't believe he is."

Mr. Hsu holds my gaze with such intensity I know I can't break it. Because if I do, he'll *know.* He'll know the Thing-I'm-Not-Sure-I-Know. "I swear! Ren's never mentioned anyone to me." A heaviness sinks inside my chest, because it's true. For the first time, Ren hasn't told me about any boy. "Why? Do *you* know something?"

I ask this mostly out of genuine nosiness, and because I read the best way to get someone to back off is to put them on the defensive.

And it works. Mr. Hsu steps back, shuffling his weight foot to foot. "Margaret," he starts. "Last night, she heard..." Mr. Hsu trails off and flexes both his hands by his sides. He's nervous. If I wasn't here, he'd be spinning his arms like windmills.

I need to know. Because the love bites, the secrets, the dreamy far-off looks—they are clicking into some kind of sense. "What did she hear?"

Mr. Hsu just shakes his head. "Someone. In his room. At first she thought it was you, maybe, on the speaker. But she said it didn't sound..." He side-eyes me. "She said the voice was deep." Then he adds, "No offense."

"None taken," I hear myself say as another thing clicks into place. Mrs. Hsu heard a deep voice. Didn't I hear one, too, at the chapel? I couldn't see from where I was standing, but is it possible Ren was talking to his phone with the speaker on? When I don't say anything, Mr. Hsu waves his hand to the side like that settles it. Ren isn't dating. He can see the truth clear on my face.

"Colin," he says. "You know Margaret and I like you. You and Ren—you're good for each other. Keep each other accountable, diligent. Especially in your studies. We're even fine with all this." *This.* He gestures to the shoebox and the gay contents inside, but he may as well gesture to me. "All that said," he continues, "Ren is far too young to be dating."

"But he's eighteen."

"*Far too young,*" Mr. Hsu repeats. "He should be focusing on college."

I can tell Mr. Hsu wants me to fill in the silence, assure him he's right. But we both know the truth—that had it been a girl, not a boy, that Margaret had overheard Ren calling last night, he wouldn't be *too young.*

"I'll take that," Mr. Hsu says, and to my horror I realize he means the shoebox. He sees it as trash—all our gay hopes and dreams. I pull the box out of his reach and hug it to my chest, practically crushing the smoldering man's face into my heart.

"Actually, Mr. Hsu...can I have this?"

By the time I've successfully crammed the box into my knapsack, crumpling my perfect notes on radical functions, Ren flits out of the house.

"About time!" he says, threading his fingers through mine. As he drags me into the foyer, he asks, "What were you two talking about?"

I look over my shoulder at Mr. Hsu on the lawn. He's bending over his garden. "School stuff."

Ren leads me up the stairs. "How many of these do you think we've had?" he asks over his shoulder. He means slumber parties.

I shrug. "More than enough."

Ren and I had our first in seventh grade, around the time everyone else started having them.

Mom wasn't thrilled about her only child sleeping over at a friend's house, especially one she hadn't met (she didn't realize Ren was the same megaslut who sassed her that day on his bike). But Mom weighed her concerns for my safety against the prospect of me securing an actual guy friend.

Still, she aired her concerns.

"Make sure the dad's not a pedophile!" she growled as we pulled into the Hsus' driveway. Ren and his parents were waiting for us on their lawn, their arms wrapped around each other like in those movie posters about happy suburban families before the murders begin. Mr. Hsu flashed us a wave and a tight smile. Mom flashed him a tighter one.

"Men are bad, Colin," she muttered, still fixing that smile. "They make you feel safe, then they take from you. You are now old enough to know." Most parents might have framed the warning in more whimsical terms—big bad wolves preying on kids. But Mom didn't do whimsy. "Just keep an eye open tonight. If that man tries anything—if he looks at you funny or asks for a weird massage, call and I'll be right here!"

Then she looked out the windshield and blinked at Ren, like she was trying to place him somewhere, and I sort of ran out and yelled bye.

Now, Ren takes me into the Strawberry Milkshake Room. The first thing I notice are his walls. They're bare and white.

"Whoa," I say, looking around. All his artwork is down. Even his linens—blushing with flowers or cherries—have been replaced with dull gray ones. The only pink left in this room is from the bike hanging by the window. It's like Ren saw the heterosexual pride flag, with its black and white stripes, and thought, *I like this prison look. I want to mood-board this.*

"I'm too old for pink" is all Ren says. "Dad's gonna help me take down the bike next."

I run a finger over the thumbtack holes in his wall. "But what about your artwork?"

"Oh. They weren't very good."

"What are you talking about? I love your artwork. *You* love it—"

"Colin," Ren pleads. "Just drop it. Please?"

To kill time before dinner, Ren and I sit cross-legged on his rug and do homework. I want to bring up Dave. I want to ask Ren if he's okay. But it's hard to ease our conversation into self-mutilation when Ren isn't talking to me. He just sits there, hunched over the sketchbook cracked open in his lap, scribbling. The book's cover is tilted up so I can't see what he's drawing, but his brow is furrowed in concentration. Or maybe he's thinking about someone. Dave? Or some other boy.

*Is Ren dating?* Mr. Hsu's question wraps around my chest so tightly I can't concentrate. I gather my spread of European history index cards and stack them carefully into a deck.

Then, just as carefully, I ask Ren, "Is there anything you want to talk about?"

Ren looks up at me through glassy doll eyes. "What do you mean?" He closes the sketchbook, but his finger is still bookmarking a page.

"Just checking in. You've been awfully quiet."

Ren lifts his pencil. "Art class."

"Please. You're all caught up with art. Last week you said you were behind on Shakespeare. You said you had a mountain of reading to do."

"Maybe I did it."

"*Taming of the Shrew.* What's the plot?"

Ren deadpans, "It's about a field mouse."

"*So close*," I joke back, pinching the air to show by how much. "But wrong story. Now, if you'll let me take this so you can *actually* read the play..."

I reach over to grab Ren's sketchbook, but he snatches it away and hisses, "Can you *not*?" Ren lays the sketchbook next to him, face down. "Don't touch my stuff again without asking."

Everything inside me shrinks. I mumble a sorry.

Ren softens. "No, it's..." He rises from his rug, only to plummet face-first into his bed. "I'm being a bitch," he says into his pillow. "Just got a lot on my mind."

I sit next to him and poke his arm. He flinches like my finger just broke skin.

"Is this about what happened...in class?" I don't say Dave's name, in case it's another sharp object.

Ren rolls to his side, facing away from me. He fixes his eyes on his bike. Or maybe he's looking out his window. "He won't even talk to me. It's like..." Ren presses a palm to his chest. "Like I can't even feel him right now."

"Maybe that's for the best?" I say gently. "For you and Dave to have some distance?"

Ren sits up and faces me. "Dave?" He blinks. "What about him?"

I don't even know where to start. "Because he—*you know.* Right in front of us."

"So?"

*"So?"* I wait for Ren to hear himself.

"Who cares? What does Plopping Dave have to do with anything?"

"It was your name," I breathe, almost in a whisper so Mr. and Mrs. Hsu can't hear. "What Dave—*carved*. On his arm. *Your* name."

"And that's my fault?"

"No. That's not—" I stagger over my words. "I'm not saying that. What happened was—"

"Pathetic?" Ren's eyes gleam with a meanness I don't recognize. "He just wanted attention. And even then, all Plopping Dave could think about carving was my *name*? Like I said..." Ren mimes lifting a spoon and turning it over. "Plop."

My forearm stings and I realize it's my fingernails digging into it. Even then, I don't stop. I can't. I want the pain to wake me up, to learn this whole conversation was a dream.

"Ren," I hear myself say. *"What the fuck?"*

Which is when Mrs. Hsu knocks and enters. "Food's here!" she sings. "But they mixed up our tomato egg for another fried rice—so, Colin, I hope you don't mind us double-carbing it. And, Ren..." She stops and looks between us. "Are you two... okay?"

"Perfect," Ren replies sunnily, without taking his eyes off mine. "Mom, did they get my order right?"

"One egg drop soup."

"Zero salt? Zero MSG?"

"Zero flavor." Mrs. Hsu sighs. Then, to me, "Ren's on this bizarre no-sodium diet. Do you know anything about this?"

I shake my head. Normally, Ren drenches his sushi in soy sauce, even after reading about how people in Japan call that barbaric.

"Anyway," Mrs. Hsu says, turning to go. "I hope you're both hungry."

"Starving," Ren says, still leveling my gaze.

I OPEN MY EYES AND SEE A CLUSTER OF STARS. PINK, WHITE, winking. *Strawberry cheesecake stars.* Then my vision adjusts to the dark, and I remember where I am.

Ren's room, on Ren's bed. The stars are just fairy lights, twinkling around his bike. Suspended by the bay window, the bike looks like it is wheeling through the night sky, flying on fairy dust.

I roll over and there Ren is, lying next to me with his back turned, fast asleep. He barely said a peep to me during dinner. He sat there in silence with his sad-looking egg drop soup. Meanwhile, his parents prattled on about office politics and some lady in HR named Louella. Then Mr. Hsu said, "Speaking of China" (even though no one was speaking of it), and he segued into a long celebration about the country's technological accomplishments. The whole time I was staring at Ren, expecting him to roll his eyes and smirk in that *classic Dad* way. But

Ren never looked up from his bowl. I don't think he was even listening.

Now, I roll onto my back and stare up at the popcorn ceiling. Before I woke up, I'm sure I was dreaming, though I can't remember most of it. Just glimmers. A forest. A field of bluebells. The longer I stay awake the more details flicker away from me, like tiny fish swimming out of my cupped hands.

Wasn't there one more thing in my dream? I squeeze my eyes shut, the better to picture it. And just as I make out the outline of something—was it someone's face?—a floorboard creaks outside the room.

I turn to face the door leading into the hallway. The light out there is off, so I can't see anything in the gap under the door. No shadow. Still, I feel someone standing out there. I'm about to nudge Ren awake so we can giggle about it, because it's so obvious who it is. But then I remember I'm still mad at him.

On the first night I slept over—back when Ren and I used to lodge a throw pillow between us to make a plushy barrier—Ren hushed me mid-story and pointed to the gap under the doorway. At the very conspicuous shadow. Mr. Hsu was out there, listening in. He wanted to make sure there were no kissing noises. So, Ren did them to mess with him—wet sounds squelching his inner arm. Then Mr. Hsu barged in and Ren dove face-first into his pillow, cackling, and I squealed, "REN, WHY?!!" and wanted to die.

Now, in Ren's bed, I hear another creak outside. Then a faint jiggle. It's the door handle twisting, clockwise, slowly. Someone wants to get in.

"Mr. Hsu?" I whisper.

The door handle freezes at five o' clock. Then it snaps back into place. Did I surprise him with my voice? I wait and wait and wait, but he never replies.

But Ren does.

"Please?" He turns to face me, and his eyes are pinched closed.

"Ren," I say softly. "You're dreaming."

"Please," he murmurs again into his pillow. He sounds scared. "Please..."

Ren never talks in his sleep. Perhaps it's a nightmare, conjured by a guilty conscience for being such a bitch. But Ren's brow unfurrows, and he gives a long, dreamy sigh. Then he stretches, which tugs his shirt up and causes the top button to slip loose. Where his shirt parts I see those love bites again, scattered across his collarbone.

But this close, under these lights, I see the hint of something else, red and purple, blooming from the area where Ren's shirt still clings to his chest.

A bruise. Or it looks like one.

How did he get it? Who left it there? Could it be the same person who left those love bites?

If Ren is dating someone, is this person hurting him?

No. It's not a bruise. Or if it is, it's from something innocent. Like a contact sport.

Ren doesn't like sports.

Or from carrying something heavy. And it slipped.

Ren doesn't like carrying things!

I stare up into Ren's popcorn ceiling again and resolve to ask him about it tomorrow. But tomorrow comes too slowly, because now I can't sleep. I don't check my phone because I can already feel the time—late enough to be called Too Early—and assigning it a number will make my anxiety worse.

I reach for Ren's kaleidoscope on the night table and peer through its fish-eye lens. When I direct it at the bike, I see those pink and white stars again. But this time it's a field of them, a whole galaxy spinning. Then something squeaks and I realize the spinning isn't from the kaleidoscope.

It's from the bike. The spokes on its wheels.

They're turning.

Before I can lower the kaleidoscope, more lights flicker on. Not pink and white this time, but sapphire—hundreds of them, burning in pairs. Blinking. And not in the way fairy lights do, on-off-on. These lights fold in on themselves like eyes. Because that's what they are.

Eyes. Hundreds of pairs of them blinking at me from a hundred faces—identical and pale and leering at me with their blue lips, blue as those eyes.

The kaleidoscope slips out of my shaking hand and tumbles into my lap. Suddenly, my naked eyes are staring at a boy.

Crouched behind the bike, he watches me through the front

wheel, his fingers threading through its spokes. He examines me from behind a chain-link fence, or through the bars of a cage. But the way he tilts his head, eyes wide, lips parting in wonder, makes me feel like *I'm* the one in the cage. I lower my eyes from his eyes. He's wearing gray trousers. Short shorts. His skin is so white he must be dead. I recognize this boy from that night on the field.

"You're not real," I hear myself say.

The Boy in Short Shorts cants his pretty head. *Oh?*

My throat is a desert. I must be dreaming.

I fumble in my lap for the kaleidoscope to prove it. In a book on neuropsychology, I read that even the most accomplished lucid sleeper can't read in their dreams. Something about altered cognitive functions and decoding letters. I turn the kaleidoscope—*this is a dream, this is a dream*—and my breath snags when I see them, shining in the dim fairy lights, every fine, spidery letter. The engraving.

*Wondrous.*

I look up. The boy is still staring at me. He doesn't blink. I don't think he can.

Without a word, he reaches out and spins the front wheel with a flick of his dainty wrist. This time, the wheel doesn't squeak. It just winds the silence around us so tightly until it cuts off all the air. I need to break it, this silence, before it strangles all the air out of me. Makes me as dead as he is.

"Ren?" I barely whisper his name. I don't move, don't take

my eyes off the boy for a second. He spins the wheel again with more force. It creaks like an old Ferris wheel at an abandoned theme park.

*"Ren."*

An annoyed rustle of the sheets. But Ren is still asleep. I'm about to shake him out of it when the Boy in Short Shorts steps forward and ducks under the wheel. His feet are bare and his toes are blue with frostbite. They make no sound as they pad around the bed, past Ren, bringing the boy closer to my side, until he stops by the footboard and looks over it at me.

"Ren," I try again. "Wake up."

*Please.*

The boy raises a hand in front of his right eye and pinches the air, as though he is holding something small and looking through it. Then he lowers the same hand to his mouth and presses a finger to his lips.

A secret between us, sealed.

Absolutely not.

"REN!" The kaleidoscope rolls onto the rug as I crawl all over him, shaking him awake. "REN! A PERVERT IS WATCHING US SLEEP!"

Ren snorts awake. His eyes go from confused to scared to furious as he groans, "What the fuck, Colin? What are you—"

"Someone's here! Look!"

Ren's eyes become orbs and he sits upright. He reaches across his bed to his nightstand and switches on his lamp, filling the room with warm yellow light. Ren trains his eyes to where my finger is pointing, to the foot of the bed, where the Boy in Short Shorts was just standing.

Where he isn't standing right now.

"I *swear.*" I crawl out of bed and march around to the baseboard, keeping a safe distance between my feet and the gap under the bed in case a pale hand reaches out of it to grab me. "He was standing right here!"

Ren shushes me so his parents don't hear. But I want them to. Maybe *they'll* believe me. Maybe they won't do what Ren is doing to me now: dismissing me, as husbands do to their wives in every haunted house movie ever made.

"I *swear,*" I reiterate. Maybe repeating myself will convince him. "He was behind the bike. That boy I told you about, the one we heard crying in the thicket—"

"We *thought* we heard crying—"

"And he was wearing that same pair of—"

"Please," Ren begs, raking his hand down his face. "Please don't say 'short shorts.'" He takes a deep breath. "Colin, I need you to hear what you're saying: An evil twink broke into my room and just vanished?"

*Not an evil twink,* I want to clarify. *A GHOST twink.*

"Please. Just…believe me."

Ren's expression softens. I can tell he wants to believe me. Maybe some part of him does. "Okay," he starts. "What if—"

He cuts off. I wait for Ren to finish his thought—*What if what?*—but he just stands there, catatonic. "Ren?"

Slowly, his eyes circle the room, gliding past me, his bike, his desk, until they land on his door. Ren stares at that door for a long time, as though he can see through it. As though he knows someone is standing on the other side.

"What are you—"

Ren covers my mouth. Before I can give a muffled protest, he leans close to my ear and whispers, "Not now." Ren hoists himself out of bed and shushes me so his parents don't hear.

I don't join him. *"Ren."*

I need him to believe me. I need him to talk to me. But he doesn't even look at me as he reaches over to the lamp on his night table and clicks the switch, steeping us both in darkness.

# 15

In the morning, I cross myself. "Dear God," I start, then stop because that sounds like using the Lord's name in vain.

"Dear *Lord,*" I try again. "I know I don't pray to you often"—or at all—"but I need your help, so I'll cut to the chase: I think Ren is possessed. Demonically."

A locker door slams around the corner. It's third period, meaning all the students should be in class—Law for Ren, Chemistry for me. Instead, here I am in the corridor on the third floor, my ears perked for the sound of eavesdroppers or hall monitors or, worst of all, Ren.

When I confirm it is just me and a Higher Power, I continue: "Or maybe it's not a demon. Maybe it's the ghost of some gay kid who likes watching people sleep. Whatever it is, it is definitely evil. In theory, you're omniscient, so *you've* seen what Ren's been acting like. He's so cruel, and he's moving to Vancouver and eating a no-sodium diet, and I know some of those things don't sound supernatural, but it's the pattern I'm addressing. *The pattern of strange behavior.*" I take a deep breath.

"When someone asks you for help you don't charge right in. You move through other people—like in that parable where you sent that fire-person to save that guy from the flood. Please, help me help Ren by moving through the right people. Like an exorcist. Amen."

I cross myself one more time, then add, "And please forgive me for what I'm about to do."

I break into Ren's locker.

66-86-22.

*Click.*

I tug on the door, but it's jammed. *This is wrong*, a voice tells me as I attempt to pry it open. *What you're doing is wrong.* I remind the voice I've used Ren's locker a thousand times. But now, for some reason, it feels like I'm about to enter a stranger's home and touch their things. I'm not even sure what it is I'm looking for, what constitutes evidence of demonic possession. I muster all my upper body strength and give a mighty pull.

The first thing to hit me is the smell. Turpentine, oil paints, pencil shavings.

The second thing to hit me is Ren's binder. His purple one for Pre-Calculus. It slips out of a mountainous stack of textbooks and loose-leafs and three-ring binders and whacks me in the nose. I barely process the sting before everything else in the locker tips over, and I rush to lean my whole body against the tower to stop it from crushing me. Ren's locker has always been a hoarder's paradise, in spite of my best efforts to organize it. But it's a strange relief, this chaos, because it's familiar.

I begin my investigation by scanning Ren's door. First, there's the photo-booth strip held in place with an avocado magnet. Ren and I took this picture at Claw and Grab, the claw machine arcade at Pacific Mall. In the top frame, Ren is sticking out his tongue, but in the next his jaw is clenched, unimpressed, while I try to duck away from the camera. In the last frame, he's forcing me to hold still.

Next to the strip is Ren's score sheet from the driver's test he took last summer. After his first class, he texted me, in all caps:

THEY MADE ME DRIVE ON THE ROAD, COLIN. WITH OTHER CARS!!! 😭

I stop myself from chuckling. Memory lane can wait.

Then I notice the locker door. There should be a magnetic mirror below the score sheet, with Hello Kitty's friend on the frame (the bunny friend—who can ever remember her name?).

Both the mirror and Hello Kitty's forgettable friend are gone. This is noteworthy because Ren loves looking at himself.

A book slides out of the stack and lands on the floor. It lies splayed open by my feet, with its cover facing up. Ren's sketchbook, with the collage cover. The one he spent all that time scribbling into last night and didn't want me to see. I kneel and turn it over in my lap.

It's a black-and-white drawing, done entirely in graphite. At first it looks like a cloud, with thick, swirling tendrils. Then I see the outline of a face and two piercing eyes, and I realize it's a person. A boy in the smoke. No—not in it. He's made of it. With his vaporous limbs, he reaches out for something. Another hand.

It's the last drawing in the sketchbook, the one Ren was finishing last night. Why was this worth hiding?

I flip to the page before it. This time, the boy is facing me—at least, I think it's the same boy. It's a close-up of his face, so his features are clearer now. He looks to be around our age. More than that, I can't shake the feeling he is real. That I have met him before, though not at St. Brandon's. I leaf through the rest of the sketchbook, flipping backward, and my heart seizes when I see the same boy, the same face, leering back, page to page. Looking over his shoulder one moment, staring down at me the next. One portrait is so realistic I can feel the stubble along his jawline scratching my skin. In another, he's a rough sketch, scribbled onto the blank page in wild crosshatches, like Ren was in a rush. Like the subject of the drawing had vanished, and Ren drew him from memory before he could forget. Who is this boy? Why is Ren so obsessed with him?

That sinking feeling inside my chest burrows deeper the more I see of him, and I realize it's because of his eyes. From whatever angle I hold the book they're following me. Hunting. That's when I remember.

I have seen these eyes before.

Wolf eyes, vodka, cigarettes.

A bubbly glob of spit.

Duke One.

Those eyes pierce through the page and bore two holes in me. His lips are tugging up, baring his teeth, and I imagine those lips moving now, speaking to me.

*Nothing worse than a Chinese—*

My breath hitches.

I read something before, about trauma responses. How while some people flee from danger or fight it or freeze, others fawn. It's a coping mechanism. You trick yourself into thinking the person hurting you isn't so bad. You might even fall in love with them. Is that what this is? Ever since that night, when Duke One spat on him, did Ren start fawning?

I take a deep breath but it's not enough, because now that sinking feeling is bottomless and all the air in the world won't fill it. Still, I force myself to look at the drawing again, to look at it harder. Like maybe sheer will can change those features, transform that face into someone else's. Then I find the date scratched into the bottom right corner of the page, hiding under Duke One's chin.

October 25.

The sketchbook shakes in my hands.

This drawing was made months before we ran into the Dukes. But that's impossible, because that would mean Ren knew Duke One all this time. How would they know each other? And if they did, why didn't Ren tell me?

*You know why,* that voice says.

Maybe I do. Maybe I've known for a while, or suspected. Didn't I sense something on that night, between them? When Duke One's eyes lingered on Ren's lips; when he stepped forward, closing the gap between them, near enough to kiss Ren?

*Is Ren dating?*

My fingers pinch the corner of the page, trembling as they turn it over. There is one more drawing.

Duke One, his arm draped over Ren's shoulder.

Duke One, resting his hand on Ren's waist. No, not resting. Pulling Ren into his side, holding him there, possessively.

# 16

It's nine in the morning on a Saturday. Mom's already up, clinking through drawers in the kitchen.

"You're up," she says as I blink back at her from the doorway. It's unusual for Mom to still be here on her day off, instead of with her friends. Maybe she's about to leave, a possibility that, in the moment, only makes me mildly sad. Ever since I found that drawing of Ren with Duke One, there is no real estate to care about anything else. Not Mom's disappointment in me or Ferris breaking my heart or even beating Blair on our upcoming biology test.

Mom grabs two teaspoons and brings them to the table, where her iPad is waiting. She's playing *Panda Bubble*. "Your tea's in the microwave."

"Oh. Thank you." I flip open the microwave and take out the Finn and Jake mug, brimming with milk tea. A star anise bobs to the surface. Mom is still watching me, so I make a big show of draining the mug, to show her everything's fine. No gay ghosts haunting *this* boy's bestie. "Mmmm." The chai sears the roof of my mouth, burns the back of my throat. "Fragrant."

Mom nods and returns to her game. Every time a bubble pops it goes *ka-ching,* like magic coins spilling out of a cash register. To Mom, that might be the greatest sound in the world: the sound of money. "Ha ha!" she says with pride as a mountain of green bubbles explodes.

I'm about to leave with my mug when Mom asks, "Where are you going? Sit down."

I freeze in the doorway. When was the last time Mom asked me to have tea with her? Any other day I might interpret this as progress, as our relationship mending, but not now. Now, this is just a distraction. I think of the notebook waiting for me on my desk, the bullet journal Ren bought for my birthday, with fat strawberry engravings on the hardboard cover. I dug it out of my drawer last night and, on the first page, scribbled *Why Ren Is Possessed* in Sharpie. And underneath that, *A Theory.*

I filled the following pages with mind maps that looked like murder boards, linking every floating point. *Duke One. Bluebells. Haunted thicket. Boy in Short Shorts.* Then I streamlined the chaos into a working argument, like Mr. Di Marco taught us in Philosophy.

*Proposition 1: Ren used to (or continues to???) date Duke One.*

*Proposition 2: Duke One is definitely homophobic (e.g., spat on Ren and called me a f—). And he is <u>possibly</u>*

*racist (more a feeling than fact). So probably he is a terrible partner.*

*Supporting evidence: Ren is behaving unlike himself and has bruises. In addition to change in behavior, there is a change in his diet (no salt) and choice of college. Also: obsession with bluebells. Related to Duke One?*

*Question: What does any of this have to do with the Boy in Short Shorts?*

*Conclusion: The trauma of dating Duke One manifested a gay ghost, who in turn possessed Dave to cut himself and is now possessing Ren.*

I stared down at the page for five minutes, willing the words to rearrange themselves. But when it still read like bullshit, I crossed everything out.

"I really should get back to my work," I tell Mom.

She waves off my excuse. "You can study later."

I try not to look annoyed as I plunk into the chair across from her. Mom continues playing her game on her iPad. *Ka-ching. Ka-ching. Ka-ching.* A stalactite of bubbles closes in on Mom's avatar, a little panda scrambling to pop all the bubbles before they crush her cubs. Mom pauses her screen. Silence fills the kitchen.

"So." I drop the word on the table. It's meant to be an invitation. But it just sits awkwardly next to the plastic container of toothpicks. "Any cool plans today?"

"Not really." Mom takes a sip. "Colin," she says, glancing up, "I got an email from the school about prom."

My stomach tightens. "I'm not going."

Mom knits her brow. "Isn't prom a big deal?"

Why does she care? Prom feels like a whole universe away. I need to return to Ren, figure out what's going on with him. "Maybe I'll consider it," I say, hoping it's enough to close the topic.

But Mom leans forward, her eyes flashing with an idea. "What about your suit?"

*Who cares about my suit?* I think. Instead, I say, "I'll wear the one I wore to Ah Gee's wedding."

Mom brightens even more, like I've given her the best news of her day. "I can help you buy one! Last week, I won the jackpot at the slots. Fifteen thousand!" Mom beams, which is my cue to beam back, to encourage her gambling. "Why don't we go out today? I'll buy you one."

Mom looks hopeful. I can tell she just wants to do something kind. A wave of discomfort washes over me. "Thanks, Mom, but that's okay." I try to keep my voice gentle.

Mom's face goes slack. She huffs and unpauses her iPad. "*I just wanted to do something nice for you,*" she mutters in Hakka, dark clouds gathering behind her eyes. I can almost hear the rumble of a storm coming, and I brace myself, knowing if she gets going, if she explodes, she won't stop.

"Fine." The words tumble out of me before I can take them back. "Let's go."

The storm clouds clear from Mom's eyes. "Really?"

"Sure," I say, though all I can think about is getting back to my notebook. I drain the last of my tea.

"Box of Delights?" Mom asks when I read her the address. "Isn't that where they sell used things?"

"A consignment store," I say brightly, hoping my tone will offset Mom's mistrust of such places. *Never buy jewelry someone else used to own,* she once told me. *It could be possessed.*

I can feel that wariness in the car as we pull onto the main road.

When Mom rolls to a stop at a crosswalk, she reaches for the peach wood talisman hanging from her rearview mirror. "Who's even heard of buying secondhand clothes?" she asks, running her fingers along its red tassels. "So what if you save money? What about lice?"

Patiently, I point out it's not just about money. It's about preventing waste and fighting consumer culture. And sometimes thrift-store shopping is like looking for treasure. The more excited I get the more Mom's eyes glaze over until she gives a great yawn.

When we reach Queen Street, Mom asks, "Is Ren going to prom?" It's just a question, but hearing his name squeezes a wet sponge, wringing cold dishwater inside my chest.

"I don't think so."

"I see," Mom says. Her eyes scan around us for street parking.

The windows are cracked open, so the silence slips out onto the open road and whips itself away with the rushing air. And that's when I realize that for once Bryan Adams isn't here with us in the car, singing about sixty-nines or things not worth fighting for. The radio is off. It's just Mom and me, talking. When was the last time we—

"Shit, man!" Mom suddenly yells as she slams on the brakes. The tires screech in protest, and I jerk forward as a Kia darts into our lane. The driver, a bald guy who looks like Mr. Clean, tries to steal our parking spot, even though Mom signaled first.

Mom honks and honks as they have a standoff, and I sink into my seat. Then Mr. Clean yells, "Learn to drive!" and sticks out his middle finger, and Mom's eyes do that cloudy thing again.

"He just effed me," she says quietly, more to herself. She stews in the injustice for one microsecond before she rolls down her window.

"Oh no, Mom. Please don't—"

"How dare you!" Mom screams this loud enough for the whole street to hear. A lady wheeling her stroller, a young couple with their kid. "Did you just eff me?"

The man in the Kia yells something back, but Mom isn't done. "You try to steal my spot and *you* eff me? You wanna eff? Let's eff!!!"

It occurs to me Mom may not know what *eff* means. Still, Mr. Clean flips another bird and, miraculously, putters off. After Mom backs into our spot, delighted, she turns and finds me still shrinking into my seat. "What are you doing?" Again, she runs her fingers along the red tassels of her talisman. "Guan Yu protects us."

I sit up. "I don't do well with conflict. Plus, everyone was watching. Weren't you a little embarrassed?"

Mom shifts her gear into park. "Nope. Never let people walk all over you, Colin. I learned that with your father."

Box of Delights is a maze of racks overflowing with worn leather and faded fabrics. The tables are lined with rustic lamps, mismatched baskets, and dishes piled high with glittering mood rings and sachet bags of potpourri.

"How do you find anything here?" Mom asks. She picks up an avocado-colored decorative ball that looks like a dragon egg. "And look at that guy," she whispers, eyeing a ponytailed man in sunglasses as he lurks through the shoe aisle. "Is he stealing those?" The ponytailed man sheds his own sneakers, kicks them aside, and slides on a pair of retro loafers. He looks around like he's about to make a break for it—oblivious to the security guard making his way over.

Mom and I drift to the back of the store, where they keep the formal wear. Mom lights up a little when she pulls out a Ted Baker suit. "Colin, look at this!"

I look, but my mind is still back in our car, where Mom made that comment about Dad. I haven't seen him in years, not since

I was four. Mom never kept any pictures of him, so I don't know what he looked like. I only remember him in pieces. The smell of smoke clinging to our apartment walls. The jingle of keys in the lock late at night when he came home, and Mom's hushed voice urging me to go back to sleep. I remember how she shook me awake one morning, and hissed, *We have to go now.* After that, I never saw him again.

"Sir?" A man wearing Coke-bottle glasses and a leopard-ear headband drifts our way. His name tag says, *I'm Stephano. Pronounced Steph-FAWN-no.* "Can I help you?"

"He's looking for a suit," Mom answers. She gives the cat ears a once-over, and I'm about to step in between them, shield Stephano from Mom's snide remarks. But Mom doesn't say anything.

Stephano pulls a plum suit off the rack. "This one just came in."

I like the color. It reminds me of Ren's lips whenever he eats handfuls of blueberries. But Mom wrinkles her nose. "No, no, no. Something classic."

Stephano crosses his arms and studies me, like he's analyzing if I'm a fall or a winter. My shoulders instinctively wilt forward until my chest shrinks into itself so there's less of me to examine.

"How about this one?" The hangers squeak on the rack as Stephano digs in between the suits. He finds it at the back.

When he pulls it out for me to look, I can't help it. I say, "Whoa."

From far away it looks like a boring guy suit—navy blue.

But up close I can make out the lace floral patterns stitched along the sleeves. Blossoms that shimmer baby blue under the light.

"Hm," Mom says, which is not a no.

"This way," Stephano says brightly. And, draping the suit over his shoulder, he leads us past the racks of vintage dresses to the changing area at the back of the store, tucked behind a display of retro furniture and a bookcase stacked with VHS tapes. "Let me know if you need anything," he purrs, unlocking a fitting room. He hangs the suit on a hook and totters off.

"Try it on," Mom says.

"Can't wait."

Ugh.

"Trying it on" is hands down the worst part of shopping. Any fantasy I have about me being cute shatters when I see the horrible truth in my reflection. Especially in a stall like this, with so many reflections. There's a mirror in front of me and another one behind me, and their reflections bounce off one another and create an infinite hallway of mirrors spanning both ways. It is impossible to avoid looking at myself when there are so many me's looking back.

They all have my squinty eyes with the shadows under them (too many hours at night poring over the blue light of my screen). They all have that same blobby swollen nose no amount of contouring can sharpen. Same ashy complexion. I look at these infinite boys and I wonder if this is how everyone sees me. The Big Spoon Boys. The Dukes.

Ugly.

The word echoes in my head, repeating for as long as the hallway of mirrors will go, for eternity.

"I'll look for a tie," Mom says as I shut the door behind me.

I tear my eyes away from my reflection and face the door. Mom's shadow moves in the gap underneath it, and before it can disappear, I call out, "Mom, wait. Can I ask you a question?"

"What?"

For a while I stare at the door, grateful neither of us can see the other's face. I'm scared to ask the question, but I need to do it. For Ren's sake. "When did you realize you had to leave him?"

"Who?"

"Dad."

Silence. It stretches on and on, and if I couldn't see Mom's shadow right there, underneath the door, I would have thought she had left. I wouldn't blame her if she did.

"What do you remember about him?" she finally asks.

I think about it. "Not much. Just that I always had to pretend to be asleep when he came home. But I didn't understand why. All you said was—"

"His temper," she finishes, remembering. "He was always mad about something. He hated it when I went out. Didn't like seeing me talk to other guys, even at work. He could be…a cruel, awful man."

My heart sinks, hearing Mom talk about him this way. Not

out of loyalty for him, but because of what it means for her. I was young, and I don't remember Mom being scared back then. She was too good at hiding it from me. Or maybe I wasn't paying attention.

I fidget with the hem of my shirt. "Did you ever tell anyone? Like your friends?" I think about Auntie Carmen, Auntie Rose.

"I couldn't." Mom is standing just on the other side of the door, but her voice sounds so far away. "I didn't tell anyone."

"Is it because you didn't think they'd believe you? Is it because you didn't trust them? Why didn't you tell them?"

"Because if I said it out loud, it would have been real. And it couldn't be real." Mom swallows. "If it was, I would have to leave him, and what would that mean for..." Mom trails off, but I know what she was going to say.

*What would that mean for you?*

A knot ties in my chest when I picture Mom, facing him alone, for me. Did Ren feel alone, too, when he dated Duke One? And what if, by some wild chance, they're still dating? Is Ren still afraid now?

"But say they found out. Somehow. Your friends." I lean into the door, and my words bounce back at me. They sound desperate and scared, the words of a child. "How could they have helped you?"

"They couldn't help me."

"*What do you mean?*" I press, even though I know I shouldn't. Even though I know I'm pushing too far now, past the point of triggering her. But this is the first time we've ever talked about Dad, about how he was a Cruel, Awful Man, about how Mom stayed with him—for me.

"They couldn't help me," Mom repeats with a huff. Not in an angry way. Just tired. "If my friends told me to leave him, I would have pushed them away."

"But—"

"Colin," Mom says sharply, and she switches to Hakka, "there is nothing anyone could have said to me. Nothing to make me see him for what he was. I wasn't ready."

My eyes get blurry, and I realize I've been crying all this time. "What made you ready?"

Mom's shadow is completely still. After a long pause, she says in a shaky voice, "I'll look for your tie."

I watch as her shadow leaves.

I take off my clothes and stare at my many reflections for a long time. Their eyes are red, and they're all chewing their lips. If Mom is right, none of them can do anything to help Ren.

I wipe my eyes and pull on my pants first. Then the white shirt and the navy blue blazer.

When I'm brave enough to look up, I'm surprised by what I see. The reflection-boy closest to me doesn't look ugly at all. The suit fits well, maybe a little loose near the legs. But the shoulder pads make his build look a little broader, and the white collar of the dress shirt Stephano picked wraps snug around my neck.

Moments later, when I see Mom's shadow slip under the door again, I tell her, "I'm sorry."

"For what?"

"For bringing him up."

A sigh. "You just want to help Ren."

My hand freezes over the bolt.

I never mentioned Ren.

"Did you ever stop to think," continues Mom's voice, "that Ren doesn't need you anymore? That he wants the company of a real man. Not a half man like you."

I stare at the gap under the door.

The shadow is gone.

"Mom?"

The doorknob twists to the right, slowly. I jump forward and slam my hand into the slide latch again. It's already locked, but my fingers squeeze into the bolt until they turn white.

"Open the door, Colin," Mom singsongs, though her voice changes, gets deeper. "Before I get mad." The door pounds and shakes on its hinges. *"Open the fucking door!"*

She pounds on it again, harder, so hard it might burst out of its frame. Then something above me crackles, and it's the speakers turning on and a guitar strum and now—even now—under the relentless pounding, I recognize those first notes, I recognize that song—"Invisible" by Clay Aiken—because Mom used to play it all the time in the car. Then the door goes *boom* like Mom threw her whole body into it, and she shouts *Open up, open up,* and it sounds like Mom but it isn't her. Then I trip over my legs and send the back of my head slamming into the wall, and everything goes white as the pounding gets louder, and Clay Aiken croons on, oblivious—

*If I was invisible*

*Then I could just watch you in your room*

I might die. I think this while staggering to my feet. I might die, and the last person I'll hear is Clay Aiken.

Then it stops.

Not Clay Aiken's song, but the pounding. The shouting.

The door is completely still. Even so, I keep my back to the wall, a safe distance away from it.

"Mom?" I call out. When no one responds, I ask, "Are you still there?" I feel stupid for asking it. My heart knows already it wasn't her.

I won't open the door until Mom—the real Mom—or Stephano comes knocking.

*If I was invisible. Wait…*

I notice the mirror.

*I already am.*

The endless hallway of mirrors is still there. But only the mirrors. My reflections inside them, at one point stretching on into infinite Colins, are gone, like somebody took them. I blink and blink, but I don't appear.

Instead, I see *him*. Deep inside the corridor, in a distant mirror, a man pokes his head out, as though he is peeking at me from around a doorway. For a moment we just stare at each other. Then he bares his mossy, rotten teeth, and I realize he is smiling.

A scream builds inside my throat. I cover my mouth. He does the same. In the gesture of him raising his arm I can make out his sleeve. *With flowers sewn into it.* That's when it occurs to me:

Those are my features, exaggerated horribly on his face. My bloodshot eyes, ringed with yellow crust. My sloping forehead, shiny with sweat in the naked light bulb. The man runs his bony fingers through his wiry hair and pulls out a bristly clump. The roots of it drip with something and my chest heaves when I lean in and see it is blood. The man tips the sopping clump to me like a top hat.

This man is me.

He is me, but terrifying.

He is me, but dying.

Grinning, the man extends a long leg and steps into frame. Then he squares his shoulders back and, slowly, turns to face me head-on.

I need to get out of here. I need to move. Why can't I move?

I stand here, frozen, as the man takes another step forward and taps the glass in front of him, like he's only just noticed he is trapped in a mirror. Then he stretches out both his skeletal hands and grips either side of his mirror's frames. With a mighty, exaggerated heave, he pulls himself through the glassy barrier.

One mirror closer to me.

*He wants to get to you,* I think as he steps through another mirror with the horrifying ease of someone tiptoeing through a doorway.

I back into the mirror behind me, then spin around to make sure he isn't also there. By the time I turn back, the man is already taking another, jaunty step forward, through another mirror. He is playing with me.

I cross myself. "Our Father, who art in Heaven—"

The man gives a soundless gasp and cups it inside his rotting hand.

Then he runs forward.

I throw myself into the door and reach for the sliding latch. It's jammed. I bang and bang and bang as the man keeps running, scrambling through mirror through mirror through mirror. No, not scrambling. Scuttling. With wiry, nimble limbs, like a spider. He is only a yard away.

"*Mom!*" I scream through the door, and tug and tug on the bolt, but it's still jammed. And now the man is close, close, close, he is coming too fast. He will explode through the mirror any second, or his arm will phase through the glass and grab my neck, pull me in there with him.

Then the bolt slides and clicks like a miracle, and I slam into the door, burst through to the other side where Mom arrives with my tie.

“What about this one?” she asks. She cuts off when she sees me on my knees, breathless. “What are you doing?”

I look over my shoulder, into the changing room, where I expect to find the ugly man, grinning. But it is only two blank mirrors, facing each other.

“Mom. Can you drive me to Ren’s?”

REN!" I BANG ON HIS BEDROOM DOOR. I DIDN'T EVEN ring the doorbell after Mom dropped me off. I just tore straight inside the house. "Ren! Open up!"

The door cracks open and his face appears in the slit. He has dark shadows under his eyes. "Colin?" he croaks, like he just woke up. "What—"

I barge in, past Ren, into his bare room with its stark white walls. His mirror on his dresser has a blanket thrown over it.

A hallway of mirrors and infinite me's.

A hallway of mirrors and a man with rotten teeth—

"What is this about?" Ren sits on his bed. He's still in his pajamas. "Colin, now's really not the best—"

"I know about him."

A flicker of worry in Ren's eyes before he catches it. Then he breaks into a smile. "Who?"

I level Ren's gaze. I have to come clean. "I saw your sketchbook. The drawings. I know about Duke One."

Ren's face turns purple. The bed creaks as Ren slowly rises from it. As he pads forward, eyes gleaming, he asks, "What do you mean, *you saw my sketchbook*?"

"Uh, well—"

"Did you break into my locker?"

"I always use your locker!"

"So, after I explicitly told you not to look at my sketchbook, you do the opposite?" Ren marches over to his door and pulls it open like he wants me to leave. "Get out."

I plant my feet. "This isn't just about *you* anymore! I just got assaulted by the Crypt Keeper!"

"What are you talking about?"

"Everything has been weird ever since that night your boyfriend attacked us!" I take a deep breath. "I don't know how he's doing it—if he put a curse on you and he's some dark wizard. But I know you know something. And I was going to give you time to come clean but, Ren, people are getting hurt. Like Dave! You have to talk to me."

*"Why?"*

"BECAUSE I'M A GOOD FRIEND. Now break up with your boyfriend!"

Ren opens his mouth. But then his eyes widen at the sight of something over my shoulder. I turn around.

Mr. Hsu is standing right behind me.

*Shit.* Maybe he didn't hear anything.

"Boyfriend?" Mr. Hsu repeats. He sounds lost. "Ren, are you seeing someone?"

Ren throws me a venomous look before stomping out of his room, past his dad. "I don't have time for this."

Mr. Hsu storms after him. "Ren, I just asked you a question. Are you seeing someone?"

Ren spins around to face him. "So what if I am?"

"You're too young!"

"I'm eighteen!" Ren spits, getting in Mr. Hsu's face. "I can do what I want."

"Not if you live in this house."

Ren gives his father a cruel smile. "Kick me out, then. I don't fucking care."

"Disrespectful. Ungrateful. Useless!" Mr. Hsu jabs a finger into Ren's chest with each word. "If there's an award for the world's biggest disappointment, it would go to you!"

*"Mr. Hsu."* I squeeze past him and lay a steadying hand on Ren's shoulder in case he sways and falls apart, as I might, if Mom had said those things to me. "That is verbal abuse!"

But Ren just throws his head back and cackles. "Oh, thank you! I get an award? Is it a trophy?" Then, with an exaggeratedly heartfelt wave, like he's just been crowned Miss Universe: "I couldn't have done this without my homophobic dad, who made me doubt myself my whole life and *still* refuses to pay for my therapy! Thanks, Dad! This is for you!"

With that, Ren spins on his heel and storms off again. Mr. Hsu follows. "We're not done yet!"

The two of them take their argument to the top of the stairs. I shift here uncomfortably, wondering if I should get in between them, or call Mrs. Hsu at her work, or just slip away. But then my fingers brush against something in my pocket—a bulge. I reach in and feel something smooth and metallic. I pull it out.

It's Ren's kaleidoscope. I don't remember pocketing it. But as I hold it up to the light, pinching it between my fingers, I suddenly remember the Boy in Short Shorts doing the same, pinching the air in front of his eyes, as if he was looking through something.

I don't know why I do it, but suddenly I'm raising the kaleidoscope to my eye, peering through its fish-eye lens. Through the swirling patterns, I see hundreds of Rens arguing with hundreds of Mr. Hsus.

And then I see something else. A flash of white. A hand.

When it comes down, I hear a sharp yelp, and I lower the kaleidoscope in time to see Mr. Hsu lose his footing and tumble down the stairs. Ren screams and my heart races as Mr. Hsu lands at the bottom with a crack.

# 18

The PA buzzes the end of first period. As chairs scrape and bags rustle around me while everyone leaves, I stay seated, checking my phone. No new messages from Ren. I text him:

Is he okay?

Mr. Hsu landed on his wrist in the fall. Ren called the ambulance, and they took his dad to a unit in the hospital for observation. The doctors said it was just a minor fracture. Still, Ren didn't come to school today.

"Mr. Ong," Mr. Frank says when I approach him. He doesn't look up from his laptop. "I haven't updated your grades yet."

"Oh, I'm not here for that," I say, which is only half true. "I wanted to talk to you about something else. All this." I gesture to the Psalms quotes plastered on the walls. Passages about hellfire and brimstone. Normally I find it obnoxious, but not today. Today, the Word of God makes me feel safe. "Mr. Frank... you seem to know a lot about hell."

"Thank you," he says, tip-tapping on his keyboard. "Is there a question?" *Tap tap tap.*

I open my trusty notebook to the dog-eared page, to the question I penned last night. "What do you know about demonic possession?"

This gets his attention. Mr. Frank tears his eyes away from the screen and leans in to whisper jokingly, "Why? Is someone possessed?"

I peek at my checklist, titled *Why Ren Is Possessed*:

1. *Haunted by Boy in Short Shorts*
2. *Dave: Carved his name into arm*
3. *Me: Assaulted by Mirror Me (Not a coincidence. Happened right after I asked Mom for advice—almost like this thing knew I was getting close to it.)*
4. *Mr. Hsu: Pushed down stairs*
5. *Obsession with bluebells, hiding mirrors or covering them, no-sodium diet*
6. *Related to trauma of dating Duke One???*

"Colin?" Mr. Frank probes.

"I'm writing a review on a horror movie," I lie. "About Hollywood and how it portrays our faith."

"Like *The Exorcist*?"

"Precisely." I uncap my pen and poise it over my page, like a professional journalist. "First question—and I'm sorry if this sounds too basic, but it's important—what is demonic possession?"

Mr. Frank scratches the bristly hairs on his chin. "To start, demon possessions take place when one or more evil entities take complete control over a person's body." Mr. Frank pauses as I scribble *complete control* down into my notebook. "And possession manifests itself in myriad ways. Strange behaviors"—I check off point 5—"contact with mysterious entities"—I tick off point 1—"enhanced physical abilities."

My pen hovers over point 2. "Like making people hurt themselves? Can the possessed do stuff like that?"

Mr. Frank leans back into his chair to get a better look at me. I consider taking that question back, because maybe he heard about Dave and now he's making connections. But Mr. Frank just stretches out his arms and legs. Does everything but yawn to indicate boredom. "I don't believe I've heard—"

He stops, however, because Blair enters with a knapsack so stuffed with papers it might explode. Blair pauses at the sight of me.

"Mr. Prince," Mr. Frank says in greeting as Blair joins us. Blair plops his backpack onto the desktop and unzips the main pocket. "Since the staff printers are out of order, Blair has kindly offered to photocopy my handouts in the yearbook room."

"Very kind." I pretend to agree, wondering how much longer

Blair will be here. Blair must hear the question in my voice because he holds my gaze as he reaches into his bag to pull out the handouts. Slowly. One by one.

"Where were we?" Mr. Frank continues, bringing my attention back to him. "Oh, right. Signs of demonic possession." I'm only half listening now, hyperaware of a third person in the room—who smells a little like flowers today. And gingerbread. "Based on scriptural data," Mr. Frank says, "we can infer that demonic possessions target unbelievers. Children who forsake our Father and refuse to bend to his will."

*Do all Catholics have daddy issues?* Ren's voice mutters in my ear.

"It's no joke," Mr. Frank frowns. I didn't realize I was smiling. "You've asked me how a demon possesses someone, but you haven't asked me why. The why is just as important."

At this point, I hear Blair give a particularly loud tug, forceful enough to tear the seams of his knapsack.

"The why," I repeat. "Because demons want to hurt people?"

"They prey on a very specific kind of person," Mr. Frank replies. "Someone who is spiritually vulnerable."

I underline my final point on the checklist: *Related to trauma of dating Duke One???*

I postulate, "Like, for instance, if you're in an abusive relationship? Could that person be considered spiritually vulnerable?"

Mr. Frank nods. "They could. But I meant more along the lines of people whose, say, *lifestyle* is contrary to Christlike teachings."

Maybe it's the way Mr. Frank's eyes glide past mine as he says this. But something—something makes my pen stop. "What do you mean," I say carefully, "by *lifestyle*?"

Mr. Frank throws his hands up into the air. He wants me to know he is uncomfortable. Whatever it is he doesn't want to say, I can tell he's already decided to say it. "You know. Sins. Both deadly and venial. Drinking, drugs. Choices that weaken our relationship to God and so leave us weak to Satan's influence. Oh, and of course there are the sexual sins, too," he adds. "Promiscuity being one of them." Then, for the first time all day, he looks straight into my eyes and holds my gaze. "Among other things."

His eyes glide over the gold star I pressed next to my eye. And maybe it's because of this star, my shiny armor, that I don't wilt under his gaze. Maybe this is why Mr. Frank's eyes flicker back down to his laptop. Why his fingers go *taptaptap* on the keyboard like he's trying to hit backspace on this whole conversation.

"Any other questions, Mr. Ong?" He clears his throat. "I do enjoy these chats, you know. And truly, even the most spiritually lost can find their way back—"

"Mr. Frank," Blair interjects. "Please stop."

Mr. Frank's face blanches in the blue light of his screen. "I beg your pardon?"

"No one asks to be possessed," Blair cuts in. "No one chooses to invite evil into their life." He is speaking in that same matter-of-fact cadence he used for his medieval torture presentation for

European History: each point about iron maidens and brazen bulls whittled down to the bare and grim facts. "In *The Exorcist,* Pazuzu would have possessed Regan regardless of whether she drank or had sex or prayed before supper."

(I make a mental note to google *Pazuzu*).

Blair plows on. "So, if the why is so important, then what about the demon? *We can infer*"—here, Mr. Frank flinches—"that to fight a demon, you need to learn as much about it as you can. Its patterns. Its motivations. You can't do that when you're only focusing on what the possessed person did wrong."

Blair pauses. I realize it's an invitation for Mr. Frank to interject.

When he doesn't, I chime in, mostly because I can't stand awkward silences. "What Blair just mentioned—didn't they do that sort of thing on that old show *Mindhunter*?" I give Mr. Frank a quick look, to make him feel included in the conversation. This is a friendly debate, after all, and no one needs to feel emasculated (especially if that means I'll get a lower grade). "Don't people in the FBI create profiles for criminals? Using, um... psychology?"

Blair ignores me and digs through his knapsack. He pulls out the last handout.

"It's important to think critically about these things, Mr. Frank," Blair says as he flattens the paper over his chest. "What you're doing is called victim blaming."

And with that, he leaves the last handout at the top of the pile and storms out.

I expect to hear the tapping of keys again. I don't.

"Well then," I say at last, looking at anything other than Mr. Frank. I imagine he must look like an eggshell, all hollowed out on the inside, where his manhood used to be. "I think it's super productive when we have these discussions."

Blair waits for me in the hallway. "So. *The Exorcist*, huh?"

"Class project," I lie. "For English."

Blair tugs uncertainly at his dissent collar. Almost shyly, now that his TED Talk is over. "Strange," he says. His glasses reflect the fluorescent lighting humming above us. "I figured you were asking those questions because Ren is possessed."

# 19

I DIDN'T KNOW WHAT TO MAKE OF IT, WHAT I'D FOUND," Blair says. He turns on his desktop, and its fan whirs to life. "And then I overheard you talking to Mr. Frank."

We're in the yearbook room, just the two of us. I've never been in here before. We're sitting at Blair's workstation, both huddled in front of his computer monitor. Unfortunately, this also means every time Blair uses his mouse, he leans in close enough for me to catch more of that gingerbread smell. And a whiff of something cool and minty.

"Takes a while to load," Blair explains when a tiny hourglass appears on the screen. He doesn't say anything more to break up the silence. I have nothing to fill it.

So, I distract myself. I look around Blair's workspace, which is basically *Tetris*. There's a color wheel hanging over the monitor, a blending guide for Photoshop. Next to the wheel is a monthly calendar with jewel-bright stickies in every block (citrine reminders for team meeting; lapis deadlines for spreads). I see another guide on his wall called *The Art of Mixing Fonts*. Blair has underlined the one called Franklin Gothic. I would have picked Garamond Italian.

Blair leans into his monitor. He scrolls through the photos Baby Gap took for yearbook. Jordan Russo mixing chemicals in the lab. Puppy Chow holding two basketballs before him like a pair of enormous orange breasts.

There are pictures of St. Brandon's athletes: guys batting birdies in badminton; guys with melon-size biceps lifting weights; guys in Speedos slipping out of the pool during swim practice. Blair scrolls through these more quickly.

"Here we are," Blair finally says. "Now, I think it's fair to warn you: This might be a little scary."

He clicks.

And I can't help it: I flinch.

It's a picture of me and Ren in Bio. Ren has a fake smile fixed on, the bluebells tucked behind his ear. And me—

"I took this of you two in Biology. For yearbook? Remember?"

My finger twitches. I want to turn the monitor off. Blink this image out of existence, forever.

I forget the exact moment I resolved never again to take a photo. But I'm sure it must have been a moment like this. It hurts to look at him, this Colin. Not because I'm looking at myself through another's eyes, but through truer ones. A crooked nose that bends too far to the left. That sloping forehead.

*Bristly hair pulling out in wet clumps.*

*Lips pulled back, revealing mossy, rotten teeth.*

I turn away from the image. Blair did say it would be scary.

"Why are you showing me this?"

"You mean you don't see it?" Blair asks. He leans in again to zoom on the picture. *"Look."* He drags the cursor over to the window behind me and Ren, the one overlooking the main road.

At first, all I can make out is white, like a glare of fluorescent lighting bouncing off the windowpane. Blair zooms the image to 150 percent.

"What is that?" I ask. But I already know.

It's a face. Reflected in the glass. At least, I think it's a face. The image is so pixelated I can only make out two blurry eyes looking through a flare of white.

"At first, I thought it was a glitch," Blair says. "But..."

Blair clicks through more pictures. I see trees, a trail, and immediately recognize it as Birchmount Forest.

"You'll remember I mentioned doing some research on floral diversity in local parks"—I roll my eyes a little as Blair says this (we're in high school; we don't do *research*)—"and I kept finding these."

Blair stops at an image of bluebells. "These flowers are everywhere."

"And that's weird?"

"Bluebells are common in Ontario, but we grow *Mertensia virginica*." When I stare back blankly, Blair continues, "This is *Hyacinthoides non-scripta*. The English bluebell. It shouldn't be able to grow here. The climate, the soil. The conditions aren't right. But if you walk along the trail, you'll see them everywhere. And that's not all."

Blair clicks to another picture. A sun-dappled clearing, dotted with a sea of bluebells. And there, wading in it—

I lean in. "Is that Ren?"

He's bending slightly, gathering the delicate flowers into an arm.

Blair leans over me and points to a white haze lingering at the edge of the field, obscured partially by tall grass. "See?"

It's that figure again. Blair zooms in, and this time the features are crisper. I get a flash of strong jawline. A straight nose. *No money in a nose like that,* Mom would say. But to me, that nose is perfect.

"You recognize him," Blair observes. "Don't you?"

I do. I've seen this man before. I've met him. I've looked into that face, years ago. Ren was with me, the two of us splayed out on his bed. That night, we cut bits of this man out of magazines and stuck them together.

*I like watching you sleep. I find it fascinating.*

"What?" Blair asks.

"Blair," I start, but then I hesitate. Because it's impossible. We were fourteen. We were two boys playing a game. We used scissors and glitter and glue and the magic in our hearts to bring someone to life. But none of it was real. How can something that isn't real appear in a photograph? How can something that isn't real stare back at you?

I take a deep, steadying breath. Then I ask Blair a question I never thought I'd ask. "Does this demon have Robert Pattinson's nose?"

# 20

I CRUSH THE SHOEBOX AGAINST MY CHEST AND PUSH Blair's doorbell. *Please,* I think when I find some dandelion fluff clinging to my shirt. *Please let me be wrong about this. Let everything be normal.* I pinch the wish and blow it off my thumb.

The door swings open, and Blair pokes his head out. "You found me," he says, though there's no hint of a smile on his face, no delight in his voice. Not that I expect Blair to *want* to see me on a weekend. In an ideal world he would have been studying or doing more "research".

What *does* surprise me is how Blair looks right now. There's no collar ruffle on his neck, or cat-eye glasses on his face. Blair is wearing a plaid shirt, checkered a deep forest green. "Why do you look like a basic straight guy?"

Without missing a beat, Blair snaps, "Didn't feel the need to dress up."

I hold Blair's cool gaze. "Thank you for making time for me." Blair holds the door open in response and I squeeze past him, into his home. The wrinkles in my shirt brush up against the wrinkles in his.

"Thirsty?" Blair asks.

I give a tight smile and shake my head no. Blair shuts the door behind me, and we both stand in the foyer, waiting for someone to take the lead. Other than Ren's, I don't visit people's homes, and I don't get the sense Blair has many visitors. I take in the house. There are green marble tiles on the floor that match Blair's shirt, and a staircase that leads to the second level, where his room might be. Everything here smells like gingerbread—probably because Blair is an alluring but evil witch.

"So," he says. The word drops and rolls on his green tiles like a penny. "*Riverdale*, huh?" I realize he's looking at my box.

I tell Blair I used to watch the show ironically. Blair gives me a polite smile and says, "Interesting."

Before I can respond, a flurry of yellow breezes past me. "Blaaaaair," a girl whines. She can't be more than six or seven. "You said to wait for two minutes, and it's already been ten. The brown butter's all cooled."

I smell something heady wafting in from the kitchen, underneath the gingerbread smell. Caramel?

"We're baking," Blair explains. "As for you," he says, turning his attention back to his little sister. "I said *twenty* minutes, Bethlehem, not two. And it's only been five. So nice try." And with that, Blair swans past his scandalized sister, up the staircase. I take this as my cue to follow.

We arrive at the door at the end of the landing. As Blair reaches out and turns the chrome handle, it hits me.

I'm about to enter a boy's room.

A boy who isn't Ren.

"Blaaaaaaair." Bethlehem weeps somewhere downstairs. "You're not filling my cup of love!"

"Cup of love?" I ask, following Blair into his room. Because that's way more interesting than Blair's patchwork bedsheets or the clothesline he's tacked over his desk to hang his photos. Or the one photo in particular of him in a graduation gown, cheeks round and squishy, lips pinched into a grumpy cat frown. Or the way everything here smells like lavender. Even Blair. "So, uh, is it a literal cup?"

"It's this thing she says lately," Blair says with a sigh. *"You're ignoring me, Blair. You're not filling my cup of love."* He ambles over to his desk. "She's gotten so...whimsical." But there's a flicker of a smile on his face as he says it.

While Blair starts up his computer, I spot the glossy lilac cover of our Latin textbook on his desk. *Discoveries,* fifth edition. Three editions older than the one I had last term. "You kept it? Does Mrs. Reid know?"

"Oh," Blair says when he sees what has caught my attention. "She let me, since it's super old. Look inside."

I flip open the cover to find a list of student names along the tangerine endpaper. All the previous Brandon boys who owned it. About four names from the top:

*"Isaiah Brackert."* The name sounds familiar. Then I realize, "Of the Brackert Memorial Prize?"

The Brackert Memorial Prize is St. Brandon's most prestigious, and valuable, graduation award—given to the top student. You get a shiny medal with the school logo on it and a thirty-five-thousand-dollar stipend, which if I won would definitely go to university, but really you could use it for anything. The Brackerts named the prize after their late son.

"This was his book," Blair says proudly. "Good omen, right?"

I offer a tight smile and remind myself that while Blair and I are partners at the moment, we are still enemies. I walk over to his nightstand. There's a paperback copy of *The Last Unicorn*. "I still can't believe Mr. Frank didn't catch you."

"You make it sound like I cheated."

I pick up the book and flip through its pages. There are pencil scratches in the margins. A book well lived. "Well, we were supposed to talk about God's Grace."

With a squeak out of his chair, Blair marches forward and snatches the book from my hands. "Unicorns are related to God. In medieval Christian art, they symbolized purity." Then, as he saunters back to his chair with a careless wave of his book, he says, "I'm surprised you didn't know that."

*Maybe I did,* I'm about to lie. But Blair plops himself into his chair and drones, "So did you bring more evidence, or what?"

I shake my shoebox at him and reply in my coolest voice, "Here."

As Blair unlids the box, I drag over a beanbag chair from the corner and sink into it.

"So, is this it?" I hear Blair ask. He lays the three faces onto his desk, then the old copies of *Seventeen*. From my beanbag chair, I crane my neck up and recognize my old flame Cheddar pouting back at me through Tom Hardy's lips. Suddenly, I can see the box through Blair's eyes, and it all seems so juvenile. So unlike anything normal boys would do, even the gay ones.

Blair doesn't say anything. He pulls out Billy next. Then Marshall. "Why are you waiting until now to compare the faces?"

"Because I need a more objective pair of eyes" is my answer. But it's a lie. The truth is, I didn't want to look at the faces again, not on my own. Last night, after Blair showed me the photos, I went home and stuffed the box into the back of my closet. It felt like there was something living inside that box, a big hairy spider, all eight legs scrunched into a corner, waiting to spring once the lid opened.

Blair clicks on a file, and Marshall's face appears on his monitor—the same image he showed me in the yearbook room. I hold up Ren's collage and compare the faces, side by side. They have the same nose, but the rest of the face is different. The jawline is too square, eyes too expressive, more bone than meat on the cheeks.

A knot between my shoulders loosens. "They're not the same," I say. I want to laugh. "We didn't conjure anything." I turn to Blair, who at some point has started flipping through the old copy of *Seventeen* Ren and I tore through to make the collages. "So maybe this face in the yearbook photo is just a glitch. Right?"

Blair ignores me. He's still leafing through the magazine's glossy pages.

*"Blair."* He looks up at me, bookmarking a page with a finger. "The pictures don't match. Which means we're wrong. Right?"

Blair lays the magazine onto his desk. "Colin," he finally says. "Have you ever heard of omission neglect?"

I haven't. But I won't admit it, not to *this* smug asshole. "Vaguely."

"It's when we neglect information because we assume everything we can see, touch, or hear is all the information we need. It's when we focus so much on what's here"—Blair boxes this word: *here*—"that we forget what's *not here.*"

Blair must register the blankness on my face because he says, "It's the *same nose.*"

"But the rest of the face—"

Blair rolls up the magazine and places it in my hand. "You're only comparing the rest of the picture to the faces you *do* have. But what if there's a face we're missing? What if there's a face that's not *here*?" He gestures to the collages on his desk.

I flip through the magazine. I see articles about toxic friendships and how coconut oil is comedogenic. I'm not sure what Blair wants me to see.

"The holes," Blair explains. "You told me yesterday you and Ren made three faces, right? You planned each one. Face shape. Nose. Mouth. Eyes. That means you would've cut out twelve models from the magazine—four to each face. Right?"

"Right."

“There are *sixteen* faces missing,” Blair says. “I counted.”

My fingers tremble as I leaf through my copy of *Seventeen.* Each glossy page feels like shed skin. Hole after hole after hole. I mentally tick off each one.

Blair is right. There are sixteen faces missing. Meaning there might be one more collage.

“I don’t remember making a fourth.”

“Then he made another one after you left.”

The dread flaps back into the room and digs two claws into my shoulders. It wants to sweep me away.

“There are details about those pictures on the bottom of each page,” Blair says. “Model, photographer, date. I bet we can find these pictures online.” Blair clicks his browser. “We can re-create the face to see if my theory is right.” Blair pores over the magazine and begins his search.

We spend the next half hour doing arts and crafts.

We find a full spread of Noah Centineo, his trademark mop of tousled curls spilling over his eyes. He’s spooning a teddy bear in bed. Then we save a picture of Dave Franco leaning against the graffitied walls of a subway station, reading a Penguin Classic. There’s Timothée Chalamet, too, first as a king in shining armor. Then a poet, then a shy lover gazing, heartbroken, into the fire. So many boys blink back at us through sleepy eyes.

We lay out the sixteen faces. Some combination of them might give us Marshall.

Bethlehem raps on the door and walks in. “Blaiiiiiir,” she says. “The butter’s ice cold now.”

"We're doing a science experiment, Beth," Blair says. He matches Chris Hemsworth's squinty eyes with the ones on Mr. Thicc. "Give us ten more minutes."

"This isn't science." Bethlehem waves a hand in my direction as I slide more celebrity pictures into our discard pile. Dave Franco reading Virginia Woolf. Noah playing the big spoon. "You two are just looking at pictures of celebrities pretending to be boyfriends. What happened to filling my cup of love?"

"Ten. *Minutes!*" Blair grinds the words between his teeth.

Bethlehem's mustard dress ruffles as she spins and stomps off. "All those guys look the same!" she informs us from the hallway.

When she's out of earshot, Blair whispers, "She's not wrong. This is, like, almost entirely white boys."

"In my defense," I say defensively, "I grew out of that phase."

My fingers land on another picture. It's Shawn Mendes grinning, nose scrunched up like I've just shared with him the funniest, most amusing anecdote in the world.

I slide Shawn to the left.

"You actually believe in this stuff?" I ask Blair. "The supernatural? Because of one blurry photo?"

Blair places Bill Skarsgård into the discard pile. "Spirit photography's always been huge. But the pictures were grainy back then. It was easier to falsify things. A ghostly face in the mirror. A woman in a veil." We hear Bethlehem in the living room, blasting *Summer Camp Island* on full volume. "Same with those radios ghost hunters use. All that flimsy equipment that never works properly, yet we believe they capture things in this world no one else can detect. Like a ghost leaving some message in the static."

Blair gets up to shut the door. "But these days, when technology is so good—when all the bugs are worked out—and you *still* see something..." Blair stops. Because he realizes he's been talking too much, that he hasn't stopped. Or maybe it's the way my body is leaning in too close, because I don't want him to stop, either.

"Although I guess there's deepfake," he says at last. He tries to trample that orange flame in his eyes. Pretend it was never there.

I turn over what Blair has said about grainy photographs, about how the ghosts have been faked. I look at these photos, gathered into two piles spilling into each other. I think about how these boys look so unlike me for so many reasons—so much whiter, handsomer, so much more boyish. None of them shrink away from the camera.

"Maybe they're just scared." I bring my knees to my chest and scrunch my toes. "The ghosts. Scared of the cameras. Of how good they've gotten. Maybe they're afraid because they show too much of them too clearly."

Blair is looking at me now. Holding my gaze—but not in an intimidating way. Like he's actually holding it, the way you'd hold someone's hand when you're helping them cross the street.

I sputter. "Like, with a grainy photo or a staticky radio, it's easier to manipulate how someone can see you? You can still hide, in a way. Show them only what you want to show them. Just enough for the viewer to know you're still there." I hold Dylan Minnette's face up to Blair's window. Squint as the orange sun bores light through his eyes. "Maybe ghosts prefer to live in the static. Maybe they feel safer in it." Someone on the television bursts into a belly laugh downstairs. I expect Blair to laugh with them, just to soften the silence that has landed in this room.

I brave a peek. He's still kneeling across from me, looking. "Why haven't we talked until now?"

I feel the heat rise to my face. It's just a question, Colin. God.

*Different circles,* I want to answer. Or maybe it was shyness, or a rivalry that, I'm beginning to suspect, was only ever one-sided. The truth is, even before coming here, before talking to Blair, really talking like this, I could always tell Blair was the sort of guy who pays attention. When he looks at something, he pulls it apart in his head and examines it from every angle.

Blair is doing that with me now. I'm not blushing, but I want to bury my face into my knees just in case.

"I'm an introvert." I dig through the discard pile. "So. Do we have our faces?"

"Here they are." He raises the four faces left over.

Blair and I each peel two faces off the floor and bring them to his desktop. With a push of his mouse, the image on Blair's monitor blinks back to life. And even before we press Troye's pink, pink lips onto the desk under Timothée Chalamet's eyes and map both features onto Dylan Minette's oblong face with Edward's nose, I can already recognize these boys in Marshall.

Four years ago, Ren pieced him together out of glossy pages and misguided dreams and our gay boyish hearts. Four years ago, we made a demon.

"But how? We stole these supplies from a teacher's closet!" And that spell—didn't Ren get the idea from an old movie? "Did we summon something?"

"Maybe not." Blair cups the pieces of our collage into one hand and pulls open a drawer. "It's what demons do: take the form of something else, something their victims trust. That way it's easier for them to wriggle into someone's life."

I pull out my phone with a shaking hand. The cold metal feels dead in my palm. "So do we hire an exorcist?"

"The Catholic Church won't count this as evidence."

"Then why are we doing this?"

"Because now *we* know. We know something is targeting Ren. And we know, for some reason, *this* is the form it's taking."

Blair lifts himself off his chair with a squeak. He starts pacing. "There are three stages of demonic possession, of course. Infestation, oppression, and possession."

*"Of course."* I chuff like a prissy pink pony. "How do you know all this?"

"I'm well-read." But when I cross my arms, Blair throws his arms up. "And I've watched all the *Conjuring* movies—whatever! So, infestation is the first stage—when the demon makes its presence known. Flickering lights. Stuff like that. Oppression is when it wears down its victims, makes them scared and weak enough to—"

"No."

Blair stops pacing. Something about what he just said feels off. I think about Dave grazing Ren's arm before cutting into his own. I think about Mr. Hsu, pushed down the stairs in heated mid-argument. I think about me and the mirrors, after I asked Mom for advice.

*Protective.* The word explodes into a hundred tadpoles that pool into my cupped hands. They nibble at my fingers. Ren scribbled that word into our list of Good Boyfriend Qualities, in long, loopy cursive, electric pink. *Protective.*

Ren isn't possessed by a demon.

He's in love with one.

# 21

I TEXT REN:

Sup, slut. How've you been?

I wait barely five seconds before three dots appear next to his profile pic, the No Image Available Guy. Then, *ping*.

I'm fine.

Sitting on the edge of my bed, I stare at Ren's text bubble, expecting more of them to populate my screen. But it's just one lonely gray island.

*I'm fine.* Why does it feel like people write that only when they're not? I thumb a response:

How's your dad?

He's healing. Mom's with him now. It's... tense around here.

Well my mom's out of town (surprise surprise). Wanna come over?

The dots bounce and bounce and I use all my mental power to will them into words. *I would LOVE to come over,* these words will say. *I have something important to tell you, Colin. A secret. Because you're my best friend and I trust you most.*

Mom's voice drifts into my room like a scratchy recording.

*They couldn't help me.*

*There is nothing anyone could have said to me. Nothing to make me see him for what he was.*

And when the dots disappear, I think maybe Mom is right. Maybe Ren doesn't want my help. Which is when the three dots reappear. Then a giant thumbs-up.

Ren doesn't like to feel ambushed, so this won't be an intervention. Just two boys, hanging out. I flick the electric kettle on and pull out a tin of honeysuckle tea sprinkled with rose petals, Ren's favorite. I bring out his mug, too—the ceramic one shaped like a strawberry, with its crown of green leaves and sepals for a lid. I dim the lights to make the living room softer, more sleepy. The point isn't to expose anyone. I don't want Ren to feel judged for his poor boyfriend tastes. I want him to open up. From there, we can heal.

The doorbell rings.

I find Ren on my doorstep, hugging himself in the cold, even in his thick, woolly sweater. Seeing him there, shivering...I want to cry. Not because he has that frail-dandelion-fluff look about him again, like the lightest breeze can blow him away. But because he's smiling at me like everything is normal, when everything's not.

Ren sinks into our couch and digs into the tray of pink mochis I leave out for him. He doesn't eat the mochi. Just holds the squishy thing up and watches it melt. He pinches the rice skin like it's sticky tack.

Mom and I don't have a television in the living room, so I turn on my laptop. "Wanna watch something?"

"Like what?"

I grin.

"Damn," Ren says later. He's watching through latticed fingers as Prince Endymion kicks Sailor Moon in the gut. "I forgot how brutal this episode was."

We're watching the season one finale. Japanese version with English subtitles on. Ren isn't wrong. Prince Endymion is full-on beating up Sailor Moon like an abusive boyfriend because he is corrupted by Queen Beryl's magic. When he raises a sword, ready to cut Sailor Moon's head off, I wonder if this is all too triggering. I wonder if Ren is thinking about Marshall.

I lean over to pause the show. "We could watch something more recent. *Sailor Moon Eternal*? *Cosmos*?"

Without looking at me, Ren mutters, "Colin, I know why you invited me over." I blow into my mug and shoot him a look like, *Whatever do you mean?* But Ren sighs. "You want to ask me about him. So just ask."

I sit up. This is going faster than I want it to. And I was so busy stressing about whether or not I could open Ren up, I didn't plan a single question for him if I did. So, I hear myself ask stupidly, "How did you two meet?"

Ren fixes his eyes on the frozen screen. Sailor Moon is on her knees, holding out her star locket to us like a bleeding heart. "At a bus stop. The one on Sandyhook."

The story sounds so ordinary I realize he's not talking about Marshall. I try to cover my disappointment. This information can still be useful. "Duke One?"

Ren nods. "His real name..." Then Ren stops, like maybe it hurts just to think it.

"When did you meet? Over the summer?" That would make the most sense. Ren said it would be *his* summer. Salacious Summer. Bad Boy Summer.

"No." Ren frowns, remembering. "It was first semester, around midterms. October?"

I nod as the timeline clicks into place. Not Ren's Sexy Summer. His Fall from Grace. "How long?"

"Not long. Maybe a month?"

One month. Ren was seeing Duke One, calling him, messaging, for one month. If I never found out, did he ever plan on telling me? Why didn't he, when I told him about Ferris, Puppy Chow. I even told him about that guy at the bookstore who smiled at me. Because that's what friends do. That's what—

I catch myself. For now, none of that matters. "So you met at the bus stop."

"I needed to get downtown. To 510. Remember?"

I nod. 510 is a men's health clinic downtown. Last semester, every Thursday after school, Ren volunteered at their front desk, taking phone calls, filing, grabbing coffee. He needed to complete his forty hours of community service—all the students in Ontario have to do it.

"Anyway, I kept seeing him at the bus stop without noticing him. This was right in the middle of university applications. And I felt so behind. I didn't start any of my personal essays, or finish my portfolio. I was scrambling."

I remember. There were weeks when I barely saw Ren outside of school hours, and on the rare occasion we met I steered clear of school talk. One time Ren called me, crying. What if he would have to stay back a year?

"At the bus stop, I'm doing this gesture drawing—the scribbly ones you have to finish in thirty seconds. Then this guy asks me what I'm drawing. And when I show him, he breaks into this huge smile and says he's impressed. And so I hand him my portfolio and he flips through it, gaping, and he says it's amazing, says any art school would be stupid not to accept me, and I want to burst into tears, because I needed to hear that."

"And you started dating?"

"Don't make that judge-y face at me."

"I'm not!" I fuss. Though I can't help it. I kind of am.

I ask in my most casual tone, "Was there anything"—*supernatural? evil? demonic?*—"off about him?"

Ren huffs. "Off? No. He was so...regular. He always wore a regular hoodie with a regular baseball cap, and had on these boring, regular shoes. Even when he took me out, which didn't happen a lot, and never in our neighborhood, where anyone would recognize him—we'd go to diners and fast-food places."

"So, he never brought you anywhere weird"—like a haunted house?—"or did he ever give you a weird trinket? An amulet, maybe, or a tiny statue?" Blair called it a conduit, a physical object tethering a demonic entity.

"Maybe that's what I liked about him," Ren continues, lost in his own train of thought. "That he was regular. That he balanced me out. Colin." Ren sits up and turns to me. "You know when we're together? And people sort of stare at us? Even on the days we don't dial it up, when we're just wearing eyeliner, people stare. Because there's two of us, so people notice us more. As if we highlight each other's strangeness." Ren cuts off, catching himself.

*Strangeness.* I dry-swallow the word and pretend its jagged edges don't tear at my throat. "Go on."

"With him, people didn't look as much. Or if they did, it was different. More like...approval. Like I stood out less with someone so regular. And I didn't realize until then how much I wanted that, something regular. Something plain and familiar and—and sturdy."

By now, the mochis have melted in their tray, their pink skin deflated, drowning in their insides.

*Did you love him?* I stop myself from asking, though I'm not sure what's stopping me. Maybe because it's irrelevant to Marshall. But Ren seems sad, and I know he wants to talk about this more. "What else did you like about him?"

Ren fixes his eyes on the laptop screen. He smiles a sad smile. "He liked my art. There were little things, too. When you like someone—*really* like him—you start noticing things about him in freaky detail. The way his eyebrows raise, barely a millimeter, before he smiles. How he clears his throat when he's nervous versus when he's irritated, that difference in sound that is so small no one else can tell but you. You can tell them apart the way some people can tell apart different kinds of snow. And over time you notice he doesn't do these things with other people—the person at the counter, the server flirting with him—only with you. And you think maybe this means those little smiles, that nervousness, is only *for* you, because you bring this side out of him. And it sounds clichéd, but we could be in a crowded room and I'd still feel alone with him. Because there was this dome around us, and it didn't matter that his friends didn't know, because I had this thing that was just mine."

I smile at Ren, even though everything inside me hurts. Not because I've never experienced this for myself. In a way, I have.

With Ferris. And the first thing I wanted to do was share it with Ren.

Now, he hitches up his legs and tucks them underneath his bum. "One time, he brought me to this diner. We were in line and this girl turned and whipped her ponytail in my face, and I felt him get close behind me, and I don't know how his face looked, but the girl glanced at him and muttered, 'Sorry—sorry' to me, and I felt his hand press into my lower back for a second. I liked that. I liked feeling protected. And I liked having to look up at him because he was taller.

"That was the fun part of falling for him—falling for me, for the person I got to be around him. I guess I was always those things. Small, soft, fem, but for once I felt safe. I could be those things freely. I felt new."

I hear a bell go *ding-ding* and Mr. Voiceover announcing: *Ren in Love—New Character: Unlocked!*

Ren looks at his hands. "You know how in the movies, when people break up there's, like . . . a blowup? Or tears or an argument. At the very least, a *conversation*. He didn't give me any of that." Ren catches me looking at his hands, and this makes him fold them into his lap. "He just . . . disappeared."

My heart hurts for Ren. Duke One pulled a Ferris. What is it with boys and their avoidant personalities? Why do we fall for cowards?

"And that sucked," Ren goes on. "Because I didn't need him to stay with me. I just wanted to talk. Because if we talked, that meant I was worth the time. That what we had *happened*."

Ren looks around us like there's so much more to say, and it's scattered around us like sharp Lego pieces, but there's too much of it, and he doesn't know where to start without stepping on one and hurting himself. "The next time I saw him, I was with you."

My fingers grip into my mug so tightly it could break.

Duke spat on Ren.

They were together and he *spat* on him.

"Ren, I'm so sorry. That must have... How did that feel?"

"It felt..." Ren grabs the cushion next to him and snakes his arms around it. He hugs it with a viselike clinginess I can feel pressing into my own chest. After Ferris ghosted me, my heart hurt so much—especially at nighttime, when I tried to sleep—that I started stacking things on top of it. Pillows, weighted blankets, my hands. The only way to dull that ache was to smother it.

Ren tries again. "It felt like mitosis."

Um.

"That last phase, when the cell splits. Like the breakup pinched me in half, leaving a Me Before the relationship, and a Me After, and the Me After had all the same memories, the same DNA, meaning I should feel like the same person, right? But I didn't. I felt like a copy. And all the things I used to do for myself—reading by the window, watching *Hot Ones* interviews and imagining myself as a guest—all the things I used to love, I suddenly couldn't. Because I poured all the love I had into this one person who left. And you know the worst part?" Ren lays the cushion in his lap. "It wasn't when he stopped messaging me or stopped showing up at the bus stop. It was after all that, when I gave up hope. When I tried not thinking about him. Those quiet moments, on my way between classes. Lying in bed for so long I never thought I'd fall asleep. First thing in the morning. Sometimes I'd wake up, and before anything I'd feel that hurt. It became a part of me, an organ, and I had to keep moving, talking, blasting music to numb my eardrums, numb everything, to forget it was there." Ren stops. The silence is so loud it hums. "You know?"

I do, I think. When everything inside you is empty and quiet but *hurts*. God, how that loud quiet hurts.

"Did you two ever..." I start. "I mean..."

Ren shakes his head. "We only kissed. My first." Ren chuffs at the ceiling. "He took it."

I imagine Duke One slipping the kiss into a baggy coat, easy as a thimble or a button. I imagine the kiss in his pocket, tumbling with every stolen, forgotten thing he was too stupid to cherish. "Did you love him?"

Ren doesn't respond. He draws up his legs and hugs them into his chest.

"Well, who cares about that poop-head! You're so much better than him. You're the best. That's why so many boys like you."

Ren squints as though I've just said something ridiculous and he's not sure if I'm joking. "Colin, no they don't." He says this slowly, like it's obvious.

"What do you mean? There's Dave, and those guys at the club. Guys are always checking you out—"

"That doesn't matter."

I stop. Ren is glaring at me. He draws in a rattling breath. "Colin, checking someone out isn't the same as liking them. Sure, guys are interested at first, but then they lose it. They take what they want and they get bored."

"But, Ren, he was just one boy. There are others."

"There won't be. No one will ever like me because..." He stops. Then it slips out of him, lifeless. "No one will ever love me because there's nothing inside me worth loving."

I sit here, stunned, unsure what to say. Unsure if I just imagined Ren saying that. But then he closes his eyes and his face twists in pain, like his own heart is hurting him. Like it's bursting out of his chest or pumping dark energy into his veins.

I want to get rid of it, this monstrous pain. The way Sailor Moon might with a flick of her Eternal Tiare. I would yell, *Starlight Honeymoon Therapy Kiss!* and blast the self-loathing out of Ren in an explosion of pink light. And when the magic faded, when the monster was gone, there Ren would be, as he was before.

But I don't have magic. All I've ever had are my words, and even as I say them now I know they won't be enough. "Ren, I don't want you to feel like this."

Which seems to make him feel worse. He folds his arms over his chest and hunches over, as though he's trying to crawl into himself. My chest seizes, seeing him get this small, because in this moment he reminds me of me. And he can't be me. Ren is so much better. He *has* to be better. I don't know why it's so important to me that he is.

We sit there in gloomy silence for about a minute.

Then a memory bobs to the surface, gasping for air, and I'm breathless, too, when I cry, "The gay whale!"

Ren puckers his lips into the perfect O. "The what?"

"Remember in our first year, when we were super stressed about exams—*our first exams ever*—and we went downtown to study? And you found that little coffee shop on Queen's Quay, along the waterfront?"

"Bean Me Up, Scotty." Ren furrows his brows, unsure where this is going.

"And there was this signage, stuck on the giant column. A whole history of the quay. And some of the letters were peeling off."

Now Ren is smiling, too, and I see the memory brewing in his brown eyes, like he can smell the dark roast. Then we're both hurtling backward in time, through the doors of Bean Me Up, sinking into their pleather armchairs.

"And on the sign, there was this one part, about a whale sighting ten years ago, along the waterfront. It was so unusual some say it probably never happened. A gray whale. Like, what was a *gray whale* doing there? But someone scratched out the *r* so it said *gay whale*. And you laughed because the sign said, 'A magnificent gay whale swam into Queen's Quay.' And I laughed, too, even though it wasn't that funny. It was so juvenile. But maybe we were so tired from all the studying, and we should have been stressing, but we just kept laughing—"

*"Okaaaaaaaay."* Ren rolls his eyes, but his cheeks have turned pink and now he's full-on grinning. He sits up. "But how does this excellent story have anything to do with *me*?"

"Because you always notice things. Like, we'll pass a gas station and you'll see a rosebush and a rose will be poking through the chain-link fence. And you'll stop so we can smell it. Or, you'll see a MISSING poster on a lamppost, and it'll be for someone's chameleon. Then we'll spend the rest of the day on the lookout for a lizard tail. You notice things all the time, especially when they're small. I don't notice that many things, maybe because I'm always looking down, or too stressed out. But it's like you're looking up and noticing things for the both of us. And that means I'm *lucky*, Ren. That means I'm the luckiest. Because if you didn't, if you weren't there, I would've missed the gay whale."

Ren turns away from me and makes this choking sound. He's crying, but in a good way, and his voice is high and shaky when he says, "Oh."

"He isn't worth it." I remember Ren's words to me, about Ferris, that day in the chapel. I remember them, and for the first time I believe them. "Duke One. He isn't worth it. Neither of them are."

I expect Ren to throw his arms around me and bawl into my ear about how wise I am, but he gets rigid. "What do you mean," he asks, "neither of them?"

I take a deep, shuddering breath. "Can we talk about Marshall?"

Ren doesn't say anything. He just turns his face down to the tray of melted mochis, like he wishes he was small enough to squirrel into one of them, hide under its skin. Then, finally, he speaks. "He told me not to tell you about him."

And that's when I realize: Ren isn't nervous. He's smiling. He giggles into a cupped hand. "Colin." Ren leans forward. "I'm sorry I kept it from you for so long, but he said you wouldn't understand. He made me *promise*." My wrist shivers, and I realize Ren is brushing his finger along it. All that sadness when he talked about Duke One is gone. Now his eyes light up like this is any other conversation we could have in my room or on the bleachers. Any other conversation about a boy.

I whisper, "He hurt Dave. You realize that?"

Ren glances away. "He only hurts people who hurt me."

"Dave didn't hurt you."

"He touched me."

"He *touched*—?" I must sound delirious, because I feel it. "Ren, he tried to hurt *me*! He hurt your dad!"

"My dad..." Ren's voice wobbles. He rises from the couch. He walks over to the sliding door leading into the backyard. He looks outside. "You heard my dad. He just wants me to be alone."

I realize something. "That night in the woods—was that *him*?" I know I shouldn't make this about me, but I can't help it. Ren lied. He lied and lied and now he's sitting here, smiling. "You told me I imagined it."

"I told you nothing in the forest would hurt us. That was the truth." Ren doesn't turn back as he says this.

I get up from the couch and join his side. "He *is* hurting you. I saw the bruises. The ones on your chest."

Ren shakes his head—like I don't understand. I want to snap at him. I want to scream. "He's a monster, Ren. He's scary."

"You know what's scary?" Ren asks, still looking outside. "Guys heckling you late at night. Guys calling you names. Looking at you like you don't deserve to breathe the same air. My dad, who I can't talk to about any of this because he'll use it as more proof I need to change. Because I did this on purpose, right? The way I am—I invited all this into my life. *That's scary.*"

In Ren's voice, I can hear the tinkling of the same jagged piece Mom left inside me after I came out. I had no idea Ren had one, too.

"At least with Marshall," he continues, "he's there for me. He understands. And he doesn't want me to change. He likes that I'm softer. Does he lose control? Yes. But that's why he needs me." Ren's voice gets all soft. "I can teach him how to love properly. I know I can do it this time. Even though I couldn't do it with…him." He means Duke One.

"How much do you really know about Marshall?" I wait for Ren to look up but he won't, so I continue. "He only shows you what you want to see. It's called omission neglect."

Ren glares at me. "*You're* telling me about omission neglect? What about you?"

"What about me?"

"You want to talk about toxic relationships? Do you know how exhausting it is, being friends *with you*?" Ren's eyes are misty now. So are mine. "You still cling on to me. I see it in your eyes when I even *mention* doing something without you...this hurt. Why do you think I threw out the Boyfriend Box? Why do you think I chose Green College?"

My voice gets small. "Because Marshall—"

"I chose Green before him. I chose a university on the other side of the country to get away from you. Because I'm ready to grow up, but you, you still want to follow me around. You don't want a best friend. You want to be someone's everything, even if it suffocates them." Ren wipes his eyes. "And now that I've found it, it's like...you want me to stay with you. Choose you, the way I always have. But I won't."

I've become a scarecrow and I'm choking on straw, my insides stuffed with huge bales of it. "What are you saying?"

"I think..." Ren swallows. "I used to need this friendship. And now I don't."

I wait for Ren to take it back. But he turns his face back to the sliding doors, squinting into our backyard, at the sad, wilting cabbages our neighbors upstairs are growing in the garden. The trunk of an old birch, pallid and thin, standing just outside the porch light's reach. Then Ren's face changes, like he sees something. He lifts a delicate finger to his lips.

"What?" I ask.

Ren backs away from the sliding doors. He's grinning.

"Ren, *what*?" I look out there, too, scan for some masked

figure skulking in the garden, the bushes. Leering at us from behind the tree. "Ren—"

*What do you see?* I want to ask. But I stop myself. Because now I see it, too.

Because now I'm fully awake, and I remember.

Our backyard doesn't have a tree.

It's not a tree out there. It's a man.

He stands so still outside the patch of moonlight I can't make out his face, can't make out any of his features, other than his height—maybe seven or eight feet tall—and that he is looking at me. Not at Ren, not at both of us. At me. I am sure of it. He wants me to see him, just enough of him—enough to know he is there.

I tear my eyes away. "Ren. Is that him?"

Ren unlatches the door. I dive forward before he can pull it open. "What are you doing?"

Ren fixes his eyes on the silhouette outside as he says, "I'm going to him." And we wrestle for the door handle as the porch light flickers and dies, and then the silhouette glides forward—*Oh God, it's coming right at us!*—until finally it comes to a stop in front of the door. I fall back, hitting the wall, as the figure tilts its head down at Ren. Then it raises both its hands and they are white, stark white, whiter even than the moonlight catching them, and it brings them together into a circle and it leans in and white fog comes out of it like he's breathing smoke through a tunnel. The figure runs a finger through the misted glass, runs a graceful arc up, then down, then up, then down, down, down, until I see what he's drawing. A heart.

On the other side of the glass, Ren presses his hand to it.

Ren reaches for the door handle.

"Don't," I hear myself say.

"He won't hurt me." Ren doesn't look at me when he says this. He is looking up at the figure like a flower turning its face to the sun. Ren is drinking him in. "You call him a demon, but you don't get it. This isn't like one of those horror movies." Ren slides the door open. "This is a love story."

The crisp night air creeps into the house, but the figure doesn't enter. It extends a long hand and Ren takes it. Then he walks out and they leave together, into the night.

# 22

Two hours after Ren leaves me, I'm in my room, scanning Yelp for recommended mediums nearby. I scroll the online profiles, trying my best to ignore the hole Ren punched through my chest. Maybe Ren didn't mean it. Maybe Marshall made him say those things.

My cursor lands on another profile. This one's name is Sebastian. He's young, maybe just a few years older than me. His cheeks are rosy, and he has a mop of curly red hair. Five stars. I click on a review:

> Sebastian is a miracle! After my brother went missing seven years ago, I was severely depressed, not knowing where he could be, if he was still alive. But after one session with Sebastian, I feel lighter. Because Sebastian said he couldn't reach my brother—meaning he is still alive!

I hit backspace again. Sebastian's cherubic face stares back at me from the little window of his profile. His smile reminds me of the look a gossipy friend might slip as you share a sad story with him, like he's a little too invested in your grief. *Oh, you poor thing. And what happened next?* I return to the listings.

My screen is littered with mediums with only two- or three-star reviews.

And then, near the bottom of the page, I see a four-star-rated profile. There's no photograph on this one. Just an hourglass, its lower bulb filled with sand.

*Old Man Twink*, the profile says. *Medium by day. Harpist by night.* There's only one review:

> What a bitch. But a bitch you want on your side—especially when you're dealing with dark forces.

I click onto his page. The blurb he included is short:

> I am a medium. Specifically, I am a sana mudang of the Shinism tradition. Look for someone else in the city who can do what I do.

I make a mental reminder to google *Shinism*. It sounds specific enough to be real. I scroll farther down the page, but there's nothing. No link to a website. Only a phone number. The profile says not to call until business hours—9:00 AM. But I can't wait for the sun to rise. I have to act now.

My phone tolls like a flatline for ten seconds before he picks up.

At least, I think he does. I expect a hello or some fake cheery greeting. But instead, all I can hear are his quick breaths.

"Hello?" I ask.

"Who is this? What do you want?"

I stumble to answer. "Um, hi there. Hello. Is this Old Man Twink?"

"It is" is all he says. I make a note to take a star off for lack of cordiality.

"Super!" I reply. "I'd like to schedule a reading?"

"Name?"

"Ong. Colin Ong."

"What day?"

"Uh, this is kind of pressing. Can we do it today?"

"This is very short notice," he says. "You're lucky I'm not booked."

*What a bitch.*

I'm beginning to lose my patience. "So is that a yes?"

Something squelches on the other line, like Old Man Twink is sitting in a big leather armchair. "Your voice," he drawls. "You sound like a child."

"I'm seventeen."

"Well, the rule is that in-person readings can only be set up by someone eighteen or older. Anyone younger requires a parent or a guardian to go with them."

"But your page didn't say that!" My protest comes out nasally, like a child whining after being told there's a pop quiz.

"Most mediums have an age requirement," Old Man Twink snaps. "Did you not do your research?"

The phone throbs in my hand. I had seen that requirement on some of the profiles, but I didn't realize it was a rule.

"Next time you call," he continues, "call with a parent, or don't call at all."

I know he's about to hang up, so I squawk, "Wait!" That squelching returns, like he's shifted his weight again. He must be annoyed, but he hasn't hung up. "Please, Mr. Twink. I don't know who else to turn to."

"Why do you want me to read for you?" he asks. "Hmm? Is there some dead celebrity you wish to contact? Or maybe you have a question about your love life? Which Ivy League college to attend?"

"You know what?" I force my voice to hold steady. "Shouldn't you already know why I'm calling?" The medium doesn't respond. I let all the anger shake out of me. "You're not a psychic. You're a bully. With a dumb stage name and a shitty website!"

I hear his weight shift in his chair. He is quiet for such a long time I wonder if he's hung up. "Um...hello?" I try, all my righteous anger deflating. "Mr. Twink?"

"You're calling for *him*," he finally says. "A brother, maybe? A lover? No. A friend. Someone in danger. Caught in a web—

latched on to—like the others. I see something else, too. A deep, dark wood."

Spit clumps in my throat. I swallow it. "You can't see all that."

"I never trust what I can see," he says. "Sometimes I question what I remember. You do, too."

A thousand mayflies scuttle across my skin. "What is this thing that's latched on to my friend? Do you know?"

"No," the medium responds. "For that, I'll need to speak to him."

The little dangling hope in my chest snaps like gossamer thread. Ren won't speak to this man. My chest lurches. *He won't even speak to me.*

"I need to know what this thing is so I can fight it. Can you help?"

Another long, infuriating pause. Finally, he says, "I just need three things from you."

"Okay." I clamber to open my notebook and grab a sparkly purple pen. "What do you need?"

"First, I need you to bring your parent. That's the rule," he says sharply before I can protest. "Any client under eighteen must have a guardian. This is dangerous work. Do you understand?"

"Yes," I reply, wondering how on earth I can talk Mom into coming. "What's the second thing?"

"A promise." His voice stretches each syllable out. "*To the head it brings madness. To the heart it brings death.* The spirit around you won't stop chattering. I could hear its voice the second I picked up. It's not a bad spirit," he adds, sensing my question. "They're afraid of it. That grit you showed me earlier—that fire. You need more of that."

I write down *fire*.

"That's two things," I say.

"What?"

"You said you wanted three things, but you only mentioned two."

There's a pause. "Right," Old Man Twink says dryly. "Do not attempt to contact this thing on your own. Do not challenge it. Courage is not stupidity. This thing is ancient. It will respond. And it will be more powerful."

The phone presses against my moist cheek.

"I will text you a time and place, Colin. Wait for it." He hangs up.

# 23

In the morning, I wake up to the sound of my phone dinging on my nightstand. It's Blair.

You're visiting a medium.

No *hi*. No emoji. And he ended his text with a period. Do all boys suck at communicating?

Heeeey! Yeah. He lives in Bayview LOL

And you're visiting him. Alone.

Nooo! I'm asking my mom to take me

And if she says no? What then?

Three dots appear as Blair texts something else. Each dot feels like a land mine, judge-y thoughts in hiding. I thumb a response before he can finish his:

If she says no, I'll go by myself.

As I slip on my pretty panda socks, my phone dings again.

Colin.

*Ding.*

DON'T.

*Ding.*

Do NOT visit the home of a stranger ALONE.

I message him back:

Turning off phone now.

Three little dots tell me Blair is texting a response, but I power off my Huawei before he can send it.

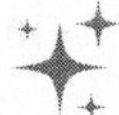

When I enter the kitchen to talk to Mom, she's having tea with the aunties. Auntie Carmen, Auntie Fa, Auntie Rose. They used to come over all the time for gossip and chai. Sharing the misfortune of other Hakka families in the community over the clinking of mahjong tiles. They all go for the same look, hennaed ringlets rolled tight into their scalps.

"Colin!" Auntie Rose bellows. She rises and pulls me into a Mom-perfumed hug. "What a handsome boy you've become. Isn't he so handsome?" she asks in Hakka.

*"So handsome,"* Auntie Carmen coos.

"Your mom is very proud of you, you know?" Auntie Fa simpers. She alone speaks to me in English. Mom always said she was the most whitewashed because before Canada she lived in New Zealand.

"So, Colin," Auntie Rose starts as she sinks into the chair next to Mom. "Do you have a girlfriend?"

The other aunties lean in with matching grins. Mom freezes like a statue as I fix a smile and mutter, "Nope. No girlfriend." Then, "Mom? Can I talk to you for a second?"

As she joins me in the hallway, I wonder how on earth I can convince her to take me to the medium. Maybe I can say it's for a research project? But before I start, Mom leans in close and whispers, "Don't tell them."

I blink. "What?"

"About you." Mom doesn't elaborate, but she doesn't need to. What else could she want to hide from them? "And these women are judgmental, okay? They *talk*. Once they know about you, everyone else will. So keep your mouth shut."

Mom spins on her heel and walks back into the kitchen. I hear her flip-flops slap against the tiles while I stand here, dumbstruck, looking at my socks. There's a tiny hole in the left one.

The aunties beam when I join them again. "No girlfriend," Auntie Fa repeats, picking up the subject where we left off. "Unbelievable. You're becoming so handsome."

The others nod their condolences. *Oh, it'll happen soon*, they gush. *You're a catch.*

And that should be the end of it.

But seeing Mom sitting there, smiling down at her mug—smiling as though she hasn't just ambushed me, when my guard was down, when I wanted to trust her—seeing my mother smiling makes me snap.

"Actually," I continue. "I *am* seeing someone."

Auntie Carmen winks at Mom, who raises her face.

Auntie Fa whoops. "I knew it."

Auntie Rose asks, "Is she Chinese?"

"Oh," I say, matching Mom's venomous gaze with poison darts of my own. "He's not."

The aunties look from me to Mom. Mom to me. *He?*

"Don't say such things," Auntie Carmen finally says with a *Bah!*

"Don't be closed-minded," Auntie Rose chastises her. "It's a different age, you know? Last week I got a wedding invite from Jennifer's daughter. She's marrying a woman."

"But they're *Jamaican* Hakka," Auntie Fa says wisely. "They're more progressive."

I drown them out. The disapproval of all the world's Asian mothers is glaring back at me through the whites of Mom's eyes.

The aunties don't seem to notice. They're too busy chatting, and when the doorbell rings and Mom and I are still having a standoff, Auntie Fa takes off to answer it.

*You're a disgrace,* Mom's eyes are saying.

*Welp,* my eyes say back.

"Sorry to interrupt," a new voice says. I look up.

It's Blair. He's wearing his signature collar ruffle again, and his eyes look uncertain as they peer around the table through his cat-eye glasses: from me to the gobsmacked aunties to Mom, who has no idea who this boy is, what he is doing in her house.

Blair gives a sheepish wave to each of the aunties, who continue to stare back at him, open-mouthed. "I'm Colin's friend," he says, still waving. I want to tell him to stop waving. "From school."

Auntie Fa and Auntie Rose exchange a knowing look. Colin's *friend.*

Auntie Carmen cups her hand over her mouth.

I give Blair a look that says, *What are you doing here?*

*You weren't responding to my texts,* he looks back.

*"Colin,"* Mom cuts in, sharp enough for both Blair and me to wince. "Who is this boy?" She turns to him. "Who are you?"

"I'll just come back when y'all are done," Blair says, backing away.

But I'm already leaping out of my chair. "Wait for me." I grab Blair's hand and drag him toward the front door. We're already walking through it as I hear Auntie Rose say, "Whoa! He was so pretty!"

Once we're on the front lawn and enter precious silence and the still, open air, I drop Blair's hand. "Okay, seriously. What are you doing here?"

"You should be nicer," he replies as a car drives by. "I came all the way here to make sure you don't do anything stupid. Like visit a stranger's home in the middle of nowhere by yourself."

Blair walks ahead and I follow. I'm not even sure where we're going, but I don't care, as long as it takes us farther away from this house. "How do you even know where I live?"

"I asked around."

"That sounds very stalker-y. Anyway, you didn't have to check in on me. I told you I was asking my mom."

"Didn't look like she wanted to go anywhere with you."

I kick a pebble. "Whatever. I don't care what Old Man Twink says. I'm forcing him to help us."

Blair and I stop at a stop sign. "Wait," I realize. "Are you coming with me? You know you don't have to, right?"

Blair frowns. "Oh, I know I don't." I try not to notice how the sunlight kisses his sharp cheekbones and strong chin. Auntie Rose was right. He is pretty. "And because all the red flags are telling me not to meet a stranger alone in his house, we're bringing muscle."

"Muscle?" I squint because Blair's pearly grin reflects sunshine. "Who?"

# 24

LOOK AT US!" BABY GAP SINGSONGS FROM BEHIND HIS wheel. "Just three hot bitches out on the town."

Baby Gap merges his SUV onto the 401. From the back seat, I watch as the dial on his dashboard shoots up to ninety-five per hour. I catch Blair's reflection in the side-view mirror: catch him looking at me before feigning interest in the yellow lines on the highway. He must be trying to gauge how annoyed I am by this surprise tagalong.

"Ooooh, let's listen to music," Baby Gap chirps. "Anyone listen to K-pop? My ult bias is—" But before he can finish his sentence a rocket-red beamer peels to our left. The driver spits expletives out from his window. *Drive faster!* his fleshy lips mouth.

Without taking his eyes off the road, Baby Gap flashes the man his middle finger. "Or Pink Sweats," he continues as though there was no interruption.

Baby Gap is so characteristically breezy about everything I feel the need to speak up. "Baby Gap?" I ask. When I sit up in his leather seating it squelches like a fart. "How much did Blair tell you about what we're doing?"

"Oh, you know." Baby Gap checks his rearview mirror. Signals left. Checks his blind spot. "Ren met a new fella. Bad news. Demonic intentions, et cetera, et cetera. Blair gave me the full update. There was a prezi and everything." When Baby Gap catches my amazed look in his rearview mirror, he adds, "Look. My mom's got stories from back home. About ghosts and stuff. Now, I'm not saying I believe any of this, but a reading sounds like a cool way to spend the night."

I gasp when it hits me. "Tonight!" The others eye me through the rearview mirror. "*Prom* is tonight!"

Blair tilts his head. "And?"

"And instead of doing prom things, you're here with me!"

"And?"

"And..." I flush and stare at my hands. "I really appreciate your support, but...you're missing a huge milestone."

Blair cranes his neck so he can face me. "What are we missing? I have no desire to see three hundred boys wearing the same boring navy suit"—I wince, thinking of the navy suit I bought from Box of Delights—"and their dates will have that wet-hair look."

I turn to Baby Gap. "But you organized it. Don't you want to see how it turned out?"

Baby Gap sighs. "I don't have a date."

Blair pats his shoulder. Then, "Okay! Just so we're all clear on our objectives tonight," he says as though he's outlining a presentation. "Our goal is twofold: figure out what this thing wants and how we can fight it. And this is all assuming the medium knows what he's talking about."

"Oh. We're fighting it?" Baby Gap pouts. "I just don't think we should rush to judge something we don't understand." With that, Baby Gap clicks his volume dial, and the SUV explodes into eight-bit music. Suddenly we're all characters in an RPG game. "It's like *Frankenstein* says: Some monsters are just misunderstood."

Blair groans. "I hate when people use *Frankenstein* to make that argument. The monster reads Wordsworth and picks flowers. Of course people sympathize with him. But what about Freddy Krueger? Pennywise? Make the same case with them."

"You are insufferable," Baby Gap replies. He flashes me a grin in his rearview mirror. "Blair always gets up his own ass. Did you know he likes his own comments on YouTube?"

"Just drive!" Blair sits up straighter in his seat, and I realize he's grinning—I've never seen him this comfortable with anyone.

Baby Gap bows his head in deference. "I'm just saying, if we were all more compassionate, we'd create less monsters. Maybe Leatherface would stop wearing other people's faces if he just learned to believe in himself."

Blair catches me grinning at him in the side mirror. He shakes his head.

I crack open my window and let the spring air and sunlight touch my skin. I wonder if Baby Gap and Blair talk like this all the time. I imagine them together on the weekends, streaming B horror movies on websites itching with spyware.

They make me think about me and Ren, and how maybe he was right. Maybe we were mostly afraid and desperate and lonely. Maybe the world forced us to need each other. But we had moments like this, too, didn't we? Inside jokes. A private language. A smaller world, inside the scarier one, scrapped together out of magazines and cheesy quotes and Sailor Moon references.

"Anyone want a doughnut?" I hear Blair ask over the *Tetris* song.

Baby Gap *ooohs* and signals right. "Pee break."

As Baby Gap waits in line for our orders, Blair and I take a seat at one of the sticky tables near the windows of Tim Hortons.

"So," Blair says. "Your mom." His chin is cradled in his palm. When I don't reply, he treads with caution. "I take it she's not the most supportive."

My seat is the round kind that twists around. I take advantage of this function, squeaking and swiveling my seat this way and that. "I don't want to talk about her."

"Fair."

I watch Baby Gap up ahead, holding a tray with three coffees. He's still waiting on the doughnuts. He catches us looking and winks at Blair. When Blair winks back, something occurs to me.

"So, you and Baby Gap," I start, casually. I fix my eyes on the pockmarked wall behind Blair. "Did you two ever..."

Blair stares. Then his eyes widen. "What? Date?" He sounds like he wants to laugh. "No. We're just friends." His attention flicks back to Baby Gap. "I guess he'd make a good boyfriend."

"Oh?"

"He bakes."

"So do I," I lie. Why am I lying?

"Huh." Blair tilts his head like he's reexamining me. "Baking? You?"

"You don't believe me?"

"I took you more for a cooking guy."

I'm surprised Blair took me for anything. I grin. "You mean like someone who barbecues? Someone butch?" Blair's mouth pinches into a smile and it's kind of amazing, so I keep going. "Oh my gosh, do I seem like a sigma? Someone who cooks steaks on the grill?"

Blair lays a hand on my elbow for a fluttery second, theatrically horrified I could ever think I'd pass for straight. "Oh no, Colin. *Absolutely not.* I meant more like quiches and pasta salads and cheese plates." Then Blair checks his phone to look up how much farther away Old Man Twink lives, and I'll check on my phone, too, I will. As soon as I stop smiling. As soon as my elbow stops tingling where Blair touched it, gentle-soft, a butterfly's landing.

Baby Gap joins us with our tray and a comically large box of doughnuts. He lays everything down. "School just emailed us," he says, pulling out his phone. "Details for that scholarship. The Isaiah something."

"The Isaiah Brackert Memorial Scholarship?" Blair and I say in unison. I sidle up to Baby Gap's left. Blair to his right. The three of us read off his phone.

Baby Gap opens the email and taps the blue link to the memorial website. The website loads a grainy black-and-white photo. It's a boy of about seventeen. This must be Isaiah Brackert.

A tendril knots in my chest when I realize I've never actually looked into this boy before, or his family who created this grant. For so long, the Brackerts have only been rich people with money. Never a grieving mom and dad and their lost boy, who died so young.

In the photo, he's ducking his freckled face into a shy smile. It's the same move I use to avoid exposing too many features. I wonder if he's doing the same thing, trying to hide his long and sharp nose.

The rest of the photo loads down his body. His slender, girlish neck. His white button-up dress shirt and the maroon tie (maroon must have been our school color back then). Gray khaki shorts. Black dress shoes, scuffed at the soles.

*Fingertips hold the shoe up delicately like it's brittle. Made out of glass.*

I've seen this boy before.

"The Boy in Short Shorts."

Baby Gap looks at me. "The boy in what?"

"I saw him in Birchmount Forest." My voice squeaks, and Baby Gap looks at the table of middle-school boys a few feet away, daring them to laugh. "Then I saw him at Ren's."

"But he's dead," Blair says carefully. "He died twenty years ago."

"Reported dead," Baby Gap corrects. "Says here he went missing."

"*Last seen on campus late at night,*" Blair reads from his own phone. "He was heading home."

Quickest route home is through Birchmount Forest.

I'm aware of how quiet the two middle-school boys have gotten, but I don't care. Not when, finally, it feels like something has clicked.

Baby Gap asks, "So this is our guy? The spirit haunting Ren?"

I bite my lip. All this time Isaiah has been warning me about something.

He was heading home.

"I think something in the forest got Isaiah. Thirty years ago. I think this same thing is now after Ren."

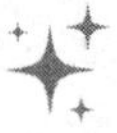

The medium's house waits for us behind a wrought-iron fence. He lives at the top of an old split, five stories high.

Baby Gap takes note of the chipped white clapboards. Creeping ivy, withered and brown. "Looks like somewhere you'd live," he tells Blair.

Blair squeaks the gated fence open, sending a Saint Bernard lumbering out of the lowest apartment. It runs at us, goofy tail wagging, and Baby Gap tenses beside me until we hear a woman call "Winnie!" and the dog spins around and trots back inside.

"You okay?" I ask Baby Gap, who has a hand pressed to his chest.

"Dog fear," he says between breaths. "It's why I could never get into sexy werewolves."

We spiral up the staircase to the topmost roost. A peeling red door greets us. "Ten bucks says his lampshades are made of human skin," Blair mutters. Then he gives the angel-head knocker three raps.

There's some rustling behind the door, like a plastic bag, and then the door creaks open. A locked chain goes *clink*. A single eye peers back at me through the crack. It swivels across the three of us, like Sauron in Barad-dûr, scanning his base for incoming enemies.

"What do you want?" the evil eye spits. "Who are you?"

Neither Blair nor Baby Gap speak, too disarmed by Old Man Twink's bitchiness.

I clear the ball of saliva in my throat. "It's Colin Ong? We have an appointment, remember?"

"And your mother?" the eye says. "Where is she hiding?"

"She's not—" I start.

He cuts in: "Then no reading." Old Man Twink clocks Blair, who folds his arms. "Look, I've already told your friend before. Channeling the otherworld is dangerous work, and no way am I doing that without a parent's consent. That is the rule. And you should be suspicious of any medium eager to break it. Consider this a life lesson."

"But if you could just—"

"Ta. Ta," he enunciates. And then he shuts the door.

Somewhere below us, the dog named Winnie pines for a treat. Baby Gap looks to me, then to Blair. Looks to someone to do something. I bang on the knocker. Six, seven, eight times before the door swings open and the chain clinks again.

*"What?"*

"We're not leaving until you help us." I jut my chin out, do my best not to wither under his gaze.

Baby Gap steps in front of me. Grinning, he says, "Listen. Old Man Twink, is it? Can I call you Old Man?"

"You may not."

Baby Gap winks. "Understood. Look, my friends and I came all the way here because none of the adults in our lives will help us. They don't care. Truly, you're our last hope."

The eyeball's glare softens a little, and suddenly I understand why Baby Gap was voted our year's social rep two years in a row.

"You remember what it's like," Baby Gap presses on, words dribbling with syrup. "When you were once a young person like us, did you have a friend who you loved, and they were in trouble? And didn't you wish someone else who *could* help you would care enough?"

Again, Old Man Twink slams the door in our faces. But then we hear the chain slide off on the other side, and the door flies open.

"Twenty minutes," he barks.

"Whoa." Baby Gap takes in the medium's long silk robe, a jade serpent's tail swishing behind him as he sweeps across to the living area. He slithers between the potted delphiniums and teetering stacks of books. "He's... orange." Baby Gap's observation doesn't sound judgmental, though. He sounds impressed.

We all are. First, Old Man Twink isn't old at all. Maybe a bit over sixty-five. His hair is a shock of white but his skin, lightly wrinkled around the eyes, has been spray-tanned so bronze his whole body looks gilded with gold. Like a trophy that sprung to life on a display case.

He glances at us over his shoulder. "Shoes off." Old Man Twink leans over his couch and takes a wad of clean, unfolded laundry. He throws it onto his rug. The apartment smells like a temple, with incense burning somewhere, though I can't see his shrine.

I sit between Blair and Baby Gap. Old Man Twink eases himself into the leather love seat across from us. "Do you have an object of his? Your friend."

I stare at him blankly. "Why do you need that?"

"Well, I need something if I want to read him."

"You never said that!"

Old Man Twink crosses his arms, and I think and think.

Wait.

I scramble to unzip my backpack, digging past my notes until I feel the thing at the bottom, the size of a lighter. When I hold the kaleidoscope out, Old Man Twink takes it from me in a polished hand. I catch a flash of five black glittering dragon scales. I hold my breath as Old Man Twink surveys it. Holds it up to the light. Then he presses it to his chest, eyes closed. Thin eyebrows knitted.

"Anything?" I finally ask.

"It's strange," he says, looking back at me. "I can see your friend in class, in bed, at a café, scribbling something. But the rest...blank."

"Blank." Next to me, Blair purses his lips. I can tell he wants to say more.

"I mean the man is blank," Old Man Twink explains. He holds out the kaleidoscope for me to reclaim, but I don't take it. Not when taking it means defeat. Old Man Twink sighs. "Our auras graft parts of ourselves onto the things we love. Or that bring us joy. They give little windows into our hearts, our memories. But this...it's like parts of it have been wiped clean. Like"—his wrist rolls circles into the air—"it seems whatever has taken control over your friend can white itself out of his memories."

"So, you can't see anything?" I ask. "You can't see what it is?"

"This thing is clever. It doesn't want to be seen. Most things don't, when they have that much power."

Blair scoffs. "How convenient."

I feel Baby Gap's whole body seize on my other side. Old Man Twink's heavily lidded gaze lands on Blair. "Come again?"

"How convenient," Blair repeats more slowly. "These arbitrary rules—from no traceable belief system."

Old Man Twink folds his hands into his lap. "Your friend seems to believe in my gifts, or you wouldn't all be here."

"He's desperate," Blair replies. Then, turning to me, "I'm sorry, Colin. But you are."

Old Man Twink squares his shoulders back. "Just what are you implying? That I'm taking advantage of him?"

Blair levels his gaze. "I've watched the YouTube breakdown videos on mediums. They're called cold readings—dropping breadcrumbs to get a reaction. Some go so far as to research their clients."

"You think I'm a fraud."

"I think you're a grief vampire."

Blair's words drop like a paperweight. For a moment, no one says anything. Then Old Man Twink stirs in his conch shell, and I expect him to fly at Blair, talons tearing at his beautiful face. Instead, the medium lifts his birdlike shoulders into a shrug. "I prefer Grief Succubus."

Blair slings an arm through the leather strap of his messenger bag. "Let's go, guys."

Baby Gap gives a shy wave and squeezes past me. He follows Blair to the front door.

Old Man Twink watches me, penciled eyebrow raised. *Well?* it says. *Aren't you leaving, too?*

"What if we do one more reading?"

"Colin—"

"Just one, Blair." I'm so hasty in my march over to him I nearly knock over the leaning tower of books. "Can I see your bag?"

"My bag?" Blair coils its strap around his hand. "Why?"

"Trust me."

Blair tugs his dissent collar, like I've seen him do so many times before.

"Thanks," I say as I take it and rummage inside. I find what I'm looking for. Of course I do. Blair never leaves home without his homework.

"*Latin Odyssey*?" Old Man Twink reads when I plop the textbook into his lap.

I sit across from him. "That aura-memory thing you talked about. Do the dead leave them behind, too?"

"In death we see truth," Old Man Twink responds, though I'm not sure that answers my question. His polished hand grazes the cover. "Isaiah." The name shudders out of him, sending a chill to everyone in the room.

Blair steps forward. "What did you just say?"

Old Man Twink says, "He's cold, this boy. Always outside. Lost in rows. Rows and rows of eyes. So many of them."

The seat next to me sinks in as Blair reclaims his spot.

"He is calling," Old Man Twink whispers. "For Mom. For Dad. But the sound dies in his chest, eaten by the hole. This terrible, terrible hole this thing has left. *Can you hear me, Colin? Can you hear me?*"

Those last words to come out of Old Man Twink were not his own. He spoke them in another's voice. Not husky or tired, but light, cracking with uncertainty. A boy's voice. My stomach drops like the time I was downtown and turned my face up until I could see the top of a skyscraper.

"Who are you?" I ask, but somehow I know, without knowing his name. The Boy in Short Shorts.

"Isaiah," the voice answers. "My name used to be Isaiah."

I feel Blair rustle next to me, and then Old Man Twink lunges forward and digs his dragon-scaled fingers into my wrist. "Beware," he chokes.

"Whoa, hey!" Blair tries to pry the medium's hands off. But I'm too stunned to help him. Too stunned to do anything other than lose myself in the milky whiteness of Old Man Twink's eyes, rolling back.

"Beware the One with the White Hand," he breathes. "To the head it brings madness. To the heart it brings death."

And with a fish-mouthed gasp, Old Man Twink's fingers loosen their grip, and his arms go limp. The medium's head slumps forward, chin bumping into his chest.

"Oh my god." Baby Gap tiptoes over to him. His face blanches. "Did we just kill him?"

His face still downturned, Old Man Twink raises a limp arm.

Blair asks, "Are you okay?"

In response, the medium crooks a gnarled finger, and something horrible cracks open the silence in the apartment. A creak and a bang. In the corner of the flat, a closet door has swung open, laying its insides bare. Wigs and old dresses trail down from a rack like glittering entrails. On its hanger, one of the dresses sways back and forth. Something is hiding in there.

*"In."* Old Man Twink does not raise his chin, and his eyes are still closed.

"What?"

"In," he croaks again.

I take in the closet. It's small, barely a walk-in.

Old Man Twink sways in his chair. "He has more to say." His words are raspy. "But only to you."

Like an open maw, the closet waits for me to climb inside.

"Don't," I hear Blair say. He doesn't get up to stop me.

"I also vote against this," Baby Gap chimes. "In the closet? *Really?!*"

But I'm already crossing its threshold. I kneel down, nestling my back into glittering veils and garments that smell like freesias. "Isaiah?" I call out to him. I brace myself for a pair of white fingers to slide out from a pair of puffed sleeves. "I'm here. Did you want to talk?" If I can make myself sound like an old friend, maybe he'll believe it. Maybe I will.

A rustle behind me. A scrape of metal on the iron rack. The smell of something dead, and wet soil.

Blair's eyes linger on something over my shoulder. He whispers, "Oh my god" before the door swings forward and slams a wall of black into my face.

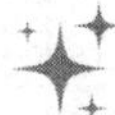

We're not in the closet anymore. We're sitting in a clearing, the two of us, in Birchmount Forest, and it is night. The air is cool and crisp around us. I smell damp earth and pine and wildflowers.

The Boy in Short Shorts bends down, plucking a bluebell from the grass. He brings it to his nose. "He used to pick these for me," he says, breathing it in.

"Who?" I ask.

The Boy in Short Shorts looks up at me. "You know who," he replies. "I was once like you. A student at St. Brandon's, and I had no one. Until one day, in the forest, a man came for me through the trees." His eyes fix on the tree line behind me. "He came out of the shadows like he was made of them. He promised to keep me safe from the others. The other boys. My dad. The whole world. Everything felt... softer when he held me. Like the whole forest was cradling me."

Then his expression darkens. "But sometimes he would disappear. Just like that. And it was like choking, when he was gone. I'd sit there, waiting, fading away."

I lean in, drawn to the pain in his voice.

"And that's when I realized: I wasn't living when he wasn't there. I needed him. I knew I had to do everything to keep him by my side." He talks faster. "One day, he told me he needed something, something of mine. Something important to keep the magic alive between us. To keep the flowers alive, and if I didn't, they would die, then he'd be gone forever. He asked for it, and I gave it to him."

My voice is barely a whisper. "What did you give him?"

The Boy in Short Shorts looks at me. Then, with a hand, he slips off the top buttons of his shirt and pulls it apart.

My breath catches at the hole in his chest, spilling with bluebells. Petals and stems and leaves of them cascading down like a bouquet.

I stare at that hole in his chest where his heart should be, and I want to cry. Cry for what Marshall did to this boy. Cry for what he will do to Ren.

The boy cants his chin. "Oh, Colin," he whispers. "Don't be sad. Such wondrous things live inside me now." He inhales like he is breathing in an idea—getting high off it, exhilarated. It blossoms in his eyes. "Would you like to meet them?"

He seizes my wrist and plunges my open hand into his chest.

*Pull out.* I try to pull out. But his grip is strong; it drags my hand deeper inside him, past the flowers, wilting with each second, dry, rustling leaves—past the damp roots into his cavity, his heart, where it used to be. My hand clenches into a fist, but I can feel all of him on my knuckles, soft, cold.

Then I feel the legs. Thousands of them, skittering along and between my fingers, scuttling up my arm. Beetles, roaches, spiders, centipedes, millipedes. Wiry, bristly, wet, living. Climbing, chittering, clicking. Eyes, many eyes, blinking. I want to scream, but I can't open my mouth because they mean to crawl inside. They mean to tear into my skin with pincers and claws and burrow until my body is just tunnels. Until they make a home in me, too, like they have with—

"Isaiah!" His name, not even a whimper on my tongue. And it is not his face leering back. It is Ren's, his cheeks blue, bloated, eyes cloudy white as a dead fish. And he is rotting, that smell, and his skin is wet tissue paper, bloating in a sewer, falling apart. His lips, or what's left of them, are pulled back into a grin. He's rotting in ecstasy. Someone screams. Is it me? Am I the one screaming? When I look around, I'm not in the closet. I am dry and warm on the couch where my spirit left me, and the bugs are gone and Ren is gone and there is no rotting, just a pair of strong massive arms holding me in place. Holding me as I keep screaming into Baby Gap's chest, a name.

# 25

WHAT ABOUT THIS AMMIT GUY?" BABY GAP SAYS, peeking over a book. "Says here he's the devourer of hearts."

From the couch, I watch as the medium pulls out a book from his bookcase, considers it, places it back. "Or an incubus? Seductive creatures." His dragon-scaled fingers click along the spines of other hardcovers.

Old Man Twink flips the tome open and puts on the pair of reading glasses hanging from a pearled chain around his neck. He and Baby Gap haven't been at the research long. But they're trying to make do with the few breadcrumbs Isaiah left for us in his story. Earlier, Blair stepped out for fresh air.

I wish I could join them, but the medium told me to catch my breath. "Spirit channeling is exhausting work," he said with a wink. Then he gave me an animal cracker. "Physically, but especially emotionally. Ghosts have so damn much to moan about."

Now, Baby Gap is curled up in the love seat across from me,

a tome cracked open in his lap. "I can't find anything about demons and bluebells."

"The forest," I say. "Is there anything demonic that lives in a forest?"

"I don't think that narrows it down. Hey, *easy*," Old Man Twink says when he catches me sliding off the couch. "Can you stand?"

I can. This time, the world doesn't tilt under my feet.

"I'll check on Blair."

He's out on the front deck, chest pressing into the wooden railing. It's not dark yet, but I can make out a sliver of moon pinching the gray sky. I breathe in the crisp air and smell damp grass and something else.

"Violets," Blair says when I join him. He breathes in the scent, too. "Sorry," he says, though I'm not sure what he's sorry for. "I needed some air. That was . . . intense."

I think about how the others scrambled to slide me onto the couch, keep me hydrated, stuff my face with complex carbs. The whole time, Blair was frozen, too afraid to move, like maybe touching anything might make it more real. I hate that none of us thought to ask Blair if he was okay. "I'm sorry I brought you into this."

"I was the one who wanted answers," Blair says. He's looking down at the gated front yard. Blair cups his chin in a hand, and

I glance at the Ares tattoo, shining red on his inner wrist. For a moment, the wooden floorboards pulse beneath my feet. Is it the vertigo of looking down or the realization that, when last I saw that tattoo, Blair and I weren't friends? We were two boys sneaking into a gay club. Too shy to talk to the men by the bar. Too shy to speak to each other in a way that mattered.

From below, a stray Nebelung cat slinks across the yard. It turns its gray whiskered face up at us. I lean my shoulder closer to Blair's until they're touching. "You can leave all this behind, if you want. Go back to a normal life."

Blair is quiet. Then: "A while back, just after Beth was born, before we moved to Markville, my folks and I had a fight." Blair's chin presses deeper into his palm. "I don't even remember what the fight was about. Dad didn't like the way I walked or something stupid. So, I went to the library. And I met someone there, on the other side of the stacks. He—um—he said I was beautiful." Blair flushes.

I smile at this pink story of young love. Maybe this was Blair's first boyfriend. Blair presses on:

"The thing is, Colin. I was just a kid when he said that. He wasn't."

The Nebelung cat is gone. Blair's voice becomes soft, becomes so Un-Blair, as he shares this with me. "I wasn't dumb. I knew grown-ups shouldn't be saying things like that to kids. And I don't know how that man could have gotten there, behind the stacks. It was at the back of the library, and no one was there when I'd last checked. It was like he had come out of the books, crawled out of one of the stories. It was weird, but I didn't run. I stayed there, on the other side of that bookcase, listening to him." Blair's shoulders hunch forward. He's trembling.

I want to hold him, make the shaking stop. But I don't know if Blair wants to be touched.

"He said he'd been watching me for a while. Could tell how sad I was. A nice kid like me." Blair moistens his lips. "And then he asked about her. My baby sister. He seemed so curious when I brought her up. He asked for her name and—I gave it to him. I was so stupid. Why did I give it?"

I lay my hand on top of his. He doesn't move it. With his other hand, he wipes his tears away with a sleeve.

"That night, I couldn't sleep. I just had this feeling. So, I went to check on Beth in her crib. And in the dark, I swear, I could see him, the man. Hunched over her. Smiling. I heard him call her name."

"Blair." His name barely leaves my mouth. "Oh, Blair..."

"Dad checked the whole room. The house. He said it was a nightmare and I shouldn't get scared by stuff like that. After that, I became obsessed, you know? Obsessed with that man no one else could see. I looked into all this ghost stuff because...I needed to prove it was real. That it wasn't all in my head. I felt like I owed Bethlehem that."

"Why?"

"Because I let it in, Colin. I brought it into our lives—into hers. And if it ever came back, I had to find a way to stop it."

Suddenly, we're back in Mr. Frank's classroom. What did

Blair say? That getting possessed wasn't Regan's fault? Now I realize he didn't say it for my sake. "It's not your fault." I resolve to say these words again and again for as long as Blair needs them. "You know that, right?"

The fingernail moon slices more brightly in the evening sky. I can just make out a pale crater. When I turn, Blair is looking at me. A sliver of moonlight glows on his cheek. "I didn't notice until now," he says.

"Notice what?"

"You're taller than me."

Before now, I've never stood this close to Blair. Never realized he doesn't even reach my chin. Under his glasses I see a birthmark, shaped like a musical note, over his right eye. Blair doesn't blink as he continues looking at me. He tilts his head, like he's waiting for something. Before I can unpack what this look means, if it means anything, Baby Gap calls us from inside: "Guys, we could really use another pair of eyes."

Blair and I share a look before making our way inside. Right. There are bigger fish. Lives at stake.

I know this.

Just as I know, years from now, I'll never smell another violet again without thinking about Blair in this moment, and how much I want to kiss him.

"Anything?" I ask.

Baby Gap shakes his head sadly. The medium is reading while kneeling on his threadbare rug, robe spilling around him like a jade pool. "My powers lie in the sight. Not in research."

Old Man Twink rubs circles into his temple. "Maybe we're getting caught in the details. We can't see the trees for the forest."

Baby Gap frowns. "I thought it was 'forest for the trees'?"

"Eyes."

The three of them turn to me. I hadn't even realized I'd said it out loud. But that word—*tree*—sparks something in my head. I turn to Old Man Twink. "You said Isaiah was lost in eyes, right? What if he was giving us a hint? What if he was referring to a tree?"

Blair gets it first. "The birch."

Old Man Twink clicks his dragon-scale fingers along the hard cover of the closed book in his lap. Then he lifts himself up. His robe rustles behind him as he sweeps over to his bookcase. His two fingers skip along the spines until they land on a purple one. He plucks it out.

*Brigg's Encyclopedia of Faeries.*

Blair eyes the lilac cover. "Faeries. You're kidding."

"We're not talking Tinker Bell. Real faeries were assholes," the medium says, flipping through the book. "Stealing children. Cursing mothers. A faerie is no different from a demon or vengeful spirit. Or really, any other supernatural being. They all fall under the broader category of spirit."

Baby Gap's cheeks flush with awe. "You know everything."

Blair gets worked up, too. "Wait, this makes sense, Colin!

Think about it. The bluebells. Faeries were thought to enchant them. And Ren takes them with him everywhere. Maybe that's why he's acting all lovey-dovey. And this creature could use the bluebells to create illusions, too. Take a specific form."

"And Ren's no-sodium diet!" I realize, vaguely remembering a superstition. "Doesn't salt repel faeries?" When Old Man Twink nods, I try to recall all the other details. I remember the mirror Ren covered in his room. The magnet mirror he took off his locker. "What about mirrors?"

Old Man Twink scratches his chin. "If the faerie's power is tied to concealment or illusion, a mirror could theoretically interfere with that. 'Reflect away' the enchantment and expose the truth."

I dig inside my pocket for the kaleidoscope—an optical illusion created by three mirrors facing one another. Maybe that's why Isaiah wanted me to look through this. Maybe if I can show Ren what Isaiah really looks like...

Old Man Twink flips through the encyclopedia. "Birch. Birch. Birch. Ah! Read this." He holds the book out to me. My eyes land on the section marked by his thumb:

## THE ONE WITH THE WHITE HAND

*Of all the insidious spirits of the wood, this faerie is notable, though perhaps the least known. It is birthed by a felled birch tree. Once every thirty years, the One with the White Hand stalks through the forest, preying on wanderers whose spirts are similarly broken. It attacks its prey first by assuming the form of something the victim loves; then by touching their head, inflicts the madness of love. Over time it will feed on its host by touching its chest. It is only when the prey has devoted their whole heart to the faerie (and once the faerie itself has successfully isolated its prey from its kin, whom the faerie views as competition for its food source) that it consumes the victim's proffered heart. Satiated, it rests within its felled tree for another thirty years.*

*Whispers of the faerie originated in Taunton, England, where it had targeted a student in a boys' prep school. The boy's friends had vanquished the faerie by burning the felled birch from which it emerged. But its spell on the victim could not be broken.*

I flip the page to a black-and-white sketch. The pale figure stares back at us through milky eyes. Stringy, limp hair hangs down its gaunt face, flaked with skeleton leaves. Its hands are long, pale fingers—

Thin as twigs. Twisting and pulling and yanking.

A white, white hand.

"It's like a parasite," Blair says.

I picture the bruises on Ren's chest, the deep hollows under his eyes. This thing is feeding on him. And Dave, Mr. Hsu, me—Marshall is targeting anyone it perceives as a barrier to its host.

Baby Gap's voice brings me back. "Well, this is good, right? We find this magic stump and set it on fire."

"It's a big forest," Blair replies. He turns to me. "You were with him that night. Did you see it?"

I think through the fog and tell them about the thicket, clean-bone white. Wherever the felled tree is, it must be in there.

"There is no thicket," Blair says. "I've been to that forest multiple times this last week. There's nothing on the board-walk."

"Ren." My heart lurches every time I say his name. "We need him to bring us there." I should be relieved—we know what we're fighting. But my eyes linger on that last line.

*Its spell on the victim could not be broken.*

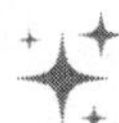

After Baby Gap turns on the engine and his SUV sputters on, a crooked finger taps against my window. I roll it down. Old Man Twink's robe flaps around him. He hugs himself in the cold. "Take this," he says. He pulls out a box of Old Firefly matchsticks.

I lean out the window to take them. "Thanks."

"I was wrong."

I pocket the matchbox. "About what?"

"On the phone, when I told you to shield yourself so others

can't get in. Isaiah chose to speak through you. He wouldn't open himself up to just anyone—not if their heart was closed."

I can hear the tinkling of wind chimes on someone's porch. "But why me? I'm not strong. I'm not..." *Ren,* I'm about to say.

Old Man Twink raises a penciled brow. "Well, if I got into a brawl you wouldn't be my *first* choice to tag in. Because you're not a wand."

"A what?"

Old Man Twink rolls his eyes. "My boy, have you never had your cards read? Wands! Fire! Passion! Willpower! Physical strength! And you, sir, are no wand."

I shift in my seat. "Great. Thanks."

The medium's eyes twinkle. "You're a cup. You feel things deeply. Love, intuition—these are your gifts. Perhaps Isaiah could sense it. So don't be a wand, Colin. Be a cup."

I fold up Old Man Twink's words like a paper crane and imagine slipping it into my pocket. I want to thank him, but he nods like he already knows.

"This was fun!" Baby Gap hollers from the driver's seat. "Maybe next time we visit, you can play on your harp."

Old Man Twink waves a majestic hand and takes a giant step back so we can leave. I wonder how many other horror stories he's heard. I wonder how many of those stories are his. "Be safe."

I try not to laugh. *Be safe?* For years, something has been living in our neighborhood forest. Something is trying to kill us.

A sad smile twitches on Old Man Twink's face, like he can read my thoughts. "Something always is. But we're still here."

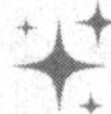

"Good evening, Auntie." A smile stretches across my face when Mrs. Hsu opens the door. I wave at the boys behind me. "The three of us were hoping to talk to Ren."

"Colin," Mrs. Hsu says. She takes in the sight of Blair and Baby Gap, who step up on either side of me. I follow her line of vision and realize Baby Gap is checking out his biceps in the porch door's reflection. I elbow him to stop.

"Where can we reach him?" Blair asks.

"What do you mean, you're looking for Ren?" She blinks. "He told me he was going to meet you."

Blair and I share a look. "How long ago did he leave?" Blair asks.

"Maybe a half hour ago."

"Did he say where he was going?"

But Baby Gap gets there first. "Prom."

We're about to turn and leave when Mrs. Hsu sighs. "Colin, I know you've been lying for him."

I turn around to Mrs. Hsu. "I don't understand."

"You promised us," she says. "You promised my husband. You would tell us if Ren was seeing anyone. You said he wasn't. You lied. You lied about...it."

I should leave, but maybe it's the way the Hsus keep calling it "it"—like the thought of Ren dating another guy is a million-legged insect, too disgusting to name. Or maybe I'm channeling the outrage coming off Blair and Baby Gap in hot sheets. Because we've all heard these arguments before, haven't we?

And that's when I see it, a faint white trail sprinkled in front of the door. A few grains caught in the cracked tiles. Salt.

"He's protecting you." I think about Isaiah and the rule. No salt in the house. "Ren's still protecting you, even though you and Mr. Hsu are both—*jerks*."

Mrs. Hsu blanches. "We love him."

"Your love is poison," I hear myself say. "Stop telling Ren you love him when you're hurting him. Just—stop!"

I feel a pair of hands pull gently on my arms. Blair wants to save me from this whirlwind. But it's too late. I lose myself in the memories, all of them. Me coming out to Mom. The crying, the disappearing.

A parent's love is like a cut. Paper-thin ones that itch along your knuckles. They tell you they love you as they ask you to change. That they'll give you this love even though there's some part of you that doesn't deserve it—even when *you're* the one hurting *them*.

"This isn't a phase. Ren isn't confused. He's eighteen and the world is fucked up and he's looking for comfort because you're not giving it to him." My voice rings on the porch. "He's hurting. Why can't you see you're hurting him more? You're his parents!"

Blair tugs my sleeve again. "Come on."

"He's right," Mrs. Hsu says. "You should go." She glances at me for a moment before shutting the door.

"That was a lot," Baby Gap says as we head down to his car.

Blair watches me. "It's tonight, isn't it? When Marshall will ask him to…"

I think of Isaiah, parting his shirt. I think of the hole in his chest, all the things living inside it. "We have to go now."

We scramble into the car, but Baby Gap doesn't start it.

"Come on," I plead, nudging his seat forward with my knees.

"This," Baby Gap says slowly, "isn't mine."

His fingers twist around something tasseled and red. It spills like blood off a wooden talisman with Chinese characters on it. *Anquan.*

Safe.

"That's my mom's." I reach over and pull the talisman into my hand. It's the one Mom hangs over her dash mirror. The one to keep us safe from bad spirits.

As I hear Baby Gap ask, "How did it get here?" I turn it over and finger the carving of Guan Yu's mean, whiskered face. He glares back at me, not in a challenge, but like he's been betrayed.

His eyes have been scratched out.

# 26

I SLAM THE CAR DOOR BEHIND ME. "WAIT HERE," I TELL the others. Blair is about to protest, but I cut him off. "It *can't* get all three of us. Call the cops if I'm not out in five."

"Shouldn't we call them first—"

But I'm already flying across the lawn through our front door, which is unlocked.

"Mom?" There's no answer, but the silence doesn't feel empty. My fingers fumble blindly along the wall for a few agonizing seconds before finding a light switch. The landing spills with yellow light. I creak into the living room.

Next, the kitchen. "Mom?" A floorboard groans in the hallway upstairs. Whoever else is in this house must be there. Before I follow the noise, I scan the kitchen for a weapon.

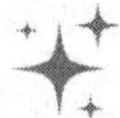

Each squeaky step on the staircase gives away my position. I hold the serrated blade of the bread knife flat against my chest. I look into the door on my left first, which leads into Mom's room. No one is there.

"Whoever is here," I hear myself boom, "I'm warning you: I have a knife!"

The walls of the house groan in answer. Expand and contract like the lungs of something enormous.

"Colin?"

Ahead, the door to my room pulls open, and I see Mom's head poke out.

"Colin!" she says. "There you are. We need to go right now." She dashes back into my room. I hear something unzip.

There's luggage splayed open on my bed. Mom is loading folded laundry inside.

"Mom," I say, kneeling by my door. I lay my weapon down while she isn't looking. "What are you doing?"

"Something attacked me," Mom says. "I don't know what it was. But it came for me in the car. It's still out there." She dashes over to my wardrobe and pulls open cupboards, drawers. Loads socks, boxers, T-shirts into one arm. She throws me an accusatory look. "It's after you, isn't it? I could feel it, Colin. It won't stop until it has you. What have you done?"

"Nothing," I sputter, backing out into the hallway. "Mom, you don't get it. This thing—it's dangerous. But I have to stop it. We can't leave."

Mom throws the balled laundry into my luggage and snaps

it closed. She sits on my bed; the mattress squeaks under her weight. “All this time, Colin,” she says, moaning into her hands. “You make it so hard for your mother to keep you safe.”

“He’s my friend.”

“You’re my son.” Mom glances up at me. “I know I’m not the perfect mother, okay? But I do love you.” Mom creaks off the mattress and pads closer to me. Her footsteps are weightless. “I’m sorry for today. Those things I said. But I want you to be happy, Colin. You know your mother wants that, right?”

Mom lingers by the doorway. I know she’s waiting for me to close the gap between us. She wants me to hug her.

Because she can’t hug me.

“Why can’t you leave the room, Mom?”

Mom’s eyes flicker down. The bread knife lies dead on the floor, next to a powdery white line trailing across the doorway.

*Use salt to guard against wicked sprites and faeries.*

*MSG works just as well.*

Mom levels my gaze. Her lips stretch into a thin smile. Stretch and stretch until it splits her whole face into a bloody slit. Her limbs crack and twist in their sockets. Her eyes roll back and convulse like milk bubbling over the stovetop.

“Hello, Marshall.”

*Pop!* The overhanging light in my room blows out, sprinkles glass onto Mom’s hair. I hear another bulb blink off and on before blowing out over the staircase.

Then another. *Pop. Pop. Pop.* All the lights I flicked on earlier die. The whole house soaks in inky darkness.

"I know how to stop you," I manage to say. It's meant to be a warning, but my fear is so plain, even in the dark. "Once I find your tree..."

The shadowy doorway is quiet at first. And then the One with the White Hand speaks. "Stop me..." His voice blows through the whole house like the cries of a thousand ghosts.

A faint rustling behind me, like a bride's veil.

Slowly, I turn back. A scream builds in my chest, then suffocates like a smothered candle before it can leave my throat.

Children. Across the hallway, they stare at me. Some are my age, some younger. Nine of them, or ten. Pale, with lips frostbitten dead blue. They're all dead.

"They can never leave me," the One with the White Hand says from behind. The steps creak under his feet as they shuffle toward me. I nearly back into him through my doorway, my feet hovering just an inch over the salt line. "I never let them leave."

The children are close now, only six feet away. I'm about to duck into Mom's room. But something shifts in her doorway, and I jolt back. A pale silhouette emerges from its darkness. One, two, three more children.

My legs crumple beneath me. I'm trapped. I squeeze my eyes shut, willing the bad pictures to go away. Those pale fingers, reaching out.

"Soon, Ren will join them, too."

Stop.

"And if you try to stop him...."

Stop.

"I'll hurt you, Colin. Same as your mother."

I bury my face in my knees and ignore the moans shaking the house. I flinch when a floorboard next to me creaks and wait for ice-cold fingers to latch on to my skin. I wait for their howls in my ears. But when they don't come, I lift my face.

The children are gone. The doorway is empty.

Still, I don't move. I don't dare. Not even when Blair and Baby Gap crash through the front door and bound up the steps.

# 27

My mom used to keep a picture of me in her wallet. It was taken on picture day. I was in second grade, back when my eyes were brighter and cheeks chubbier. My nose was still pixieish. That picture was proof I hadn't always been ugly. That I had a face you might want to replicate, save. Carry around with you.

Mom loved that picture of me more than the others. This was reason enough for me to destroy it.

This was a few months after I had come out to her. At this point, Mom had given up. Given up on the teas and the foot pads. Given up on the promise of purging her son of his gay, cross-dressing demon. Instead, she said nothing to me. Drifted zombielike from room to room, ignoring my questions, my presence.

"It's like he's not even here," I heard Mom tell Auntie Wei. From the staircase, I pictured the two of them hunched over the kitchen table. Hands clasping hands. A pat-pat on the back for comfort.

Some nights I would find Mom in her room, bent over that picture of me, letting her grief spill into his eyes, nose, and mouth. She knew I could see her, and I wondered if that was why she cried so openly. Sobbed loud enough for me to hear her in the other room. Did she want me to find her like this? Did she want me to know I'd killed something she loved?

Fine.

One day, I dug through the grave of her purse while she was out. There was that picture of me in her wallet. Pretty, pretty Colin. With a black marker, I scratched out his eyes. After blinding him, I put him back.

I did the same to my baby photos in the album. To the photo taken of me at my eighth-grade graduation, the one framed on the wall, over the staircase. I found every picture I could of me around the house and scratched all their eyes out.

Dead.

Dead.

Dead.

I waited for her to find them. I waited for the sobs, the howling. I waited all night in my room for a perfect storm that never came.

It didn't end with the pictures. That whole year I haunted that house, leaving my shameful gay secrets out for her to find. A mascara wand in the bathroom. By the remote control, a love letter to a boy I'd written (to no boy in particular). One time, I left the television paused on a BowFlex commercial, frozen on a pair of tanned, pixelated pecs—to make the homoeroticism crystal clear.

"Why are you doing this?" she finally asked me one day. She had just discovered a drawing Ren gave me that I had crumpled and left in her purse. It was a giant purple penis Ren had sketched during geography when we were speculating if Batman's dick was bigger than Robin's. "Are you trying to kill me?"

Ghosts are passive-aggressive bitches, so I said nothing. Just glided past her, back into my room.

I sit with Blair and Baby Gap in the waiting area. Everything in here is too bright, too sterile and white. The sharp smell of disinfectant is like poison when it enters my body, bleaching my thoughts, numbing my memories so I can barely feel them.

When did we get here? How long have we been waiting?

"She'll be okay," Blair says, somewhere. Just loud enough so I can hear him, over the tortured wails of an infant sitting behind us.

Three missed calls were made between four and five thirty by an officer with the York Regional Police.

There was an accident. At 1:30 PM today—right around the time we arrived at Old Man Twink's—Mom swerved out of her lane at the Douglas-Fir intersection and crashed into a traffic lamppost. (What a strange route to take, I thought. That road doesn't lead home.) No one else was hurt. But Mom would be waiting for me in emergency care at Stoufville—

"Colin," Blair says quietly. He's so gentle when he touches my shoulder, the softest nudge to bring me back. "What should we do about Ren?"

I blink. The antiseptic smell has made everything hazy. "Ren?"

"Prom starts in one hour," Baby Gap says. He fumbles nervously with the front of his shirt.

"I..." I say. They're both so far away they probably can't even hear me. "I don't..."

I leave that sentence cut open like an exposed wire. Blair leans in, each of his words careful. "I'm so sorry, Colin. For all of this. But we need to act now. Ren—"

"We can't," I say. I hope the infant's cries drown me out, because what I'm saying is horrible. Horrible and true. "We can't save him." I look down at my hands in my lap.

I can feel Blair and Baby Gap exchange a look.

"We don't know what we're doing," I say. I should be laughing—why am I only realizing this now? We're dumb boys. Dumb boys who find mediums on Yelp. Dumb boys who assemble demon facts from Wikipedia and from B horror movies.

I've seen the others. Those kids, faded whispers of what they once were. Marshall did that. He'll do it again. He'll keep doing it, long after Ren is gone.

"I know you're scared." Blair's voice sounds in my head. "But this is what he does. Isolates his prey. Makes them feel like they don't have anyone left. Ren needs you to be strong for him."

*But its spell on the victim could not be broken.*

"I was never the strong one."

A bald nurse by the front desk tells me Mom is ready to see me. Without looking back, I follow him.

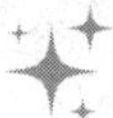

The doors give a ding and slide open. On the wall in front of us is a sign. ACUTE INJURY UNIT.

*Acute.* From the Latin *acusa,* which means "sharpness." Needles.

"This way," the nurse says. As our shoes clop down the hallway like hooves, I imagine Mom, eyes closed, hooked up to beeping machines, covered in wires and plastic tubes, tangled as a nest of thorny vines.

What I don't expect is to hear her voice. "Eurgh. Cheese! I hate cheese."

When we arrive in her room, a squat doctor with gray streaks in her hair and a clipboard in hand walks over. "Greg," she says to the nurse, who nods before heading out. Then, to me, "You must be Colin. I'm Dr. Singh."

From behind the door, Mom lies in her cot and pushes a tray with what looks to be a microwaved burger away from her on the side table. Her other arm is in a sling. Mom's eyes meet mine.

"Fractured wrist. But her vitals are fine," Dr. Singh informs me. I nod, unsure which parts of our bodies are vital or not. "We also checked for head injuries or trauma—nothing detectable so far."

"So, she's okay?" I ask, ignoring the snort of disapproval from the bed. "I mean, other than her arm?"

"Well, we'd like to keep her overnight in case other symptoms develop." Dr. Singh checks her clipboard. "Minor soft tissue damage. Whiplash. And your mother tells me about her sore back."

"Caused by stress," Mom adds, lifting a finger.

Dr. Singh purses her lips. I wonder if they've had this conversation before. "Possibly, Diana. But as I've said, it's more likely from the crash. Really, it's a miracle you're in this condition, given the state of your vehicle."

"Doctors," Mom grumbles once Dr. Singh leaves. "Think they're so smart with their medicine." She whispers to me in Hakka, "It's all bullshit. Chinese medicine is more advanced."

"So maybe I should study acupuncture instead of medicine." I slide into a plastic chair next to her cot.

"No, no," Mom says, horrified. She waves away my stinky fart of a joke. "Be a doctor. They save lives."

Eventually, I run down the hallway, to where the vending machines are. I return with two Styrofoam cups of milk tea. Mom takes one with her good hand and breathes in the steam. It's only half-filled, so there's less of a chance she'll spill it.

"You sure you're okay?"

Mom blows into her cup. "I'm fine, I'm fine," she baahs. "I told you. Guan Yu is protecting us." I feel the lump in my pocket and remember those scratched-out eyes. A shudder hatches into a hundred insects on the back of my neck. My mind zigzags outside, down the elevators, into the waiting room where Blair and Baby Gap might still be waiting.

*Ren needs you to be strong for him.*

My fingernails dig into the cup on my lap. I stop before they can puncture the sides, spill scalding chai all across my legs.

I hear Mom say, "Your face looks so much older lately. So tired."

I wait for Mom to say more. And then I realize this is her way of telling me she's concerned. "Um," I start. I fumble for a lie, but it gets buried under everything else. The house. The doorway. The children. The crash. I push down the sob that suddenly swells in my throat. "There's been a lot happening. And I don't think there's enough—" My words get so thick I can't force them out.

Mom searches my face for the rest of that sentence. Enough what? Time? Hope?

*You need to be strong.*

"I don't think there's enough in me, Mom. I don't think I'm enough."

I don't feel any lighter, admitting this. And I prepare for Mom to roll her eyes, give another *baah. So sensitive*, she might say. *All kids your age.*

But instead, in a soft voice I haven't heard from her in years, Mom says, "Colin, do you ever wish you had a father?"

I blink. "Why are you asking me that?"

Mom sighs and places her chai on the table. With a grunt, she rolls onto her side, over her good arm, so she can face me. "Do you?"

"No," I say, thinking about it. "I never think much about him." But Mom is still quiet, so I lean forward and ask, "Did you ever love him? Even though he was terrible?"

I expect Mom to release a breathy sigh. But she throws her head back and cackles. "Love?" She laughs so hard it erupts into a fit of coughs. "Oh my lord, no! He was rich, though. And Hakka. That was enough for my parents."

Mom ignores my stunned face and takes a long sip. "And I was beautiful, too, you know? Well, of course you do. That was enough for *him*." Mom stares up at the ceiling's unremarkable tiles. "Then he wanted more. My time. My joy. He didn't want to share any of me with anyone else. Just take, take, take. And Hakka women—we're strong, see. But stupid." She taps her temple. "We give, give, give. That's what we're taught. We give and we stay."

Mom doesn't sound sad. More like resolved. How many times has she relived this story? How many times has she wanted to share it?

Mom taps her head again. *Strong but stupid.* "Anyway. Then I had you. And he didn't want me to keep you. He wanted me to—" Mom breaks off. For the first time tonight, ever, I think she's ashamed. "I even went there. To do it. But before they could call me, I ran. I ran to a street corner. Ran until I was alone. And I held on to my belly and I said to it, 'I love you. I don't know you yet, but I love you.'" Mom clears the huskiness from her voice.

I want to tell Mom she has no reason to be sad. I want to tell her I wasn't even pea-size at that point, not even real. She had every right to get rid of me.

Mom presses on. "Sometimes I ask myself, should I have stayed with him? Maybe he would have changed." Mom pauses. Somewhere on the floor, we hear the steady rhythm of a stranger's heart beating on a monitor. "Maybe with him around I could have given you more."

"You give me enough," I say. And with everything lately, with her, with my life, I'm surprised by how much I mean it.

"When you were just born, we lived in a small apartment. Remember that?" Mom's eyes shine at the memory. In them, I can see that tiny kitchen. Little cracks in the walls, where the cockroaches lived. "Even then, I would get one of your aunties to drive us uptown. So we could look at those big white houses. So many. Big, big. With swings in the backyard. For the kids," Mom says, the wishing stars in her eyes blinking out. "I couldn't even afford to get you that *Sailor Moon* DVD."

My brows knit together. *Sailor Moon* season one. Hadn't I watched it a million times with Ren? "But, Mom," I said. "You bought me that DVD."

But then Mom looks at me and I remember: how we rushed out of that video store. How she grabbed my hand. How, maybe, she looked over her shoulder—did the man by the cash register notice?—how she may have kept looking back until we reached the car. Every time I played that DVD. The damn theme song.

"Sometimes, with your kid, enough isn't enough. You also want them to be happy."

I reach for Mom's hand.

"Colin," she asks, "do you know what I want for you?"

My heart clenches. *Please,* I think. *Don't mention the girlfriend. The wife.*

"I want you to have everything," Mom says. "Everything I could never give you. That's why when I see you studying, or talking to your teachers and those other smart students, it makes me so happy. My dream is one day you'll be surrounded by people like that. People who are important. People much better than me." She looks right at me. I want so much to look down, to hide the blurriness warming my eyes. I let her see it. "That's all I want for you. I don't even need you to love me back."

Mom lets go of my hand and brings the chai to her lips. "So don't ever tell me you're not enough."

I wait for Mom's snores to shake her cot before I slip out of her room.

I don't forgive Mom for what she's done to me. But I don't think she was asking for forgiveness. I think she wanted me to know I have love. Maybe, all this time, it was easier for me to forget it was there.

We love and we hurt and we spend our whole lives learning how to love someone else properly. Maybe that's all growing up is.

When I reach the waiting room, I can already hear them.

"Manny Jacinto's pecs are so underrated," Baby Gap says, scrolling his phone.

Blair turns around and catches me staring. He smiles. "Are you ready?"

As we leave the hospital, I mull over the second thing Mom's story taught me: When you choose someone to love, you protect them.

In this one, we don't die.

In Baby Gap's car, I cross this promise over my heart.

# 28

A CHIPPER ST. ANNE'S GIRL GREETS US OUTSIDE THE gymnasium doors. She's wearing a flouncy periwinkle dress with puffed sleeves. "Don't you three look handsome."

Baby Gap looks down at his polo shirt and dark jeans that have faded to acid wash. He smiles up at her sheepishly. "Guess we stand out."

Beaming, the girl clips over to the double doors. She winks at him before pulling them open. Lizzo's voice thunders into the hall, pounds against our chests. Our power levels and heartbeats raise up to two thousand. "You still look great," she says.

The gym blushes magenta and blue as a disco ball carousels stars above the overhanging streamers. Twinkly jellyfish and beluga whales cut out of Bristol boards and sprinkled with glitter. There's some Disney influence, too. Taylor Naranjan glides past the fog machine in a black tuxedo.

Boys are wearing tuxes. Girls are wearing ball gowns. It's as boring and gender normative as you'd expect from St. Brandon's. But everyone is smiling and having fun, so it's hard to hold it against them.

"It's like a prom put together by Hallmark," Blair says, eyeing the streamers.

Maybe. But I think it's magnificent.

We decide to split up. Blair goes north. Baby Gap south. I forge my way west, through a dancing throng of couples. In the chaos, I search the bobbing sea of heads for his face. I'm about to pull out my phone to fire him another round of texts when the microphone shrieks on and the music cuts off.

"Testing, testing," a deep voice calls on the speaker. It's Puppy Chow on the stage. God, he looks handsome with his hair gelled down. "Everyone having fun?"

There's one or two shy whoops and a drunk guy saying, "YEAH!"

If the stakes weren't so high, my heart might flood with something other than fear right now—love, maybe, for this whole school and all its freaks.

"Cool, cool," Puppy Chow says. He clears his throat. "Now, let's bow our heads for our prom king and queen!" A girl hands him a slip of paper. Puppy unfolds it. His eyes shine. "Well, okay!"

I don't hear the names, just the gym exploding around me into applause. They sound like bat wings. I watch as a beautiful guy pulls a beautiful girl onto the stage. I watch as they get crowned.

I hear a song, too, the synthesizers.

Someone behind me whispers "Troye Sivan" as the king helps his queen off the stage and they enter, blinking, into the spotlight. They fold their hands together in a slow dance.

*And when the lights start flashing like a photo booth*

*And the stars exploding we'll be fireproof.*

I'm lost in a sea of *ooh*s and *ahh*s. All the air strangles out of me. It feels so trivial that after everything, this moment between lovers can still make me laugh. Because after the horrors of these last two weeks, I still want it. The promposals and rainbow cakes. This thing that doesn't mirror anything in my life. It isn't crooked or howling with ghosts. It's so whole.

"Barf. I can't believe I came."

Fingertips claw over my shoulder like spider's legs.

The first thing I notice is his hair, a perfect jet black made of all the pigments in the universe. He's wearing a fitted suit, too, burgundy, with a black tie stitched with roses. The shadows are still under his eyes, but somehow he looks so perfect and so here. I worry my breath will snuff him out like a birthday wish.

I throw my arms around him. "Ren." I breathe him in. He smells like a damp forest, leaves dripping with rain. "Did he hurt you? Where is he?"

Ren's hands wrap around my waist, and for a second my muscles seize under his touch. Marshall the shape-shifter.

It takes the form of that which you love.

"Don't worry." Ren's breathy, fairy-dust laugh tickles my ear. "It's me."

Somehow, I know it is.

My eyes scan over the gym, scan through the suits and dresses. "I know how to stop him." I grab Ren's wrist and pull on it. "His tree. We—"

"Forget about him for now," he says with a sad tousled shake of his head. And, like that night at Fulcrum, Ren arcs his whole body back, dragging me with him. "Dance with me?"

I choke out, "We don't have time. Also, this song is for the prom king and queen."

"So what?" Ren says over his shoulder. He steers us through the suits and ball gowns, the pungent clouds of Old Spice and flowers trying too hard to be flowers.

"No one's watching us."

He's right. Not the boys in the tuxes, the girls in their dresses. Ren takes us to the darkest corner of the gym, next to the bleachers. Then, with an uncertain hand, Ren takes my palm into his. With a shy laugh, he scrunches a clammy hand on my waist and attempts to sway to the rhythm.

He rests his head on my shoulder.

Suddenly, I get it. Why brownies hide in rosebushes. Why Clefairy gather only at night to sing. A quiet sort of magic happens when no one outside your circle is watching. It shivers inside you and ripples out. I feel it humming right now between us, my body pressed against Ren's, his heart beating along with mine.

"Ren?"

"Colin?"

"How is your heart?"

"Tired," he says. "I'm really sorry, Colin. For saying those things at your house. About how we shouldn't be friends." He doesn't drop my hand.

"He's lying to you, Ren. He's a monster."

"I know."

"He hurt someone else. Isaiah."

"I know."

I lean back. I want Ren to look at me. "Then why are you protecting him?"

Ren buries his face deeper into my chest until he becomes a part of my heartbeats. "Do you remember that night in the woods? Before we stumbled across that thicket. Before all this. Do you remember what I asked you?"

By some magic, or Troye, I feel the fog of that night in the forest become clear in my head. I think of the two of us on the boardwalk. And I remember.

*Do you ever get tired of being brave?*

"I'm so sorry," I say, my voice getting hoarse. "I'm sorry I didn't notice how much you were hurting. I was all wrapped up in Ferris and—"

"It's not you, Colin." Ren sighs. "I'm just tired. Tired of my parents being disappointed. Tired of the stares, the comments. Tired of being called brave when I'm not. I'm scared of fighting. For once," he says, before breaking off. He takes a steady breath that warms my neck. "For once, I want someone to fight for me. And I know that's pathetic. But I want that."

I look for the spotlight. Except there is none, because Troye is done singing.

I want to tell Ren I know what he means, because I felt it, too. Even now.

"He's not real, Ren."

Ren lifts his face to mine. I've never looked at him this closely before. His lips are shaped like a heart. Then, with his fingers gripping the back of my neck, Ren leans forward until our foreheads are pressing. And in that space where our skin touches, I can feel his mind, manifesting something so hard it becomes real in my head.

*Ai love you.*

It's the two loves I told Ren about all those years ago in his room. Two loves for one boy. Except his eyes are sad. And that's when I realize this isn't a confession. It's goodbye.

The fire alarm rings.

# 29

I LOSE HIM IN THE TIDE OF SUITS AND BALL GOWNS SQUEEZing out into the hallway, then through the front doors of the school. We spill into the quad as the chaperones remind us to line up in an orderly fashion.

I call out his name, which drowns in the five or six hundred voices calling out for their own special person. Baby Gap huffs over to me. "Did you find him?"

"I did." The school's giant windows continue to flash in neon purple. Not a flash of orange, or a single tendril of smoke. "Is there an actual fire?"

"I think it's a grad prank." Blair joins us. "That's what the teachers are saying—some asshole pulled the fire alarm."

I look past the throng of students huddling close to one another, their breaths misting the chilly night, past Taylor Naranjan in his burgundy suit. I look at the gnarled branches of the towering birches, peeking down at us. This wasn't a prank.

Baby Gap turns to face the forest behind him. The eyes of Birchmount Forest stare back at us. "We still don't know how to find its tree. Colin, if Ren's already in there..."

A breeze shudders through the three of us. Blair tugs at his dissent collar. "Ren was the only one who knew how to find it."

The wind tousles my hair. I remember Old Man Twink's words. *Isaiah chose you.* My belly fizzles when I realize that, for once, Blair is wrong.

"Ren's in there!" I say, pointing to a random window on the second floor. "I saw him!"

Baby Gap and Blair swivel to look, finding nothing. "Guys," I breathe, praying that for once my face isn't open, that they can't see how much I don't want them to come with me. I don't want anyone else to get hurt. "I need you to distract the teachers, okay? While I go back in."

Baby Gap gives a salute and bounds over to Mrs. Lamb. Blair looks at me curiously, then follows him. Once he's swallowed into the crowd, I dash in the opposite direction, to that gap between the trees, where this all started. My legs feel exposed under the scarred eyes on white trunks. The trees want me to enter. They have been waiting for me all along.

"Everyone get your cameras out!" I hear Baby Gap bellow behind me. "Blair's gonna sing us a song!"

Before I can hear it, I ball my hands around the box of matchsticks in my pocket and enter Birchmount Forest.

In the dark, I call out to him. "Isaiah?"

He doesn't respond, even though I know he is here. Old Man Twink said a faerie's enchantment can be broken with a mirror. So I pull out the kaleidoscope from my pocket. I look through it.

The graveled pathway fractures into a mosaic of jagged stones, flecks of moonlight. Thorny bushes bloom into stars. I use the kaleidoscope to scan the forest until it lands on a pair of soiled socks, hundreds of pairs, then legs wrapped in gray short shorts. I lower the kaleidoscope. Isaiah is right in front of me.

I'm not afraid. "Take me to him."

He turns his head and walks in the same direction. I follow him off the path. I follow him when my shoes sink into damp earth. I follow him as he glides through a bramble, even when its twigs cut and tear at my legs. I follow him as he takes me someplace where the trees get thicker, where the overhanging branches meet and tangle together like clasped hands, where the last slivers of moonlight end.

I follow him for so long I'm not sure we're even in Birchmount Forest anymore. We've left Markville. He stops at the edge of a dried-up riverbank. Isaiah points down into its center. I look up from my phone, into the sunken grave.

The thicket sits there like a baby tooth, rotting, its hollowed entrance a cavity.

"Wish me luck?" I ask. But when I look up he's gone. I climb down into the grave.

*Moon Prism Power.*

*Make up.*

# 30

THE DIRT PRICKS MY FINGERS WITH DRIED TWIGS AND rocks. A thorny roof lurches over my head and scrapes the back of my neck. The thicket closes in on me, so I press myself down and crawl on my elbows, inching deeper, until the light stops.

I expect something wet and shiny to scuttle across my fingers. I even want it. I want to touch something alive. There's a tunnel of light on the other end. Like the sparking whites of a car's headlights or train, it gets bigger, and my head feels lighter, too. Everything is light.

My fingers close around the kaleidoscope. I feel the smooth, polished surface.

Soon the white is all around me, and I stand—somehow now I can stand, blinking as my eyes adjust to the too-brightness of this new room. Is it a clearing? Am I outside? I see grass under my feet, but it hurts to look at anything. The light dazzles and stings like soapsuds caught in the eyes.

"Ren?"

I stumble blindly in this strange world until my squinted eyes make out something hunched over in front of me. It's the tree. I'm sure of it. It bends like a crooked, snapped wrist, petrified white. Is the brightness coming out of it? And there, slumped to the side of the tree, like a bent spoon…

I throw myself down and take both his cheeks in my hands. His eyes are open, but they're two empty windows. "Ren," I say gently, feeling his pulse. Feeling for something still inside him. Even something small, a little wick of a candle behind his eyes.

The matches. The branches look dry, already dead. I was never in Bear Scouts, but isn't this kind of wood perfect for kindling? I dig through my pockets and pull the little matchbox out. But then Ren slumps forward, and his head knocks into my chest and the box falls from my hand. His loose shirt dips down by the collar, and I see something on his bare chest. A white mark of a hand.

"I'm sorry, Colin."

First, the weight of a stranger's steps. Then Marshall kneels down beside me. His finger reaches forward and tilts Ren's head, almost lovingly, so I have no choice but to look into those hollow eyes. "He's already offered it."

Ren's limbs are as stiff as petrified wood.

"I haven't taken it yet, his heart. But I will. Most of Ren is gone now. More gone every second. Even if I don't take his heart, he might die anyway."

He's lying. Isn't that what the faeries do, in the stories? My fingers close around the kaleidoscope.

"Ah, the mirror," Marshall says. "Let me guess. You want to show Ren the real me? A bit too late for that, I'm afraid. Even if you can somehow manage to force him to look through that thing, it won't make a difference. Ren has made his choice."

Finally, I look at him, this thing that calls himself Marshall, as beautiful as Ren imagined him. He gazes down on me, and I realize whose eyes Ren finally chose for him. Wolf eyes. Duke One.

"I hate you."

Marshall doesn't glower or grin. He leans in and has the audacity to look sad. "This hurts me, too. I know you don't believe that. But it hurts every time, when I have to do this. It's the kind of pain I keep with me, with every new person I love."

"Is that what this is?"

Marshall rises to his feet. He is so much taller than me, than Ren. His shadow spills over the both of us. "You don't understand. When a boy offers his heart to me, it's like…I make a home for them. Can't you see how beautiful that is? How like a fairy tale? Can't you see what this means? That Ren will live on forever, inside me?"

I sit Ren upright and press our foreheads—almost smash them—together. If Ren is fading away, he needs someone to act as his border, something solid and strong to keep everything in place. I do what Ms. Edith said all those years ago in class—what we tried to do in my room, too, with the collages. Back when we thought we were magic. I manifest something, a future for Ren.

Ren moving into a dorm room in a sunshine city. A peninsula. A grove of owls. The entire ocean. I picture him meeting his soon-to-be boyfriend in a coffee shop. Their nights, together in bed with the rain tapping outside. Tangled feet under a duvet cover.

I visualize other things, too, that Ren loves. Decorative hardcovers on his bookshelf. Shaved ice with red bean. That moment in *Sailor Moon*, the one Ren loves, that warmed his face flush with tears—when Usagi holds her star locket out to her prince—holds it out like an open, musical heart.

*Because you deserve it, Ren. All the Bright Shiny Things. Your life will be dazzling and full.*

*I don't even need to be in it.*

And I feel Ren's hand lift—except it's Marshall pulling Ren up. Up to his side, out of my arms. Marshall gently cups Ren's chin and tilts it forward until they're facing. Ren's eyes aren't looking back. I shatter right there at the sight of them.

"It's easy," Marshall says, "when they're hurt. It's easy to make them fall in love."

My fingers wrap around the match in the dirt. I want to strike its head into an orange flame and set everything on fire. But what about Ren? I imagine his body, petrified stiff as the flames lick away at his limbs.

Marshall raises a hand. And his fingers stretch. They stretch and stretch until they're wiry and long. Until they squirm across Ren's chest like blind white worms digging in.

"Don't," I say, hating how weak I sound. "Please don't."

My grip on the matchbox loosens. I should have fought harder. I should have stopped all the enemies Marshall scared off. Dukes. Ren's parents. Dave.

And that's when I realize—

"What about me?"

The worms slither off Ren's chest. Marshall turns to face me. "What did you say?"

What was it Blair said? About paying attention to the things we miss?

"You hurt any threat. Not a threat to your victim—a threat to *you*." I trip over the words and details in my head, I'm running through them so fast. "You hurt the people who threaten your food source. So why haven't you hurt me?"

Marshall's eyes glint red. His lips curl.

"You've scared me. But you've never actually touched me." I lift myself up. Square my shoulders back and stretch to my full height. "It's because of him, isn't it? *Ren*. If you hurt me, he won't trust you. And you can't take what he won't give."

Marshall lays Ren down. Then he steps forward and his face swims. His nose and lips, those wounded eyes. All those perfect, carved-out features squirm around like there's something alive rippling under his skin. He strides forward until he is standing over me, a beautiful tower. But for once I'm not afraid. Mr. Frank. Dukes. Peter Chen. How many others have forced me to look up?

"You like it, don't you?" I say. "The invisibility. That's what makes it just a little easier to control how we see you. But I have a picture. I have a recording, too, of all those kids you hurt."

Marshall's perfect face flickers—for a second. A wizened gash for a nose. Dead milky eyes. And then it's gone, and Marshall is back. But I've seen him and he knows it.

Because Marshall doesn't want to be seen.

The plainness of this fact shines like a glowing pebble. I know this feeling. Wolf eyes looking back at me in disgust; my face in those pictures, all those pictures.

"I'll send them—everything I have about you. I'll share it with everyone. And then they'll know! They'll—"

Marshall leans forward and I feel myself lift. My feet hover five or six inches off the ground. My words are choked, but they still come out. "Soon there'll be stories. Everyone in Markville will know about the ugly thing that lives in the woods. The thing that took Isaiah. And all the others before him. Every thirty years. And if I can't find every name, Blair can—"

Slithery eyeless worms twist and coil, leathery around my neck. They squeeze, but I keep going. "Soon everyone will see what you are."

Over his shoulder, I see, in Ren's blank eyes, two empty windows. And maybe a light, flickering somewhere inside him.

Then a pop and a gasp, and I realize that's me. That's the world inside me, blinking out, thinning, becoming lighter than air.

And I hear three more things. A rustle, then a *fwick.* A boy says, "Marshall."

Then everything explodes into orange.

TWO
MONTHS
LATER

# 31

WE GRADUATE IN THE QUAD, WEARING MAROON. This, Baby Gap tells me as we line up for our diplomas, is a gross injustice.

I don't mind the color. Actually, I think it's appropriate, like we're all wearing red cloaks, heading into the dark, scary forest of the real world.

"I look better in canary," he mutters, pinching the front of his robe. "So," he starts, and he does it again, dribbles the phantom ball. "Are you going to Puppy's house party? He invited our whole year."

"I might sit it out."

"You're doing it again."

"What?"

"You always smirk when I dribble. You're not even sneaky about it."

"I do not!"

Baby Gap pouts. "What would you say, Colin, if I told you I

was really insecure about my compulsive need to dribble—but I have to because it helps me process information?"

"Then I would say I feel awful for being so ignorant and I won't joke about it privately anymore."

"I'm really insecure about my compulsive need to dribble, but I have to because it helps me process information."

"I feel awful for being so ignorant, and I won't joke about it privately anymore."

I stick out my tongue. Grinning, Baby Gap wraps me into his huge arms—better than any Big Spoon Boy hug. "I'm glad we became friends. Even if you're a smart-ass."

Across the quad, I see Mom staring. She smiles, the sad-happy kind of smile you give when everything is about to change. I cling to the image of this smile even when I look away, when they call my name and I cross to the podium, when I shake the chancellor's hand. Ren isn't here. But Mom is. This is more her day than mine.

I even let her take my picture.

"Blair!"

I want to laugh when his head snaps up, lemur-like, scanning the quad for me. Graduation is over, but the boys of St. Brandon's linger around, planning for Puppy Chow's party. Half-hugging goodbye. When he sees me, Blair's smile makes that spark in my chest shine a thousand times lighter than the gold medal hanging down from his neck.

“Nice medal, Mr. Valedictorian.” I want to sound 100 percent happy for him when really it’s more like 85. We’re still rivals, and I hate coming in second—even to him.

Blair hangs his head sheepishly. “I was surprised, too.”

False modesty, for my sake. I grin.

“And how are you?” Blair asks. “Are you good?” I know what *good* really means. Lately, Ren haunts every question, every casual request for an update on my life, even when no one says his name.

“I’m good,” I say. “I’m happy.” I cup this last word inside my hand. Not because it’s untrue. I *am* happy. It just makes me feel guilty admitting it.

Blair tells me he’s looking for places in Claremont next week. Pomona starts in the fall, but he’s looking for a studio off campus.

“Dorm life.” He shudders. “No thanks.”

I smile and tell him that’s great. That it sounds like an adventure. For the last month, it’s been mostly the three of us—me, Blair, Baby Gap. At first, it felt strange, like I was an awkward ghost they’d invited into their lives out of pity. A third wheel who haunted every friend date at the board game café, or their anime nights every Tuesday at Baby Gap’s. They did it because they didn’t want to leave me alone.

But once I got over my insecurity, I found myself letting them care for me. I even had fun.

I reach out to hold Blair’s medal and trace the Latin inscription. The *S* in *Studio Gradum Faciant*. Then I realize I'm touching something that's touching Blair, though he doesn't seem to mind.

"Are you going to miss it?" he asks. "All this?"

I look around our campus. At the gravestone building, the muddy lawn. "It hasn't hit me yet. I want it to, though."

"You know what you should do?" Blair folds his hands behind his back and bounces on his heels. "Walk those empty hallways. Give yourself one last, private tour of the place. All the rooms you like best. And say your goodbyes."

I wait for Blair to grin, to give some indication he's joking. "Say goodbye to the school?"

Blair blushes. "I did. It's like listening into a seashell. You'll hear it say something back. Trust me."

I do.

We both get kind of quiet after that, but not in the way where one of us wants to leave. More like we're waiting for something. I tell the brightness building in my belly to settle down. It's been doing this a lot lately—every time Blair lets me walk him home, or when he recommends a book title or a song. My heart hums whenever Baby Gap leaves us alone, to use the bathroom or just to disappear for a bit, and he smirks over his shoulder, knowingly, then it's just me and Blair and this silence, these three feet of space between us, that weighs as much as a third person. Every time I sneak a look at Blair, I find him looking back, and a part of me wonders if it's all in my head.

But when Blair's mom and dad call him and he turns to cross the quad and join them, I step forward into that three feet of space. Close the gap between us.

"We should have dinner," I say, looking down at his sleeve. It takes everything in me not to tug it. "Some time. When we're back. Or, um, before we leave."

"Dinner," Blair repeats. His cheeks flush red. Or maybe that's the red reflecting off his robe. Maybe it's the red coming off me. "Sounds good."

"Lovely."

"Fantastic."

"Tremendous."

Blair scratches the back of his head, searching his brain for a better word. He agrees. "Tremendous."

In Latin, sometimes they leave the verb at the end of a sentence. That means you don't know what two things are to each other until you reach that last word. It dangles there, like hope or a promise. I watch Blair head back to his mom and dad, maroon cloak swishing behind him, and I realize, for now, a promise is enough.

I do what Blair said. I walk through the empty hallways of St. Brandon's for the last time and say my farewells.

*Goodbye, hallway. Goodbye, classroom. Goodbye, chapel.*

I go deeper into the corridor, past the lockers, until I reach Ren's. *Goodbye, locker.* Each farewell digs a deeper well into my chest, but I don't hear it yet, that voice, like Blair said.

It isn't until I'm standing at the front of the school, on the top step, looking up at the concrete building like Ren and I did so many years ago, that I finally hear something talk back. And it isn't in God's voice, or the universe's. It isn't rumbling and man-like, or eternal.

Just the little ghost voices of two boys holding hands.

*But what if it's not what we want it to be?* the first one asks.

*It will be,* says the second. *It'll be everything. And everything more.*

# 32

Hey, Ren.
You don't have to respond to this.
I know you want space.
And maybe that's for the best.

You were always the more cringe-y one, especially when we talk about FEELINGS. I just want to tell you about this thing that happened. With my books.

I was clearing my space of childish things before the big move to Nova Scotia. Twilight. Raven Boys. All the gay things by David Levithan. Modern fairy tales we devoured before high school started.

Because wasn't high school supposed to be like those books? Intense. Scary. The promise of a miracle love, strong enough to save you.

But lately, when I look at those books, I see them through this double vision. Because high school wasn't like that. It could be—for someone else—maybe. Someone prettier. But it wasn't like that for me. And it hurts when I look at those books, and remember how much I wanted all of it. How much I still do.

So the plan was to give them away. Shove them in boxes to be unpacked and stocked and shelved at the public library, where some other kid can find them.

But then.

I cracked one of the books open and I saw your name. It was your book. We used to swap them, remember? And you'd call and we'd talk in hushed voices about our favorite parts—the righteous anger you felt when I loved something you hated, when I cobbled together the perfect argument for why you were wrong. And then there was the thrill of discovering those moments that spoke to us both.

Was it the sparkly vampires I came back for? Or was it this sharing? Connecting?

A conduit. That's the occult term for it. Were these books, these dreams, these childish things, were they conduits?

Anyway. In the end I gave up those books—but not the one book you gave me.

I wanted you to know that.

I reread my texts in the playground, at the top of the big slide. I read them even though Ren—wherever he is—won't know they exist. But once I turn off my screen and pocket my phone, I hear something miraculous.

*Ding.*

Colin.

*Ding.*

COLIN.

"Did you really think I'd let you leave without saying goodbye?"

I tear my eyes away from my screen to find him blinking up at me in the sunlight, eyes half-obscured by his hand. It's like he's squinting at me through a pair of binoculars. Like we're both looking at something impossibly far away.

"Wait up there," he says before I can slide down. "I'll join you."

Soon the two of us are perched on the rickety bridge at the top of the jungle gym, dangling our feet over the sand. When we're sitting like this—beside each other—we can't see the other's face. Maybe this is for the best. Looking at each other will only make this harder.

"So," I start just as Ren says, "How are you?"

We both laugh, like this fumble is normal.

Across the field, a young couple walks by, hand in hand. They're strolling at turtle pace, stretching this moment for as long as they can.

"So," Ren starts again. "Excited for King's?"

"I guess. I hope there are a lot of Asians in Halifax."

The corner of Ren's lips twitch.

I tell Ren how, in the end, I decided to live on campus. Have a roommate, share a bathroom with the whole floor. Ren beams, but there's a flicker of sadness in his eyes. Or maybe they're just reflecting mine. After prom night, after Ren set fire to the birch, after I pulled the both of us out of the thicket, he stopped coming to classes. He didn't even take his exams. But Ren didn't totally ghost me. He sent me one message: Green College didn't withdraw its acceptance. We would still be going to different colleges, after everything.

I watch the boy across the field adjust his girlfriend's shirt collar. The gesture is tender, and on any other day, it might make me ache. I wrap my fingers around the chain links. "Plus you won't be there."

The bridge keens underneath our weight.

"I went back to the forest," Ren says. I look up. "After… after everything." Our legs are no longer swinging. Just hanging down over the sand, as if they've only just realized we were never really floating. "I told myself it was to make sure he was really gone, but I think a part of me still wanted to see him. But sometimes I miss him. Marshall. After everything. I miss him. And I wasn't ready to return to how things were, to see you and pretend I was all right, while wanting to be with him."

Ren clicks the heels of his shoes together. *Two times for adventure. Three times for home.* "I'm so fucked up."

"I think a lot of us are." Because this world beats you up and calls it loving. It takes and we give and we keep on giving until everything inside us belongs to this thing that will never give back, long after it's left us.

"Sometimes, it doesn't feel like it'll get better," Ren continues. "I'm realizing this now. It's still there, the missing. I think it might always be there. Maybe I'm supposed to get better at ignoring it."

We keep sitting there, talking, and for once time doesn't dilate for us. It flits off like it wants to give us some privacy. And it's nice when it's just us, Ren and me, in the playground, but without all the time in the world everything moves too fast, and the sun's already dipping into a cloud when Mom texts, Where are you flight leaves in two hours. Then we're getting up, climbing down the jungle gym, brushing gravel off our butts. We look down at the sand, at the swings; look up at the big, rickety bridge; we look at each other's toes, our kneecaps, our legs; look at everything but each other's faces. Then I mutter "Bye" and put the Claw on his shoulder, and Ren waves it off and grabs me by the wrist—like a male love interest in the K-dramas—and I joke, "So masc," and Ren pulls me into a sweaty hug.

"*They're* the lucky ones. You know that, right?" His words get crushed between our chests.

"Who?"

"You'll see."

He presses something into my hand.

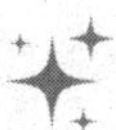

In Mom's car, I'm still holding the tube of lip stain Ren gave me. Kissy-Kissy Butter Balm. I uncap it and put some on.

Mom pulls us out of the driveway and looks into the rear-view mirror. Ren is standing in the middle of the road behind us, watching us leave. For a second, I half expect him to run along beside us, like those guys do in the cheesy rom-coms, just to give us a reason to laugh.

He doesn't. Ren stands there and we keep driving, and soon his figure gets smaller and smaller until he's swallowed by the sunlight. I wonder if a few months from now, Ren will get here before me, and he'll be on that spot, waiting—once the leaves are gone in Markville and the sun sleeps earlier. Once the snow arrives.

Mom clears her throat as we pull onto the ramp leading into the freeway. "Are you two dating?"

I spin in my seat to face her. *"Mom!"* I want to flick on the radio. Drown this awkward conversation in oldies or Clay Aiken. Mom and I have never talked about boys before. We're not ready.

"Ren's just a friend," I insist. Mom listens as I explain how we're nothing more than that. We're two boys who hang out and laugh and call each other slurs and talk constantly. Two boys lucky to find each other. Two boys who share all their secrets. Share everything.

Just friends. And anyway, I'm a college boy now—too old to believe in love stories.

"Huh," Mom says when I'm done. She signals left. For a while, the car gets really quiet. "Still sounds like a love story to me."

A passing skyscraper blocks out the sun long enough for me to catch my reflection in my window. The ghost of a smile.

It does, doesn't it?

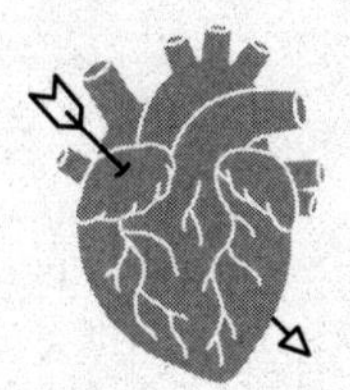

# ACKNOWLEDGMENTS

To my kick-ass editors and scream queens at Little, Brown Books for Young Readers, Erika Turner, Crystal Castro, Roddyna Saint-Paul, and editor-in-chief Alvina Ling: This novel sparkles twice as much because of your work. Thank you for your incredible insights, your patience, your passion for horror. You four understood this story's heart and, in true final-girl fashion, kept that heart beating. Much gratitude as well to managing editors Andy Ball and Esther Reisberg, to copy editor Vivian Kirklin and proofreaders Elizabeth Starr Baer and Brandy Colbert. To Jenny Kimura: Your cover art is the pastel nightmare of every boy's dream. More thanks to Martina Rethman for steering this book through production, to Bill Grace, Andie Divelbiss, and Savannah Kennelly of Marketing, and to Victoria Stapleton of School and Library Marketing and Cheryl Lew of Publicity. No one could have assembled a more perfect team—even with a magic collage.

Speaking of magic, thank you, Amy Moore-Benson, for championing the hell outta this book. You are my dream agent. To Kerry Ball, the best TV agent in the biz. Tenacious, protective, witty, and possibly a vampire slayer? To Glenn Cockburn, Olivia Chafe, Mayra Janendran, Jen McLean, Meaghan Stringer. Team Meridian Artists, unite!

Thank you to Emily Pohl-Weary and Rick Gooding, my wonderful thesis supervisors at the University of British Columbia. And to the Social Sciences and Humanities Research Council for their generous grant.

Before monsters, before horror, this book is about friendship. And so it would not exist without the small acts of care I receive from friends. Sarah Suk—one badass and talented role model. Andy Ho, for challenging me to smash those PRs. Susin Nielsen: Who chuckles at our juvenile antics harder than we? Kyrie Vermette: My baking never tastes as magical when I attempt it without you. Ren Maguire, you are *incredibly* gifted. Let's make a show together! Xine Yao: You have Ellen Ripley's heart when it comes to bettering this world and empowering your friends. Thank you for not telling anyone what I did at that screening of *Nosferatu*. Aidan Davis: for the K-dramas, the sleepovers, the name *Colin*. I still treasure the things you said about my novel. Thank God you broke into my drawer to read it.

To my Claw Crew. Valeria De La Vega: Thank you for the walks on the seawall, the witch's cackle. Thank you for buzzing me to hang out, without planning, without reason. Vancouver misses you as much as I do. Shanleigh Klassen: for our trips to the Rio and our long, healing convos about *Sailor Moon*. Thank you for giving me the first title of this book. A title so gay I shan't say it at the risk of alerting the watchdog parents.

Ugh, whatever—it was *Horny Lover Boys.* (Get a life, watchdogs!).

To my family: Emma, Tracy, Joanna, Jeanette—the funniest people I know. Any moments the characters in my writing feel most alive, most heartfelt, most electric and real, come from you. To Mom and Dad: Thank you for the never-ending love and care. Mom, you are the best storyteller I know. One day I will write you that ghost story.

Finally, to K. My first Scream Queen. This book is ours, you homo.